D0016281

buzz kill

BETH FANTASKEY

Houghton Mifflin Harcourt
Boston New York

Copyright © 2014 by Beth Fantaskey

All rights reserved. For information about permission to reproduce selections from
this book, write to Permissions, Houghton Mifflin Harcourt Publishing Company,
215 Park Avenue South, New York, New York 10003.

The text of this book is set in Dante.

www.hmhco.com

Library of Congress Cataloging-in-Publication Data
Fantaskey, Beth.
Buzz kill / by Beth Fantaskey.
p. cm.
Summary: Seventeen-year-old Millie joins forces with her classmate, gorgeous but
mysterious Chase Albright, to try to uncover who murdered head football coach
"Hollerin' Hank" Killdare—and why.
ISBN 978-0-547-39310-0
[1. Murder—Fiction. 2. High schools—Fiction. 3. Schools—Fiction.
4. Coaches (Athletics)—Fiction. 5. Dating (Social customs)—Fiction.
6. Mystery and detective stories.]   I. Title.
PZ7.F222285Buz 2014
[Fic]—dc23
2013011423

Manufactured in the U.S.A.
DOC 10 9 8 7 6 5 4 3 2 1
4500468433

To my parents, Donald and Marjorie Fantaskey—
and "my" librarian, Mrs. Elizabeth Maule

"Nancy, every place you go, it
seems as if mysteries just pile
up one after another."

—The Message in the Hollow Oak,
Nancy Drew Book 12, by Carolyn Keene

PROLOGUE
Fall, Junior Year

Head football coach "Hollerin' Hank" Killdare was having such a massive meltdown that even from where I was standing at the Booster Club's concession stand, I could see his trademark blue vein popping in his neck and the usual flecks of spittle flying out of his mouth.

Well, maybe I couldn't see the spit, but from the way demoted, one-time quarterback Mike Price—the object of the coach's rant—kept flinching as Mr. Killdare tore into him, their noses inches apart, I was pretty sure Mike was getting a shower *during* the game.

Apparently, according to the beefy, balding coach, Mike, now a lowly running back, had done something "boneheaded" and "dim-witted" that was going to cost the Honeywell Stingers "the whole *bleepin'* season."

As the student reporter assigned to cover that particular "bleepin'" game—and daughter of Assistant Coach Jack Ostermeyer—I probably should've known what had just happened on the field. But the truth was, I didn't really like sports and hadn't been paying attention to the action, preferring to focus mainly on the book I'd brought with me—*Understanding Kant: Concepts and Intuitions*—and my pack of Twizzlers.

However, even I couldn't overlook it when Mr. Killdare abruptly wheeled around and, completely unprovoked, drew back his big foot and booted our school's costumed mascot, Buzz the Bee, right in the stinger, launching him across the sidelines. Which was—anybody would have to admit—pretty funny. Especially when Buzz, stumbling and flailing wildly, careened toward the cheerleaders and smashed directly into my archenemy, Vivienne Fitch, sending her sprawling on her butt, so *everybody* got a view up her flippy little "cheer" skirt.

That really should've made me laugh, but I actually kind of winced. *If this ends up on YouTube, Viv is going to murder Mr. Killdare AND stomp a poor, innocent bee.*

As Viv jumped up and tried to act like she hadn't just been publicly steamrolled by a guy in a bug suit, I tucked my book in my backpack and took out my reporter's notebook, thinking I should at least find out what was causing Hollerin' Hank to go nuclear—which also happened way too often in the gym classes he taught.

This guy is nuts, I thought, echoing stuff my dad said all the time. *A total whack job!*

In fact, I was pretty sure my father was thinking something along those lines right then as he approached Mr. Killdare, obviously trying to get him to cool down. My dad was rabid about football, too, but at least he didn't literally foam at the mouth, unlike Hollerin' Hank.

"Come on, Hank," I heard Dad coaxing while I edged past Principal Bertram B. Woolsey, who I thought should've done something more than bite his neatly manicured nails. And, pushing farther through the crowd, I heard a lot of parents and other fans muttering about why a foul-mouthed blowhard continued to be allowed to work with kids. Sentiments I knew they'd forget when the Stingers won yet another state championship trophy for our school's already full case. "I think that's enough, now!" Dad added. "Enough!"

But Hollerin' Hank wasn't done yet. In fact, he spun around and confronted my father, actually drawing back his fist.

I knew my dad could fight his own battles—his conflicts with Mr. Killdare were pretty much the stuff of legends. And more to the point, I was only five foot two and weighed about one hundred pounds, despite a steady diet of cheeseburgers and Little Debbie products. But without even thinking, I dropped everything and started to run to my father's aid.

Before I could get there, though, the new quarterback, Chase Albright, stepped in.

Wrapping his hand around Coach Killdare's big forearm, he stopped what had seemed like an inevitable punch.

The two guys stood there for a long time, Chase's obscenely perfect, thick, dirty-blond hair riffling in the breeze, while everybody else seemed to suck in a collective nervous breath. Even the cheerleaders stopped chattering for once.

I glanced at the sidelines and saw that Viv was clutching her shivering pompoms to her locally legendary cleavage—

and glaring at Mr. Killdare like she hoped for a fight. One that would result in the coach getting *his* butt kicked to the grass. I also caught a glimpse of my French teacher, Mademoiselle Lois Beamish, who was pressing her hands to her also large, but somehow not as attractive, chest, as though she was terrified for Chase, her prize student. And I once again thought, *Ugh. She has a crush on him!*

Then I returned my attention to Chase, who was saying something to Coach Killdare—although so quietly that I couldn't hear a word. But whatever he uttered . . . It made Mr. Killdare's face fade from crimson to pink, and his hands fall to his sides.

I stared at Chase—a mysterious, reportedly uber-rich kid who'd transferred from some pricey "academy" that nobody seemed *quite* able to pinpoint—wondering, *What are you? A crazy-coach whisperer?*

Honestly, it seemed possible, because the next thing I knew, Hollerin' Hank pulled free of Chase and addressed Mike in a brusque, but civilized, tone. "Price—you're benched." Then, as Mike sat down to sulk, Mr. Killdare and my dad exchanged some gruff coaching-type words and the game got underway again, as if nothing had happened.

Retrieving my stuff from the ground—and brushing a footprint off my notebook—I climbed into the bleachers, trying to pay more attention, so I'd at least have *something* for the *Honeywell High Gazette*. But my mind kept wandering, and as the fourth quarter drew to a close, I found myself doodling a picture of the heavyset, universally despised coach with a knife in his chest and *x*'s for eyes, next to the word "Inevitable?" And just to pass the time, I inked a list of suspects, if the murder ever really did happen.

> Dad (It's true!! Wants that head coach glory!)
> Mike Price—disgraced football hero, probably losing chance for scholarship
> Mike's parents—soon paying $$$ for college for meathead son!

I glanced again at the sidelines, where Viv had resumed hopping around with a scary-false smile on her plastic face, and added her, too.

> V.F.—humiliated in bee incident + natural born killer

Then I tapped my pen against my chin, recalling a kid who'd recently been taken away in an ambulance during one of Mr. Killdare's controversial "two-a-day" football practices, and who still wasn't back in school. Rumor was, Roy Boyles had shriveled in the hot afternoon sun and might be a vegetable—or worse. I set pen to paper, writing "Roy's family?" along with

> Principal Woolsey—stuck with nutcase on staff (☹ tenure!)
> Anyone who's ever met Coach, exc. his mother (maybe)

Okay, maybe it wasn't the most narrow, practical list.

Then I also sketched a tall guy in a football uniform, with a question mark on his jersey, along with the query

SERIOUSLY—WHO IS CHASE?

I was a decent reporter when I put my mind to it, and I'd read about fifteen classic Nancy Drew books with my mom, back when I was nine, so I considered myself pretty well equipped to solve mysteries. But as I watched the enigmatic guy who was rumored to be either in the witness protection program, a teen CIA agent, or royalty slumming it to learn the ways of commoners—*seriously, folks?*—I had a feeling I'd never get *that* question answered.

Bending my head again, I retraced the question mark on Chase's jersey, darkening it, because he might not have been —as I guessed—anything more than a phenomenally snobby kid who thought he was way too good for our school, but Chase Albright definitely seemed to know how to keep his secrets.

Chapter 1

There were probably a million things we seniors could've — or should've — done on the rainy day in early September when nobody showed up to teach our first-period gym class. Such as, say, choose somebody to lead calisthenics while we waited for a real teacher. Or organize some kind of game, with a ball.

But as the minutes ticked on with no sign of Coach Hollerin' Hank Killdare or a substitute, most of us wandered back to the locker rooms, got our stuff, then sat down on the mats usually used for crunches and proceeded to text, study, or — in my case — read Montaigne's *Collected Essays*.

Only my best friend, Laura Bugbee, seemed unhappy about what most of us accepted as a stroke of good luck. I mean, I was okay with not running laps for one day. But Laura's conscience, at least, couldn't rest.

"Millie . . . Don't you think we ought to tell somebody that Mr. Killdare didn't show up?" she fretted. "Like Principal Woolsey? Maybe Coach had a heart attack in his office!" She looked toward the guys' locker room with genuine concern in her brown eyes. "Maybe he's *dying* in there. He looks like he has high blood pressure!"

Laura was probably right about Coach Killdare's constricted veins, especially since his one positive claim to fame —off the football field—was consuming, in one sitting, a sixty-ounce porterhouse at the local Sir Loin's Steakhouse—a feat I aspired to myself someday. But my friend's imagination was definitely running away with her.

"Think about it, Laura," I said, shutting my book reluctantly, because I'd been very intrigued by Montaigne's arguments *against* formal education. "If Mr. Killdare was dead or dying in his office, don't you think the guys would've noticed when they changed? I mean, I doubt the boys' locker room is a model of order or hygiene, but I don't think somebody could die in there without attracting some attention."

Laura seemed somewhat reassured, but she still scrunched up her eyebrows, scanning the gym through her wire rims. "Maybe. But we could ask one of the guys to check. Just to be safe." She frowned. "I wish Ryan was in this class. He'd do it."

She was referring to our friend Ryan Ronin, who *was* a nice guy. However, Ryan was also a football player and complained endlessly about how Hollerin' Hank treated him. "I don't know if even Ry would get off his butt to save Mr. Killdare," I noted. "I'd say it's fifty-fifty."

Would anybody *bother to save Coach Killdare if he ever really was in trouble?*

All at once—although I was still pretty sure our teacher was probably stuck in the long morning drive-through line at Dunkin' Donuts or something like that—I recalled a list

I'd made the previous year, when I'd been bored at a football game. A roll call of people who might actually want to kill the coach, and not just by failing to resuscitate him. If I remembered correctly, I'd been able to think of at least six — or possibly sixty — individuals, including my own dad, who'd probably like to stick a knife into Hollerin' Hank's overtaxed heart.

Then that weird thought was interrupted by the sound of a ball being dribbled, and I realized somebody had finally started using the equipment.

Laughing, I nudged Laura. "Hey, Chase is up and full of energy. Why don't you ask him to check the locker room?"

I believed Laura was genuinely concerned about Mr. Killdare — but obviously not enough to approach a guy she'd worshiped from afar, ever since his transfer to Honeywell. "No, that's okay!" she sort of cried, her face getting red.

"Oh, come on," I teased, grabbing her arm, like I was going to drag her over to where Chase Albright was alone, shooting hoops. He was a one-man team, sinking a shot, retrieving it, and going in for a lay-up — all with the lazy, I-don't-give-a-damn-who's-watching, but-don't-ask-to-join-me vibe that he always managed to give off. Chase was, I thought, the embodiment of aloof. Which apparently didn't bother Laura or a lot of other girls, who seemed perversely drawn to his inaccessibility — and, I supposed, the way he looked in his T-shirt and shorts. Even I — who had *nada* for Chase — couldn't deny that he filled out a gym uniform pretty well. And his face, with those blue eyes that gave away *nothing* . . . There wasn't much to criticize there, either.

My grip on Laura loosening, I studied Chase as he did another lay-up, his hair managing to gleam under the fluores-
cent lights, just as it had on a sunny day when I'd doodled his
picture with a question mark on his chest.

*And I still don't know much about Chase—except that he likes
to watch moody foreign films that no other kids go to. But I can't
seem to ask him what's up with that when I sell him his single ticket
from my claustrophobic booth at the Lassiter Bijou . . .*

"You think he's amazing, too." Laura's accusation brought
me back to reality, and I realized I was still holding her arm.
She pulled away, giving me a smug look. "You practically
went catatonic, watching him!"

"I did not," I protested, my cheeks getting warm. A propensity to blush for virtually no reason was the curse of being
a redhead. "I find him *interesting*," I explained. "How can a
guy who should be the most popular person in school—a guy
everybody *wants* to be around—seem to have zero friends, let
alone a girlfriend?"

At least, Chase had never brought a date, or anybody else,
to the theater where I worked, as required by my father, who
insisted that earning minimum wage "built character."

"I heard there's a picture of a girl in his locker," Laura
informed me, both of us again observing Chase, who'd
switched to taking shots from the free-throw line. "A very
pretty girl."

"Really?" I turned to Laura, intrigued. "Who is she?"

Laura shrugged. "Nobody knows. Probably a girlfriend at
his old school."

Interesting. And where, exactly, is that school . . . ?

I was just about to voice that question when somebody behind me butted into the conversation, saying in a super-snarky, high-pitched voice, "Dream on, ladies! Especially you, Millicent. Because Chase Albright is exactly one million miles out of your league."

Knowing that things were about to get very, very bad— probably for me—I slowly, reluctantly, turned to see who had joined us.

Oh, crud . . . Here we go!

Chapter 2

"You may have phenomenally dumb luck with some things, Millie Ostermeyer, but you will never be with *my* future boyfriend," Vivienne Fitch advised me. She towered over me, having already changed out of her gym clothes and into a pair of heels that were forbidden on the polished floor, like she was sure Mr. Killdare wouldn't make a last-minute appearance. Because, seriously . . . *heels?* He'd make her run ten laps in her stilettos, then force her to rent a power sander to buff out the scratches. "Because no twist of fate," Viv added, "short of an accident with sheep shears, can save you from that mess on your head. It's like a flag that says 'I will always be alone.'"

I wasn't sure he understood the joke, but her simian sidekick, Mike Price, snorted a laugh. Viv treated Mike like dirt —right down to openly expressing interest in Chase—but he continued to serve her like a butler and shamelessly sucked up because he was desperate to get in her pants. "Good one, Viv," he grunted. "A flag. That's funny."

Ignoring him, I peered up at Viv. "First of all, I don't give a rat's derrière about Chase Albright. And no offense, but I don't think you should get your hopes up. I seriously doubt he's dying to date a girl who just showed up on national TV getting trampled by a giant bee—in slow motion, no less."

Indeed, an amateur cell phone video of Viv getting crushed on the sidelines of a football game by Stingers' mascot Buzz had resurfaced after going viral the year before. Just when it had seemed like "Cheerleader BuzzKill" had gone dormant forever—after upward of a *million* YouTube hits—ESPN had resurrected it for a bloopers show celebrating the start of the high school football season. Talk about national exposure— of Viv's butt.

She jabbed a finger at me, a murderous gleam in her eyes. "I swear, if you had anything to do with that—"

"Viv, I do not spend my time videotaping you," I promised her. "That whole thing was Mr. Killdare's fault. He's the one who kicked Buzz. Go threaten him!"

"Speaking of which," Laura interrupted, "have you seen Coach Killdare, Viv? Because I'm kind of worried about him."

Viv seemed to think Laura'd lost her mind. "I have no idea where he is," she snapped, "and I don't care if Hank Killdare fell through a wormhole into another dimension!"

I had to admit I grudgingly admired her grasp of time-space portals.

"Not only did he humiliate me," she continued, her voice rising, "but if he gives me one more D for not climbing that stupid rope, I might not get into Harvard. I don't care what the hell happened to him!"

Ouch. That was harsh. And why was she assuming that

something had really "happened"? Had there been, say, a four-car pileup that the rest of us weren't privy to yet?

"If you'd just eat something," I suggested, not unkindly, "maybe you could climb the rope—and be in a better mood."

"Not all of us have freakish metabolisms and can stuff our faces all day," Viv countered. She glanced at my chest. "Although if I were you, I'd wish I could gain weight *somewhere*."

Ooh, a flat-chest wisecrack. Those never got old.

Grabbing my book, I finally stood up, as did Laura. "What do you really want, Viv?"

She crossed her arms. "I'm here to remind you that you have an overdue story for the *Gazette*. And I want it on my desk, ASAP."

I knew that Vivienne didn't care about that stupid story, and was, as usual, "reminding" me that as student editor of the paper, she was technically my boss for the year. One who took twisted delight in giving me the worst assignments—including this latest snoozer, about some chinks in a cinder-block wall, for crying out loud.

"Viv, if you honestly think I'm going to schlep out to the football field to look at a few cracks in the bleachers—"

"Oh, I don't just *think* you'll do that." She cut me off. "I expect to see a story about the stadium's *major structural problems* on my desk by the end of the day. And I want quotes from Mayor Jack Ostermeyer, too, explaining why this boondoggle of a school that he wanted so badly not only gives people cancer, but is already falling apart at the seams."

Laura sucked in a sharp breath because that was low, even by Viv's standards.

My dad had fought for the construction of our state-of-the-art school, but that stuff about people getting sick because it stood on the site of an old factory . . . That had all been disproved—after nearly costing Dad an election. And my mom had died of an aggressive form of leukemia, back when I was ten. Viv should never even have uttered the word "cancer" around me, after what my family had been through.

"You'll get your story when I feel like writing it," I growled, feeling Laura's fingers twine around my arm, like she was ready to hold me back. "And if you bug me again, you'll have cracks in *your head*."

Viv and I had a long history of pushing each other's buttons, but she seemed to realize she'd gone too far. I could see it in her cold, sharky blue eyes. She didn't back down, though —and certainly didn't apologize. "I'll give you two more days," she advised me. She summoned her minion. "Come on, Mike. Let's get out of here."

I'd almost forgotten Mike was there, and he was equally oblivious to me. Following his gaze, I realized that his dull eyes were trained on Chase, who was still shooting hoops.

Mike's a mean kid who's still pissed about Chase getting his quarterback spot—and killing any shot he had at a college scholarship. And he really *blames Mr. Killdare—*

"Mike," Viv snapped again, so her lackey surfaced from his trance. "Let's go."

I watched them walk across the gym, Viv's heels clicking, until Laura ventured, "Hey, sorry about what she just said,"

Bending, I grabbed my mat since class was almost over.

"You don't have to apologize. You're not the soulless psycho-path."

Laura began to roll up her mat, too. "You know she's really just jealous of you."

"Yes," I agreed. "I inspire envy in every Ivy-League-bound cheerleader with long, blond hair and what I swear is a surgically altered nose."

"You are prettier than Vivienne," Laura insisted. Before I could protest, she added, "You know she envies how easily stuff comes to you, and your red hair was the first thing she ever got jealous about. Remember how you won that costume contest in third grade, just by wearing a trash bag and making a ponytail on top of your head?"

I grinned. "Yeah, I was a volcano. While Viv's family spent, like, a thousand dollars to dress her up as Snow White."

I could still picture Viv stamping her crystal-encrusted shoes as I'd accepted a plastic pumpkin full of candy and marched down Market Street, leading Honeywell's Halloween parade.

"And then there was the time you saved that kid at camp when he almost drowned in the lake," Laura reminded me. "That was *huge*."

"I was actually begging Kenny Kaluka to stop pulling on me," I admitted. "I kept trying to pry his fingers off my arm the whole time I was dragging him to shore."

"Well, you came off like a hero—and got Camper of the Year, even though Viv had dominated pretty much everything all summer, from archery to canoe racing." Laura frowned.

"And then you won that Peacemaker thing last year . . . That was probably the last straw."

She was talking about the National *Pacemaker* Awards, which were the equivalent of Pulitzer Prizes for student journalists. And she was right about Viv having a conniption when I'd won for feature writing, for a sappy story about our school's blind crossing guard. I hadn't even technically entered—the *Gazette*'s eager new advisor, Mr. Sokowski, had filled out the paperwork—but I'd come home with the honors.

"That did tick her off pretty badly," I agreed. "She didn't even get honorable mention for her piece on bulimic cheerleaders." I shrugged. "Too clichéd, I think."

"And she's obviously still mad about your father beating hers for mayor, too," Laura noted as we walked toward the equipment storage closet. "She's got it in for you *and* your dad."

"Well . . ." I tossed my mat into a bin. "In less than a year, Viv and I will part ways forever. I'd say the odds of my accidentally shining again at her expense are pretty slim."

I looked once more at Chase. *Good thing I really don't have designs on him. Viv would destroy me if I ever "stole" a guy she liked!*

Laura was also watching the mysterious Mr. Albright—of course. But she didn't think I should keep my distance. On the contrary, she suggested, "Hey, maybe you could do an exposé on Chase and win another one of those Peacemakers. He is a total—gorgeous—puzzle."

I reached for the door to the locker room. "I'm pretty sure what I'd uncover would earn the headline 'Self-Absorbed Rich Kid Too Snooty for Small Town.' Which is not exactly a man-bites-dog story." I kind of snorted. "Let's face it. Nobody from Honeywell, Pennsylvania, will ever win the investigative reporting prize. What the heck would you look into?"

Laura and I both laughed, then, because nothing significant—not counting football championships—ever happened in our sleepy town.

It never occurred to either one of us that a question on our class's collective mind, that morning, might actually turn out to be a *huge* story. No, it wasn't until we'd had a substitute phys ed teacher for over a week, and my dad had slid into the role of de facto head coach of the Stingers, that I, at least, realized somebody might want to make a sincere effort to answer . . .

What the heck really happened to Coach Killdare?

Chapter 3

Millicent, what is that stain on your uniform?" my father inquired, shooting me a quick glance as he drove me back to school, where I·had an after-hours interview—and he had football practice—to conduct. He wrinkled his nose. "And why do you smell like rancid butter?"

"I had a little accident with the dispenser," I admitted, wiping ineffectually at the oil slick on the hideous gold-buttoned, red polyester shirt I was required to wear at the theater, where I was scheduled to work that night. The uniform was supposed to resemble an usher's getup from the Lassiter Bijou's silent-movie heyday, but I was pretty sure I looked more like an organ grinder's monkey in a fright wig. "Can we *please* go back home so I can get a jacket," I begged yet again. "I'll just run in quick—"

"I asked you, twice, if you had everything you needed before we left." Dad cut me off. "This is a lesson in responsibility."

Actually, it was going to be a lesson in *humiliation*, because all the football players and cheerleaders would be at school, too.

"Weren't you supposed to do this story days ago?" Dad added, turning on to the winding road to the high school, which was located just outside the quaint little town he ruled with an iron fist. "I remember you mentioning a 'lame article' about stadium repairs quite a while back."

"Actually, it was due eons ago," I informed him. In fact, I'd deliberately delayed another six days after Viv had given me her two-day warning in the gym. "But I can't give my editor the satisfaction of thinking she's really my boss."

Dad gave me another look. "Millie—she *is* your boss."

"Well, in that case, I'm supposed to get a quote from you," I said, without bothering to retrieve my notebook. Ever since the "cancer cluster" debacle, my father had distanced himself from anything school related except football. He could *never* wean himself off that addiction, and I strongly suspected that he wished he'd had a boy who could've played. Actually, I sometimes thought he secretly wished he'd just remained childless. "So, any comment on the bleachers?"

As I'd expected, he didn't answer. After pulling into the school lot, he parked his sensible Dodge sedan in a visitor's spot close to one marked H. Killdare—a little perk that I knew my dad would've liked and that had gone unused . . . I did a quick calculation, surprised to realize the *real* head coach had been gone for over a week.

"Dad, have you heard any news on Mr. Killdare?" I asked —not that I was eager to see Hollerin' Hank in the gym again.

His absence just seemed odd. "Like, has he called to say where he's at?"

"No. But Principal Woolsey seems to vaguely recall Hank saying something about taking time off." I could tell Dad—like pretty much everybody else—considered Mr. Woolsey completely incompetent when he confided, "Frankly, I think he's afraid he dropped the ball and should know where his head coach has vanished to during the height of football season."

"Yeah, that sounds like Mr. Woolsey," I agreed. "But would Coach Killdare really blow off the season?"

"Emergencies arise, Millicent." Dad rammed the car into "park." "Some of which trump football, even."

I opened my mouth to mention my sixth birthday party, which my father had missed because of a game, then let it go. In retrospect, there had been a lot of squealing, and Laura'd peed her pants after drinking too much lemonade. Who could blame a grown man for trying to avoid that scene? But I couldn't imagine *anything* that would keep Hollerin' Hank from football.

"Jeez, maybe Laura's right," I mumbled. "Maybe something really happened to Mr. Killdare!"

My dad didn't share my concern. He gestured to the book on my lap. "I don't want you reading while you work the concession stand tonight, Millie. That's like stealing from your employer."

How had I sprung from a father who was ambitious, followed rules, and—I studied my dad's face—was olive-skinned, and dark-haired, and had a long, narrow nose? A nose that nobody would ever compare to that of a bulldog, like always happened to me?

In fact, Dad was probably decent-looking, by middle-age standards, and I wondered, as I sometimes did, *Does he ever consider dating?*

"Millie, did you hear me about reading equaling stealing?" he prompted.

"But we're going to discuss this book in Philosophy Club," I said, holding up my copy of Hegel's *Phenomenology of Spirit* —and invoking the organization I'd founded last year because my dad was worried about my lack of "extracurriculars." Although I was still technically the only member, I added, "I need to be ready for the meeting."

Dad wasn't convinced. "Reading at work is stealing, Millie. Period."

"Fine." I tucked the book under my arm, thinking it was probably more like stealing when I ate Charleston Chews from the candy counter. But honestly, I hadn't sold one in a year and felt like I was doing the owner, Mr. Lassiter, a favor by getting rid of them. If one of our old patrons ever did purchase one and tried to sink his or her dentures through stale, rock-hard nougat, my employer might just find himself footing a big dental bill. I didn't mention that to my dad, though, and promised, "I'll find something else to do when *nobody's* buying popcorn."

For some reason, my father still seemed exasperated, and as we got out of the car, he muttered, "I am going to talk to

Isabel about when and where you read. You seem to actually listen to her."

I had one foot on the pavement, but I stopped short, surprised that Dad had just called "my" librarian, Isabel Parkins, by her first name. I consulted with Ms. Parkins on at least a biweekly basis—she was both a book recommender and something of a confidante—but I rarely mentioned her to Dad. And I certainly never used her first name.

Then again, Ms. Parkins *was* head of Honeywell's public library, a key part of Mayor Jack Ostermeyer's fiefdom.

"Millie, will you get out of the car?" Dad suggested, adding, with a rare hint of laughter in his voice, "I think your date for the evening is waiting for you!"

I slammed the door, not sure what the heck he was talking about because I hadn't had a date since . . . well, never. But when I looked across the parking lot, I spotted . . .

Oh, good grief.

Chapter 4

What a pair Head of Custodial Services "Big Pete" Lamar and I must've made when we entered the football field, me in my organ-grinder's-assistant suit and my "date"—weighing in at about three hundred pounds—lumbering along in soiled, olive-drab coveralls and heavy work boots.

We look like homecoming king and queen—at Clown College.

"Let's get this over with," I sighed, flipping open my notebook as we made our way down the track toward the far end of the bleachers. I clicked my ballpoint, ignoring the stares of the football players gathering around my dad. "What's the deal with the stadium? How bad are these cracks?"

"It's actually a mess," Big Pete said, huffing from the walk. He began rifling through a huge ring of keys that he'd dug out from some cavernous recess in his pants. "We gotta empty out a storage space under the seats and bring in a crew to do repairs—then go through a state safety inspection. Pretty big —expensive—job."

Okay, that surprised me. I'd expected him to confirm my

suspicion that the story wasn't even worth covering, and reluctantly took down his quote about the cost.

"Hank Killdare was the first to notice 'em and make a fuss," Big Pete added. "Said he didn't want the whole stadium collapsin' during a game. Threatened to go to the real press . . ." He obviously realized he'd insulted me and gave me a sheepish look. "Sorry . . . Anyhow, Killdare said fix 'em—or else."

"So these cracks . . . Are they really serious?"

"Eh." Big Pete shrugged. "Probably just cosmetic, to be honest. But when Hank Killdare gets a bee in his bonnet . . ." Grinning at his own—clearly inadvertent—pun, he jabbed a thick finger at my notebook. "Hey, write that down! Stingers coach has a bee in his bonnet!"

I wasn't laughing—or writing. I was looking at my father, who by then was surrounded by players, including Ryan, who waved to me; Mike Price, who was, as usual, doing his own lower-primate impersonation; and the always attention-grabbing Chase Albright, who stood with his arms crossed and a look of concentration on his gorgeous high-and-mighty face, now and then nodding at something my dad said.

Is this school really a "boondoggle"? Have my dad and Hollerin' Hank clashed about fixing the stadium, as well as coaching strategies?

The cheerleaders had arrived for practice, too, and I found Viv at the head of the pack, her lips frozen in what everyone else accepted as a smile, but which I always thought looked like a wolfish snarl, complete with wrinkled snout and sharp incisors.

And did Viv know how much fixing the cracks will cost? Did she know I'll have to write a story that really will make Dad look bad? Because he gets blamed for everything that goes wrong at Honeywell High.

How sick to use me against my own father . . .

"I guess you'll wanna see the storage space, huh?"

"What?" I turned around to see Big Pete heading toward a door I'd never noticed before, in the cinder-block wall under the bleachers. I also saw a bunch of fine, jagged fissures in that wall, which often bore the weight of hundreds of people, because Honeywell's nationally known football program packed in the crowds. "What did you say?" I asked again, catching up to my guide.

"I guess you'll wanna see the storage space," he repeated, jamming a key in the lock before I could tell him that, no, I didn't really need to see a bunch of old javelins or tackling dummies or whatever they kept under bleachers. Especially since, as I drew closer, I started to *smell* something coming from behind that portal.

Stepping reluctantly beside Pete, I fought the urge to cover my nose, thinking, *Jeez, what's really in there? Mascot Buzz's unwashed, sweaty bee costume? The eviscerated organs of our vanquished sports foes?*

"Look, I really don't think I need . . ."

I was just about to insist that we keep that door closed when Pete, looking confused himself, hauled it open. The stench got even worse, and we both looked at each other, like, *What the heck?*

Looking back, I'd never be sure what, exactly, compelled

both of us to walk toward that odor instead of running away from it. Maybe it was the fact that I'd come to document the whole bleachers problem, and clearly there was something seriously messed up inside that dark hole. Regardless, after a moment of hesitation, I made the first move, taking a tentative step into the shadows—only to stumble and fall against something. Something big and hard, but squishy and slippery, too, as if it was covered in nylon.

This is wrong, I thought on instinct. *Something is very wrong here.*

Then, as my eyes started to adjust and I began to recognize exactly what—or whom—I was resting against, Big Pete gave me the quote of a lifetime, albeit one that I couldn't have put in a G-rated school newspaper article, even if I'd been able to write anything down.

"Holy ****! It's a *dead guy*—on a John Deere!"

Chapter 5

L et me go!" I cried, slugging somebody—hard—in the shoulder. "LET ME GO!"

The individual who was clutching me to a rock-hard chest didn't listen. On the contrary, he spun me around, so we were in a Heimlich-maneuver position, then began dragging me so the soles of my old Adidas scraped concrete. "Deep breaths," he whispered in a low, strangely soothing voice that was at odds with the way I was straitjacketed and struggling in his arms. "You're okay. Stop screaming."

I wanted to protest that I, Millie Ostermeyer, had never screamed in my entire life—not even on Hersheypark's Skyrush roller coaster—but as I was hauled into slightly fresher air and fading sunlight, I realized that I was, indeed, shrieking and maybe borderline incoherent. And when I finally did inhale deeply—catching a whiff of very nice soap or cologne, layered on top of the smell of *rotting flesh*—I also realized who was holding me—and recalled what I'd fallen onto moments before.

Coach Killdare's CORPSE.

I just fell directly onto a dead phys ed instructor, who is inside a cinder-block TOMB, slumped over a lawn tractor with THE ENTIRE BACK OF HIS SKULL SMOOSHED IN.

Feeling my captor's grip ease, like he'd realized I was at least lucid again, I turned to face the boy who'd yanked me out of that makeshift mausoleum, and for some reason felt compelled to inform him, in big ragged gasps, "Mr. Killdare . . . His whole head . . . Bashed in!"

Then, before Chase Albright could respond—before I could even read what was going on behind his deep blue eyes—I proceeded to thank him for helping me by bending over and vomiting my entire dinner of SpaghettiOs, minimeatballs, and gummy bears onto his cleats.

And as round two came up—again onto his shoes, because, honestly, there wasn't even time to move—I felt someone else grasp my shoulders and heard my father offer, "I've got her, Chase. You go clean up."

True to his usual form, Chase didn't say a word. I just saw his puke-covered feet move out from under my face while I remained bent over, because I'd eaten *two* cans of SpaghettiOs, and I wasn't sure they were both accounted for yet.

"Millie, are you okay?" Dad asked. He helped me straighten, finally, so I could see that Ryan had joined us, too. "Did I hear you right about Mr. Killdare?"

My dad was obviously concerned about me, but distracted. His gaze kept darting toward the storage space, where Big Pete was blocking the view, warding off the football players and cheerleaders who were starting to gather around, trying to figure out what had happened.

"I'm . . . I'm okay," I assured Dad. "You'd better go help Pete, because Mr. Killdare really is . . ." I couldn't say "dead," for some reason. Not without getting queasy again.

"Go ahead, Coach," Ryan intervened, clasping my arm. "I'll stay with Millie."

That seemed to reassure my father. "Thanks."

With one last glance at me, Dad left us, threading his way through the crowd of players, managers, and cheerleaders that had gathered. Some kids were gawking at the girl who'd freaked out and lost her lunch on a quarterback, but most were craning their necks, trying to get a glimpse past Big Pete, whose bulk was coming in handy.

"Nothin' to see here," he kept telling everybody. "Nothin' to see!"

Except stuff I'll revisit in nightmares, I thought, recalling, too vividly, how Mr. Killdare's bluish-white hands had hung stiffly down at his sides, the way his face had been pressed against the tractor's steering wheel, and, of course, the caved-in back of his head . . .

"Millie, what's going on?" Ryan asked, studying my face with obvious concern. "What, exactly, is under the bleachers?"

I started to tell him, but my voice was drowned out by the wail of approaching sirens. Only then did I finally fully grasp that Mr. Killdare actually had been *murdered,* just like I'd sort of predicted a little over a year before.

And as I recalled, yet again, the list of suspects I'd made, in an exercise that didn't seem remotely amusing anymore, I realized that no fewer than three of them were right on the scene: Vivienne Fitch, who was arguing with Big Pete, as if she'd waited her whole life to see a homicide victim and would not be denied the chance to take a photograph of it with her cell phone; Mike Price, for once not glued to Viv's hip, but rather standing on the margins; and, of course, Jack Ostermeyer, who by then was at the entrance to the storage space, not taking charge, as I'd expected, but staring into that stinky crypt with a very strange look on his face. One I couldn't quite read in the dimming daylight.

And as police cars and ambulances began to drive up to the stadium, tearing across the grassy field, I also saw that Chase hadn't run off to change his shoes, like I thought he should do before semiliquefied Chef Boyardee seeped through his laces. He still lingered at the very back of the milling, excited throng, far enough away from the other kids to qualify as alone.

And the look on his face . . . It struck me as even more curious than the expression on my father's. I almost could've sworn that Chase Albright, whom I'd previously thought incapable of anything but an icy, unyielding, smug superiority, looked . . . sad.

Then I jumped about a mile when somebody clapped a firm hand on my shoulder and told me, in a weasely, sort-of-familiar voice, "Don't go anywhere, Millicent Ostermeyer. I'll need to talk to you."

Chapter 6

So, you two were the first *youths* on the scene," Detective Blaine Lohser said, pacing in front of me and Chase, whom he'd corralled on the bleachers, out of the way of other official-looking people who were bustling in and out of the storage space. Somehow, the way he said "youths," it came out as "juvenile delinquents." His gaze darted between me and Chase. "Why were you two under the bleachers?"

He managed to imbue that simple question with heavy innuendo, so it was clear that he believed the correct answer was (a) "making out," (b) "shooting heroin," or (c) "returning to the scene of the murder we had planned for kicks." Or maybe (d) "all of the above."

I knew skinny, twitchy Detective Lohser from when he'd been a patrolman with the Honeywell police force, where he'd earned zero respect, and I was pretty sure that he still struggled to remind people that his last name was pronounced with a long "o" — a battle he'd probably fought since kindergarten. However, that didn't stop me from feeling inexplicably guilty under his boring — in the sense of "soul searching" — gaze.

"Well?" he asked when neither Chase nor I answered.

It was Chase who spoke first, and it was clear that he wasn't nervous. "First of all, we weren't 'under' anything," he said, sounding borderline dismissive. "And I'm sure the maintenance man told you why . . ." He finally looked at me, like I should supply my name, and I blinked at him in disbelief.

Seriously? You sit practically behind me in French class!

He kept waiting, though, so I grumbled, "Millie. My name is Millicent, remember?"

That seemed like a revelation. And not necessarily a good one. "Oh."

"We sit two desks away—every day—in French," I reminded him. "Every. Day."

"I don't think you participate much," Chase countered coolly. "I don't think I've ever seen you get called on."

"Maybe not, but I get *yelled at*," I pointed out. "Don't you hear Ms. Beamish? *'Mee-leh-CENT! Wake up!'* Or however she says it in French."

Chase frowned. "Yeah. I guess I have noticed that—"

"Look, lovebirds," Detective Lohser interrupted, like he hadn't paid attention to anything we'd just said. Really, wouldn't a lovebird know its mate's name? "What *were you doing under the bleachers? With a body?*"

Chase returned his attention to our interrogator. "As I started to say, I'm sure the custodian explained why Millicent was there—with him."

How did it once again seem like I'd been making out with somebody? And with a custodian in dirty coveralls, to boot?

"I didn't show up until Millie screamed," Chase continued

before I could decide if I needed to clarify things. "I heard her and went to see if I could help. My role is pretty simple."

"Yeah," I blurted, finding my voice, because it seemed that I hadn't exactly been exonerated. In fact, I felt a little bit like someone who'd just been thrown under a bus, the way Chase had said *"My* role." "If you think we killed Mr. Killdare, you're completely wrong!"

As soon as the words were out of my mouth, I realized they probably hadn't been prudent, and Chase seemed to agree. He turned to me again with warning in his usually unreadable eyes, as if to say, *Why the heck did you say* that? *The twitchy cop didn't say anything like that!* Then, in case I hadn't picked up on the nonverbal message, he leaned close and whispered, "Are you trying to make us suspects?"

"No!" I took in a whiff of cologne while I had the chance. Unfortunately, Chase's shoes were starting to smell, and I gagged a little. "I'm . . . I'm just trying to help."

"No whispering!" Detective Lohser snapped. "Address me!"

Chase took a moment to lock eyes with me, silently suggesting that I shut up — or maybe wishing me luck, because apparently he was already done with the whole interrogation thing. "Look," he told Detective Lohser. "I didn't see anything, and my cleats are a mess . . ." He shot me one last glance, this one of blame, before asking, "So is it all right if I take off?"

The cop, who had to be sweating in his cheap, out-of-season tweed suit, clearly didn't appreciate the attitude, and I almost found myself silently siding with the bossy bureaucrat. Did Chase think he was above *everybody?*

"You're staying put until you tell me when you last saw

Mr. Killdare—alive," Detective Lohser advised my classmate. "Then you're going to explain, fully, how you *just happened* to discover his body."

There didn't seem to be any room for argument, and so I was very surprised when Chase stood up, rising to his full six-foot-something height and towering over the mini-detective. "No offense," he said firmly. "But you don't have any authority to keep me here. I'm not under arrest, and I don't have anything to contribute—at least not without a lawyer present—so I'm hitting the showers."

I blinked up at him, thinking "contribute" was a nice alternative to "say." But did people really talk like that outside of *Law and Order*? Tell cops they were just *leaving*?

I considered myself pretty rebellious, but Detective Lohser was a real police officer, not a powerless figurehead like Principal Woolsey, who'd also shown up and was talking with my father.

Chase was obviously going to get away with his insubordination, though. Detective Lohser didn't say a word—just vented steam through his ears—as Chase walked off. And although it seemed absurd, I couldn't help thinking, *Is Chase leaving because he has something to hide? Something that he doesn't want to leak out—at least without a "lawyer present"?*

Moreover, didn't he want to help? Because, sure, Mr. Killdare had been pretty disgusting even in life. He'd always spat in our faces when he'd dressed us down in class, and inevitably hiked up his eternally droopy khaki pants a moment too late, after you'd already glimpsed the waistband of his tighty whities and a flash of belly hair. And it had been hard to ignore his armpit stains when he'd stalked around the gym, telling us what "sorry asses" we were. But he hadn't deserved to be *murdered*. The man had, at the very least, won a bunch of football games and set a local record for steak consumption. Didn't those achievements mean *something?*

"Look," I offered, choosing my words more carefully. "I didn't know Coach Killdare that well, and it's going to gross me out, but I can tell you everything I saw today, in detail, because I do have a nearly photographic memory—"

I was ready to spill my guts—figuratively, this time—and therefore was a little offended when Detective Lohser, still watching Chase, waved me off. "Never mind, kid. Forensics will go over everything you saw with a fine-toothed comb. You can't tell me anything right now."

Then he shifted his gaze and got this creepy smile under his desperate attempt at a mustache, muttering, "Right now I need to talk to a certain person who, for as long as I can remember, has obsessively craved all the glory for Honeywell High's football program."

For a second, I didn't know who the heck he was talking about. Then I followed where Detective Lohser was looking —a little "obsessively" himself, in my opinion—and realized that, of course, he was referring to my father.

I also remembered that list I'd made, which had positioned my dad as the prime suspect in a once-hypothetical murder that had now actually happened. And how my dad had fought —successfully—to get Detective Lohser fired from the Honeywell force about three years before.

Uh-oh.

Chapter 7

T he sun was setting on Honeywell's main thoroughfare, and I knew it was almost time to leave the glass ticket booth that jutted out onto the sidewalk and head inside to work the Lassiter Bijou's concession stand, but I kept stalling, just watching the street.

Would Chase show up?

We were screening something black and white and dull all over by the master of gloom, Ingmar Bergman, and Chase always came for Bergman films. I couldn't imagine that even stumbling across a murder would keep him from *Winter Light,* which featured the most depressing poster I'd ever seen. It was simply of a glum guy sitting in a chair. The second I'd seen it, I'd mentally set aside a ticket for my classmate.

What does Chase get out of movies about suicidal fishermen, wars, and medieval plagues?

Will I ask him, now that I sort of "know" him?

Doubtful.

"I can't believe *I* have to be here," I grumbled, turning off the light to signal that the box office was closed, because it was after seven-thirty and the projectionist, old Mr. Mor-drick, would've started the film already. Clearly, murder had been enough to keep Chase away, while I, on the other hand, had to "soldier on" and "meet my work responsibilities."

"You have an obligation to Mr. Lassiter," I muttered, imi-tating my father as I ducked to retrieve the till with the eve-ning's ticket receipts—a whopping fifteen dollars. And while I was still crouched out of sight, I heard voices. Familiar voices.

Viv. And Mike.

I honestly didn't intend to eavesdrop on them. I stayed hunkered down, hiding, only because I'd more than once been compared to a monkey in a cage in my booth. I really didn't need Viv threatening to toss me a banana or calling me "orangutan"—which she sometimes did, even when I wasn't working.

As they walked past, though, I couldn't help hearing Viv tell Mike quietly, but with earnest venom in her voice, "Look, idiot. You know what happened. *I* know what happened. But nobody else will *ever*—and I mean EVER—find out . . ."

Then their voices and their footsteps faded as they moved down the sidewalk.

I kept crouching for a long time, my hand frozen on the till, because while I didn't know what they'd just been talking about, it didn't sound like anything as mundane as covering up cheating on a French test.

And while it might just've been my imagination running completely amok, when I considered the degree to which ruthless Viv and her mindless, brutish henchman Mike had both despised Mr. Killdare, I had to admit, I kind of wondered whether they weren't discussing . . . murder.

But teenagers—even heartless, soulless, cold-blooded ones like Viv—didn't do *that*.

Did they?

Chapter 8

O ne more bite, Ostermeyer! One more bleepin' bite!"
       "But I can't," I tell Hollerin' Hank Killdare. "I'm gonna be sick!"

I'm sitting at a table in Sir Loin's castle-themed steak house, and he's stalking around me, a stopwatch in his hand, a scowl on his face, and a look in his watery, bloodshot eyes that says I'm the world's biggest disappointment.

"Do it, Ostermeyer!" he growls, jowls flapping. "It's only sixty bleepin' ounces! This is your chance to achieve immortal glory!"

I feel really nauseated, but also like I have no choice, so I jab my oversize knife and fork into a steak that seems to keep GROWING, and hack off a fatty, rare slab that looks as big as a full-grown opossum.

"There's no way I can eat this," I tell myself. Yet my shaky hand is making its way to my mouth—only to stop suddenly when Coach Killdare turns his back on me, and I can see WORMS crawling out of a hole in his head—a writhing tangle of sugar-coated, neon gummy worms—and I drop the giant utensils, just as everything I've eaten . . .

"Millie."

The sound of Ryan's voice sliced through the nightmare, like an oversize knife through a porterhouse, and I opened my eyes, lifted my heavy head, and tried to focus, happy to discover that there wasn't a massive hunk of beef on the table —the desk—in front of me.

"Thanks for waking me up," I said groggily, not only because he'd interrupted my nightmare, but because I was drooling in homeroom.

At least I was grateful until I saw that Ry was holding something under my nose.

A copy of the *Honeywell High Gazette*, featuring a picture of me in my polyester uniform, bent over a fair-haired quarterback's shoes and doing exactly what I'd almost just done in my dream.

But worse than that was the headline for one of two accompanying stories, both written by Vivienne Fitch:

"Killdare Slaying: Police Question Assistant Coach."

Chapter **9**

V ivienne Fitch, you will not get away this," I snarled at
the girl who was sitting smugly in a metal office chair,
her arms crossed and wicked amusement in her eyes, clearly
not regretting publishing a libelous story about my father and
a borderline libelous photo of me. "You have gone too far this
time!" I warned her.

Then I turned on the *Gazette*'s fresh-out-of-college faculty
advisor, Mr. Sokowski, who, unlike Viv, was shaking a little in
his chair. I raised the paper, pointing to page one. "And how
could *you* let this run? I should sue this whole stupid school!"

"Millicent, please calm down," Principal Woolsey finally
spoke up, no doubt because I'd raised the specter of litigation. He peered nervously around his office, where Mr. Sokowski had wisely dragged Viv's and my argument, and it
seemed like he was afraid I had lawyers hiding behind his dying ficus plant. "Please," he begged. "Lower your voice."

"No, I won't—"

But before I could accuse Mr. Woolsey of negligence, too,

Viv took control of the meeting, advising me, "You are not going to sue anybody, Ostermeyer. The photo depicts a legitimate moment in a newsworthy event — and was the best-quality shot I got, since Fat Pete —"

"*Big* Pete," I said, defending the custodian's dignity. Maybe I was starting to think we'd really dated. "It's *Big* Pete."

Mr. Woolsey cleared his throat and absently adjusted items on his desk, including a photo of him — alone — on some kind of tropical vacation and the shiny name plaque that optimistically proclaimed him "Bertram B. Woolsey, Principal." He sounded more like a student, though. "You two . . . Please . . ."

Viv ignored us both. "It's the best image I got, since *Fat Pete* blocked my view of the actual body." She shrugged. "And as for the story, there's nothing remotely libelous there, either. Your father *was* questioned. And the quotes from Detective Lohser are all verbatim."

I checked the front page again, skimming Viv's two articles. One was a straightforward account of how Mr. Killdare had been found murdered. It seemed factual, although it irritatingly referred to me as "too distraught to offer comment." And the second story . . . I scanned it and had to admit that it was technically correct, too. My father had been interviewed extensively — but only because, in my opinion, Detective Lohser had it in for him. It was clear from Lohser's quote: "We are interviewing everyone who had access to the storage area and knew the victim."

Okay, maybe that wasn't as damning as I'd first thought.

And yet, thanks to the headline and a lead that played up Dad's on-field interrogation, my father did end up looking like an honest-to-gosh suspect.

That was purposeful on Viv's part.

"You're just mad because my dad beat yours for mayor —and I beat you out for a Pacemaker last year," I grumbled. "You can't get over that stuff—or anything else. You drown in the past like you're freakin' Kenny Kaluka in Lake Wallen-paupack."

Viv rolled her eyes. "Oh, please! Not *that* again! Who even *thinks* about that?"

You do, you grudge-carrying witch.

All at once, I recalled Viv's conversation with Mike outside the theater. The one that had made me wonder whether she knew something about Mr. Killdare's death.

Maybe YOU should be interrogated.

"This should've been my story," I said, watching her closely. Suspiciously. Then I tried to appeal to Mr. Sokowski, but he averted his eyes, like a man who didn't want anything he said to be repeated during a lawsuit, so I addressed Viv again. "I found the body."

Viv seemed confused by what I thought was practically Aristotelian logic. *I discovered the corpse, ergo the story is mine. Ipso facto. Corpus delecti. Agnus dei. Forever and ever, amen.* But Viv obviously hadn't studied Greek philosophy. Or maybe she had discovered a small flaw in my reasoning, because she cocked her head and noted, "So . . . Where's your article, Mil-lie? Hmm?"

"I didn't know you were doing a special edition—behind

my back," I pointed out. "I thought I had all week to file a story." We usually went to press on Fridays, so the paper came out on Monday morning. "I thought—"

"You obviously didn't think at all," Viv countered, without drawing any comment from the adults in the room. It seemed as if Principal Woolsey and Mr. Sokowski had faded —or maybe crawled—away, leaving me and Vivienne to settle a score that dated back to that elementary school costume contest. "Why didn't you ask if we planned a special edition, given how big this story is? Huh?"

All right. Maybe she had a point. I felt myself deflating a little, like a balloon animal a few hours after a carnival. Viv must've sensed my uncertainty and she pounced, adding, "Since you dropped the ball, I am going to cover this story exclusively, Millie. Every development." She smiled—unsweetly. "But don't feel bad. I'll let you interview me when *I* win a Pacemaker this spring. And for *real* journalism."

I tried to object.

"But—"

Mr. Woolsey finally interrupted, if only to suggest, "Are we certain that we need to get the school paper overly involved? The local media will keep everyone in the community abreast of developments, while the grief counselors suggest not dwelling on the horrific details."

For the first time ever, Viv and I seemed to be on the same wavelength. We both shared looks, like, *Grief counselors? For a man who wasn't even missed for a week?*

Then I quickly returned my attention to Mr. Woolsey —gladly ending that moment—to find him adjusting his tie with pale, almost feminine fingers. "Perhaps," he concluded, "for the good of student and faculty morale, it's best left . . . underemphasized."

I could've sworn he'd been very close to saying "forgotten," and I studied our principal more closely, wondering why he might want the story swept under the proverbial rug—and recalling, yet again, that list of suspects I'd made.

Mr. Woolsey's life was going to be a lot easier with Mr. Killdare out of his gym and off the football field. Especially since my even-tempered, sensible father had already taken over as head coach. But surely a guy named Bertram B. Woolsey, whose hands looked unfit for wielding crochet needles, let alone bludgeoning . . . Surely *he* couldn't have summoned the mental or physical strength to . . .

Right?

Then a girl who I did think had the capacity to kill gave Mr. Woolsey a dose of reality. "This is the biggest story in the school's history—discounting, of course, the fact that the place gives people cancer—"

"Hey!"

Viv spoke over my protest. "There's no way the *Gazette* —meaning *I*—am going to downplay it." Then she turned on her high heel and walked out of the room. But apparently she wasn't quite done with me yet. Apparently there were certain things that even Vivienne Fitch wouldn't say in front of a teacher and an administrator, and I found her waiting for me when I left a few moments later, after stopping to grab a handful of Werther's Originals from a bowl on Mr. Woolsey's desk.

"What do you want now?" I demanded, rounding a corner to discover Viv lurking there, like a very aptly named booby trap. "What?"

"Just in case I wasn't clear, back in Mr. Woolsey's office," she informed me. "Your streak of dumb—and I mean really dumb—luck is over, Ostermeyer. I am going to win a *real* Pacemaker—the one for investigative reporting, not lame, weepy features. And in the process, I plan to make sure that your dad doesn't walk away from this, if he's involved—as I suspect. Not like how he got off scot free for building a death trap of a school."

For a moment, I couldn't speak. And not just because I had a mouth full of candy, which I spat into my hand so she'd hear me very clearly when I advised her, in a growl, "You have just declared *war*, Vivienne Fitch. And you will be *incredibly sorry* you just said that about my father."

She didn't seem scared. She just smiled in her superior, evil way, then stalked off again, while I watched her with narrowed eyes, certain that she was underestimating me.

I *wasn't* the most ambitious student. I didn't join clubs or worry unduly about grades. I definitely wasn't Ivy League bound like Viv. Instead I planned to backpack around the world after high school. Or maybe take a nice nap.

But I really, really didn't like it when my family—or what was left of it—got attacked. My dad and I didn't have the greatest relationship. I was pretty sure some days he thought I was too much like Mom, and therefore painful to even look at. Other times, I knew I drove him nuts just by being . . . me.

And I didn't get my father, either. Didn't get why he was so into "playing by the book." But Dad was mine to complain about. And I was the only one who could accuse him of *anything*.

Standing in the hallway, I popped my candy back into my mouth, crossed my arms, and continued to watch Viv, thinking, *We'll see who controls this story, Vivienne Fitch.*

I also kind of wondered if my archrival, who knew my propensity for accidentally one-upping her, might just want to keep me from investigating because she was afraid I'd dig up some dirt on her.

Then, although school wasn't exactly over, I went to my locker and grabbed my backpack because I had someplace to go—and someone to consult about how to solve a murder.

Chapter 10

M illie, these are unusual choices for someone even with your eclectic tastes," Ms. Isabel Parkins observed, swiping her library checkout laser gun over the bar codes inside *How to Solve a Murder: The Forensic Handbook* and *Do-It-Yourself Detective*. "I can only assume this sudden interest in detection has something to do with you finding Mr. Killdare's body."

"Yes," I said, placing *Inside the Mind of a Psychopath* and *The Psycho Killer Next Door* on the counter, too. "It might also have something to do with besting Vivienne Fitch."

I could tell that my librarian-slash-confidante was intrigued. Her dark eyebrows arched over her funky, retro cat-eye glasses as she swiped two books I should've read years ago, to better understand my enemy. Even if Viv hadn't killed anyone, she was definitely, at the very least, borderline psychotic. Ms. Parkins slid the books back to me, noting, "Don't tell me you two are in a race to solve a murder!"

"Something like that," I said, holding back five books that I was suddenly a little embarrassed to be borrowing. "Viv wants to write every story about Mr. Killdare's murder for the school paper—and, by the way, pin the whole thing on my dad."

Over the years, I'd blurted out a lot of surprising things to Ms. Parkins, from my plan, at age ten, to walk a tightrope I'd strung between my second-story bedroom window and an oak tree in my backyard to my confession that I was starting to grow hair in unusual places. Inevitably, she responded with a book recommendation, be it a biography of the Wallenda family, which had probably saved me a broken leg by convincing me that I didn't know squat about "tension" and "slack," or the classic *What's Happening to Me? A Guide to Puberty,* which had spared me a talk with my father that would've been more painful than shattered limbs. Never once, though, had she looked startled the way she did when I mentioned my dad being connected to a murder.

That's odd.

Or maybe I was imagining things, because she quickly recovered and said, "I'm sure that even Vivienne"—Ms. Parkins was well versed on Viv's capabilities, as she was a subject of frequent discussion—"can't really cause trouble for your father. Especially since the *Gazette,* while definitely a quality paper, is the voice of a high school, not the whole community."

"Oh, don't underestimate Viv—or the reach of the *Gazette,*" I said. "The print version might only be read by a bunch of students and teachers. But the online edition gets about thirty thousand hits a week during football season." I shrugged, not getting the whole fascination with football, but explaining, "You know how Stingers fans are. They can't get enough of the team, even after they move away from Honeywell. We get comments and e-mail from people in, like, Sri Lanka who still follow the Stingers."

"Yes," Ms. Parkins said quietly. "Football is king around here, for better or for worse . . ."

She seemed to drift off, biting her bright-pink lower lip. She was one of those women who could successfully wear fuchsia lipstick, a lime-green cardigan, and three cocktail rings, each with a huge faux jewel. If I'd worn that outfit, *I* would've been judged psychotic and probably carted away. But Ms. Parkins could carry it off.

"Umm . . . Ms. Parkins?" I finally said, to bring her back from what was obviously a mental vacation from the library. And not a relaxing one, judging from the look on her face. "Are you okay?"

"Yes . . . Yes," she reassured me, pulling herself together and smiling. "And I'm sure your father will be fine."

"Yeah, sure," I agreed, not certain why we were talking about Dad again. Then, because I needed to get going, I placed the books I'd been withholding on the counter, trying not to seem embarrassed. "This is all for today, I guess."

It was to Ms. Parkins's credit that she didn't mock me. "Classic Nancy Drew!" she said, with genuine appreciation in her voice. "Now, *she'll* teach you how to solve a mystery."

I told Ms. Parkins a lot of stuff, but I didn't tell her that I wasn't really checking out a bunch of dated, corny books about a teen sleuth to learn how to solve a crime. I had a deeper, secret reason for wanting to revisit those old novels. A motive that I'd never confide to anybody because it was something I'd shared only with my mom.

Chapter 11

While he or she may be socially adept, the true psychopath has no genuine concern for the welfare of strangers, friends or family."

"Jeez," I muttered out loud, tossing aside *The Psycho Killer Next Door* after reading only five paragraphs. The author had already described Vivienne Fitch to a "t," so why bother with the remaining three hundred pages?

Then I fumbled blindly around on my bed for my Double Deluxe, extra Bungee sauce, from my favorite restaurant, Bungee Burger, while I used the other hand to grab *Do-It-Yourself Detective*. Opening to a random page, I took a bite of my sandwich and read, *"Methodical legwork is still the best way to solve a crime."*

Unfortunately, I wasn't a methodical person—wasn't even reading the book in order—and I ditched the detecting guide on the floor, too, in favor of *The Hidden Staircase*, the first Nancy Drew I'd read with my mother, when she'd gotten sick. That had been our thing. Curling up together and me reading the stories to her.

I hadn't thought about those books much since her death
— until I'd decided to dabble in "sleuthing" myself and impulsively grabbed a bunch at the library, thinking it might be
fun to refresh my memory about how a teenager went about
solving a crime. But as I held that old novel by its iconic yellow spine, all of a sudden I lost my appetite.

Everything about this book reminds me of Mom.

Forcing myself to choke down what felt like a hunk of
lead on my tongue, I pushed away my dinner and set *The Hidden Staircase* on my messy desk, next to my cell phone.

*I guess I'll have to do this my way, without help from experts
— or Nancy Drew.*

I didn't really have a plan, but I found myself picking up
my phone and, on impulse — maybe because I felt restless and
claustrophobic in my room — texting Laura and Ryan:

Meet me corner Arch & Maple in 15.

Then, while I waited for their replies, I started searching
a pile of clothes on my floor for a black shirt suitable for a
break-in.

Chapter 12

Millie, you know I want you to win another one of
those Peacemaker thingies—and show up Viv,"
Laura said nervously. "But do you really think this is a good
idea? I mean, *Ryan* wouldn't do it."

"Ryan has a chem test tomorrow, or he'd be here." I kind
of fibbed because while the part about the exam was true,
he'd also texted "RU NUTS??" when I'd revealed my plan to
search Coach Killdare's house. Locating a promising dark
window on the back of Hollerin' Hank's property, I led us
in that direction, explaining, "If I'm going to solve this case,
I need to understand Mr. Killdare. See how he lived, who he
was." I could tell she wasn't convinced, so I added, "It's in all
the detecting how-to books."

Well, it probably was.

"Millie?" Laura grabbed my arm, stopping me. "You don't
really think Viv and Mike could've, you know . . ."

After swearing Laura to secrecy—because even if I didn't
like Viv or Mike, I didn't want to spread unfounded, hideous

rumors about them—I'd filled my best friend in on the conversation I'd overheard at the theater. "I honestly don't know," I said. "But I can't just sit around while Viv either steals the biggest story of the decade from me or gets away with murder—or both." I resumed leading us across the yard. "I need to start investigating."

Laura trotted behind me. "Why don't we just Google Mr. Killdare?"

Okay, maybe I *had* skipped a logical step or two. "We'll do that later, of course," I said, like that had been my plan all along. "But first I need to see the milieu of his life."

"The *mildew* of his life?" Laura cried. "I don't want to see that! How would *that* help?"

"No offense, but if you're worried about getting caught, you should lower your voice," I suggested, pressing my shoulder against the window I'd selected. "And why didn't you wear black, like I told you to? Did you really have to promote breast cancer awareness *tonight?*" Inexplicably, Laura was wearing a pink T-shirt to a felony. "You know I'm committed to curing every kind of cancer, but seriously . . . tonight?"

"I didn't really think we'd do this!" She sounded close to panicked as I gave the window a shove—and it rose a few inches, like I'd expected. Nobody in Honeywell locked windows during the warm months. "I thought you'd chicken out. You don't generally do things that require moving around, or even standing up, you know. I see you in gym class!"

"Well, that's all changing." I rammed my shoulder against the old wooden frame again. Just a few more inches, and

I'd be able to push Laura—who was even smaller than me —through the gap. "You are in the presence of a new Millicent . . ."

I'd intended to say my full name—Millicent Marie Ostermeyer—but all at once, the window yielded about six inches, so I nearly lost my footing on the slippery grass, and the next thing I knew . . .

We could actually *get in.*

Chapter **13**

Y ou don't think there's a body in here, too, do you?" Laura asked, sounding even more worried than before. "It really smells in here!"

At least, I thought she sounded worried. It was difficult to hear her, since her head was in Coach Killdare's kitchen and her butt was facing me.

"I doubt Mr. Killdare was much for potpourri," I pointed out, although I had to admit that I was also a little put off by the strange stink coming out of our teacher's house. An odor that was definitely not the stench of death, yet somehow familiar. "Just wriggle in," I urged. "Then unlock the door, okay?"

Laura continued to delay. "I don't understand why you get to just walk in, while I have to do this . . ."

She was starting to complain, but was cut short as she dropped all the way into the kitchen, hitting the floor with a thud. At which point she screamed at the top of her lungs, then cried, way too loudly for a covert operation, "Millie . . . Something is *licking me!*"

Chapter **14**

I t's creepy in here," Laura whined, sticking too close to me in the dark kitchen. She looked down at her feet, where a long shadow loomed. "And that *thing* keeps following us."

"I knew I recognized that stench," I said, bending down to pet the ugliest basset hound I'd ever seen. It was so hideous that it crossed the line into being *awesome,* and I wanted to take it home, name it something like Chumley, feed it Slim Jims, and make it my permanent trademark sidekick who went with me everywhere. I rumpled Chum's already wrinkled head. "My Aunt Inez had a dog just like you, and her house always stank, too." I realized that was insulting and added, "Don't feel bad. It's not your fault. It's a hound thing."

"Can we get on with this?" Laura urged. "Before we get caught?"

"Yeah, yeah, okay." I started to move around the room, appraising everything with the beam of a flashlight I'd actually had the foresight to bring.

"What are we even looking for?" Laura asked. "And don't say mildew. Or clues."

Darn it. I had been about to utter that second word, because I still wasn't sure what I'd expected to find in Mr. Killdare's house.

Certainly not the greatest dog ever . . . Yes, you are, Chumley!
Yes, you are!

"Will you leave that smelly mutt alone?" Laura begged as I
tugged a pair of wonderfully droopy ears. "Please? Because if
I get arrested, I'm pretty sure I get kicked out of Key Club."

"Oh, fine." I again swept the light around the kitchen,
which was surprisingly tidy for a bachelor's place. In fact, it
was almost *un-bachelor-y.* I held the beam on a wall clock. *A*
guy like Mr. Killdare—a blustery, nonwhimsical football coach—
bought a clock shaped like a chicken? Really? Then I continued to
move the light around the room, noting a matching poultry-
themed key holder by the door, with all but one peg filled,
as if Mr. Killdare had been organized, in spite of his sloppy
appearance. And finally . . .

Jackpot. Well, maybe.

"You check the refrigerator," I suggested, moving to the
kitchen table, which was covered with envelopes, magazines,
and the freebie shopper paper that nobody wanted but everybody got anyway, twice a week.

All at once, looking at that pile, I realized that something
seemed . . . off.

I walked by Mr. Killdare's house all the time on my way to
the theater, and I hadn't noticed mail piling up on his porch
while he'd been missing. And he apparently got a ton of stuff,
including big items, like *Sports Illustrated* and . . . I shuffled
through the magazines. Ugh. Something called *XXtreme Sports,*

which featured a woman in a football jersey that didn't exactly fit her right. Meaning it was about seven sizes too small.

Trying to pretend I hadn't seen that, I looked down at Chumley, who was staring up at me expectantly and wagging his tail, like he hoped for a snack. But he obviously wasn't starving, even two weeks after Mr. Killdare's death. Nor was the floor covered in pee and poop.

What's not adding up here?

I was starting to think I might be onto something important when Laura broke my concentration with an inane observation that really made me wish I'd come alone. "Hey, it looks like Mr. Killdare ate a lot of Buffalo wings—and pickles. He's got kosher dill and two jars of sweet gherkins."

I turned to find Laura bathed in the dim glow of the refrigerator. "I don't know if the gherkins are really crucial."

"You're the one who told me to check the fridge." She closed the door, adding, "There's a picture of Mr. Killdare here, too. Under a magnet advertising Willie's Wing Hut."

I shone the flashlight across the room and saw Coach Killdare scowling at me, as if he wasn't exactly enjoying his time—apparently alone—in a place that looked like Florida. Sunny and beachy. Or maybe it was the palm trees on his shirt that made me think the setting was tropical. "I don't really see it as a clue," I said. "No more than the pickles."

Laura crossed her arms defensively. "Well, I don't see you doing any stellar detecting!"

"Actually, I was thinking about how Mr. Killdare's house is clean and the dog is fed." She gave me a dubious look, so I reached for some envelopes. "I'm checking the mail, too."

Training the light on a bunch of return addresses, I read a
few.

Doctor's office. Hospital. Doctor's office.

"Jeez, for a guy who was always yelling at me about 'developing some muscle tone,' Mr. Killdare went to the doctor a
lot," I mused. For the first time, I became aware of the para-
dox—or hypocrisy—of a gluttonous coach. "I wonder if *he*
could've run a lap!"

"Millie . . . maybe that really is important." Laura came
over to the table and picked up an envelope with the return
address "Cavenaugh-Beecham Clinic." "Maybe he was sick."
I saw, even in the dark, that she had an idea brewing. "Maybe
he knew he was dying and killed himself—like Hemingway.
He *was* a 'man's man,' like Hemingway."

I appreciated that literary-themed theory, but shook my
head, trying to get Laura to focus. "Nah . . . Mr. Killdare was
sitting on a lawn tractor with *his skull caved in.*" I made an
awkward motion with the flashlight, miming hitting the back
of my head. "I don't think so."

"Yeah, I guess you're right." Laura seemed crestfallen.
"But I do think there might be something to all the medical
bills—or appointment reminders . . . Whatever's in these envelopes. They strike me as sort of strange."

She was right, and I felt bad for wishing I hadn't brought
her along. Laura Bugbee might've been a goody two-shoes
who didn't like creeping through windows or—I glanced
down at Chumley—the planet's most incredible dog, but she
was also insightful. "If you really think these might be valu-
able, I'll check them out," I said, swiping some letters and

stuffing them into the back pocket of my *suitable-for-a-crime* dark-wash jeans. "Later. At home."

"What?" Laura grabbed my wrist. "You can't take stuff. That wasn't part of the deal!"

"Nobody's collecting on Mr. Killdare's medical bills or expecting him to keep an appointment," I reminded her. "He's dead. And dead men don't pay bills—or go to doctors."

Actually, I wasn't sure about the payment part. But Mr. Killdare definitely couldn't get in trouble for falling behind on some debts. What would they do? Put him in prison?

"The police probably want everything left just the way it was," Laura said, pointing out something I hadn't thought about. "This might all be evidence."

Well, it was disturbed evidence at that point, and I couldn't undisturb it. Besides, the police had probably come and gone already. *But they wouldn't clean up piles of dog poop, even if they'd found that. Meanwhile, somebody was collecting Mr. Killdare's mail before most of us even knew he was dead, because there was never anything on his porch. So who's been taking care of the place? A housekeeper—or someone else?*

I was about to mention that something about the mail situation and Chumley's being fat, happy, and relatively clean seemed weird to me when I realized that Laura was staring at the table.

Following her gaze, I saw it, too.

Then Laura and I looked at each other and said, simultaneously and with no small measure of surprise, "You don't think Mr. Killdare *had a friend*, do you?"

Chapter 15

It was just a postcard—a flimsy piece of cardboard with a foreign stamp and a pretty picture of a town called Lucerne, in Switzerland—but it was almost heartbreaking to find it among all the other impersonal mail on Coach Killdare's kitchen table.

"This makes him seem almost . . . human," Laura said softly. "Somebody actually thought about him while they were on vacation."

"Yeah, really . . ." I kept turning the card back and forth, not sure whether I should read the message. Breaking and entering was invasive. And stealing mail, like I was doing, might technically be a federal offense. But something about reading a very personal, if small, note was finally making me feel surprisingly squeamish and guilty.

Mr. Killdare wasn't just a mean, loud ogre. Somebody cared about him.

Then again, I'd heard that most murders were committed by people who supposedly loved one another, and given that the pool of individuals who'd been fond of Mr. Killdare was pretty small, it seemed foolish to overlook what might be genuinely important information.

Making my decision, I read out loud: "Having a great time but missing you. Love, BeeBee." I glanced at Laura, not sure why I'd hesitated. "Not very original, huh?"

But my co-investigator had her eyebrows in a knot. "Who the heck is BeeBee? What kind of name is *that?*" She frowned. "Do you think it's a nod to Mr. Killdare coaching the Stingers? Like, she'd call him Big Stinger, and she was his little BeeBee?"

Just the thought of that triggered my gag reflex, and I forced the image of Mr. Killdare getting "cutesy" out of my brain. "I don't know about the pet-name thing—in fact, hope to never think about it again," I said. "But I agree that it's definitely a woman's name. And the writing looks girlish to me." Moreover, the script looked somehow familiar. I couldn't place it, though, and added, "Anyway, since there's no return address, it's impossible to tell who she is."

"Not unless she's recently called Mr. Killdare, too," Laura noted, so we both turned toward a phone hanging on the wall. But the message light wasn't blinking, which might've been yet another indication that Coach Killdare had been phenomenally unpopular—or, equally likely, that Detective Blaine Lohser had gotten to any messages first.

Was there anything from my dad on there? One of his disgruntled calls?

Then Laura raised another possibility. "Nobody uses a landline. His messages are probably on his cell."

I swept the counter with the light. "I wonder if that's around here."

"I'm sure the police have it," Laura reasoned. "It was probably on him when he got murdered."

When Laura said that word — "murdered" — we met each other's eyes in the dark kitchen, both of us creeped out. "We should get moving," she urged.

"Yeah." Ignoring another look of disapproval, I crammed the postcard into my pocket, because I really wanted to study that writing when I had more time. "We'll check the rest of the house fast," I promised. "But first . . ." I bent down and shook Chumley, who'd dozed off. He grunted awake in a way that I was going to find endlessly endearing when he slept at the foot of my bed. "I want to give Chum a snack."

Laura seemed confused. "Chum?"

"Yeah, Chumley." I began to hunt among the low cabinets, assuming that's where you'd keep pet food, while the dog followed me, his toenails clicking on the linoleum floor and his tongue lolling out. "That's his name."

"According to . . . ?"

"Me. Who is going to adopt him." Locating the correct cabinet, I hauled out a big bag. "He's going to need a new home."

It was Laura's turn to make me think straight. "Your father will never let you have a dog, Millie. Especially one that reeks and that you'll dump on him as soon as you graduate and head to Europe."

I paused, sack in my arms. *Yeah, what was I thinking?*

And what had I been thinking, breaking into a brutally murdered teacher's house, because all at once we heard a car pull into the driveway, a slamming door, and footsteps on the porch, all of which happened before we even seemed able to react. The most I could do was drop the bag, so discount kibble scattered everywhere, then fumble to turn off the flashlight as a key was turned in the lock. Grabbing Laura's arm, I dragged my wide-eyed, panicked friend deeper into the house, both of us whispering in terrified, hushed tones a name that had at first sounded anything but ominous—until she'd come to kill us, in cold blood, for investigating her heinous crime of passion.

"BeeBee!"

Chapter 16

Laura and I were on all fours, hiding in Coach Killdare's den—there was a La-Z-Boy, a big-screen TV, and a hideous plaid couch, so I guessed that constituted a den—and breathing way too hard for people desperate to go unnoticed.

Fortunately, whoever had entered the kitchen was making a fair amount of noise, too, first tossing what must've been that day's mail onto the table, then calling *my* dog by the wrong name, scolding him mildly. "Baxter . . . How did you get the food out?" I heard happy whining and the thump of a hand against a dog's substantial side, along with, "You are a real glutton, mutt." There was a pause, then "Wow . . . And I have got to give you a bath *tonight.*"

I didn't want to get caught, but I couldn't help turning on the flashlight and pointing it up between me and Laura's faces, so we could see each other's confused, surprised expressions as we both mouthed silently, "Chase Albright?"

Chapter **17**

E asy there, Bax," Chase said, sweeping up the dog food
I'd spilled and dumping it into a bowl.

At least, that's how it sounded from where Laura and
I were still crouched, only half hidden by the recliner and
a small bookcase. Shifting my weight, I bumped into the
shelves and nearly knocked over a replica of London's Big
Ben clock and a plaster Leaning Tower of Pisa.

"Shoot!" I muttered, earning a wide-eyed "shushing" look
from Laura.

But Chase was still oblivious, telling the snuffling dog,
"Slow down. Chew!"

I knew Laura and I should start backing toward the front
door, which I could see over my shoulder, through a small
foyer. But something kept me there, on all fours. A question
I'd asked about a year before and that was actually getting
harder to answer:

Who are *you, Chase Albright?*

As Chase moved around the kitchen, finally turning on

a light, so Laura and I jumped, I ran down the few things I knew for certain about him.

Quarterback. Semifluent speaker of French. Fan of pretentious, gloomy movies. And now . . . Dog watcher for dead coaches?

"Let's get out of here," Laura whispered, when it sounded like Chase sat down on the floor to keep Chumley . . . er, *Baxter* company while he ate.

But I still didn't move. I was listening to Chase talk to the dog again, more softly and with obvious affection. "Sorry you're stuck here alone, buddy. Maybe somebody'll come claim you soon?"

For a second, I forgot about how Dad would object and got excited, thinking I might actually have a shot at adopting Baxter. Then I started wondering how long Chase had been dog sitting—and bringing in the mail. Was there a chance he'd known about Hollerin' Hank's demise before the rest of us? Maybe even *played a part* in the crime?

No. That's even more far-fetched than thinking Viv and Mike might be guilty.

And yet, shouldn't Chase have been more eager to talk with Detective Lohser? At least admitted that he had a key to the victim's house?

Yes. But he'd acted as if he'd barely known Mr. Killdare—

Chase's voice broke into my thoughts again. "That's enough food." It sounded like he was standing up. "Let's go upstairs and clean you up."

I glanced at the staircase—too close to us—and nudged Laura. "Come on. Let's go before he comes in here."

She nodded, clearly eager to bolt. "Yeah."

We started backtracking, then, like demented toddlers on our hands and knees. It seemed impossible that Chase wouldn't hear us. But once we got going, there was no turning back.

Fortunately for us, Baxter did not want a bath. There was a pretty big struggle going on in the kitchen as a football player wrestled a dog that had to weigh at least eighty pounds.

"Settle down," I heard Chase urge just as I turned and scrambled the last few feet to the door. Laura was hot on my heels, her frantic breath hitting my neck while I fumbled with the knob. Then we thudded across the porch and tore into the night.

I looked back only once, but I was pretty sure I saw a shadowy figure on the porch, watching us sprint away.

"You . . . think . . . he . . . saw us?" Laura panted when we finally slowed down after about four blocks.

It was the farthest I'd run in years, so I could barely talk, either. I bent over and clutched my side. "Jeez . . . What . . . do . . . you . . . think, Miss . . . Pink Shirt?"

We got quiet then, except for some wheezing, until we were within sight of my house, at which point Laura asked something that I'd been musing on, too. "Why didn't we just admit to being there?" She could speak normally by then, while I was still struggling a little. "Chase is just a kid, like us. I don't think he would've called the police or anything." She sounded sort of disappointed. "Maybe we could've hung out even."

"I don't think Chase hangs out with anybody—except my dog," I reminded her, forcing myself to talk as if my breath was coming easily, too. "And *something* told us both to hide. Some instinct we were probably smart to follow."

Because Chase might be keeping some big secrets?

Laura seemed to consider that, and we stopped talking again, me distracted by other thoughts. Memories of things I'd noticed as we'd crouched in a room cluttered with remnants of Mr. Killdare's "glory days" as a player and coach. I hadn't been able to make out details of the countless framed clippings, but many had featured images of guys in football uniforms. And there'd been a shiny plaque, too, the gist of which had been fairly clear, thanks to the moonlight streaming through the curtainless windows. I'd been able to read "Volunteer," "Appreciation," "Coaching Excellence," and "Mason Treadwell Academy."

Had there been more to Coach Killdare than I'd thought?

I ran down a mental list for my teacher, the way I'd just done with Chase, enumerating everything I knew about Hollerin' Hank.

Loud yeller. Friendless—except for the mysterious BeeBee. Former owner of world's greatest dog. Apparently, volunteer. Sticking my hand in my pocket, I checked to make sure I hadn't lost the envelopes and postcard I'd taken during what I considered an increasingly embarrassing retreat. *Man plagued by health problems? Guy with bachelor tastes—yet chicken-themed kitchen accessories . . .*

All at once, I grabbed Laura's arm, stopping us in our

tracks as I recalled one more detail from the den, which hadn't really struck me as odd until that moment.

"Do you think it's weird," I noted, "that a man who had virtually nothing you could call décor—except a bunch of guy crap, like old clippings—not only owned a clock shaped like poultry, but also had a *bookshelf full of carefully arranged European-landmark knickknacks?*"

Chapter 18

When I got home, my dad was in his favorite chair, talking quietly on the phone, so I crept up to my room, where he probably assumed I'd been all night, reading. Sitting at my desk, I shoved aside my Nancy Drew novels and drew my laptop front and center.

"You might've had a cool convertible 'roadster,'" I told Nancy, who was looking at me, wide-eyed, from the cover of *The Clue in the Crumbling Wall*. "But you didn't have the Internet." I returned my attention to the screen. "Now watch —and learn—how a twenty-first-century sleuth works."

Opening Google, I typed in "Hank Killdare"—only to discover that being unpopular enough to get murdered in real life perversely made one the toast of cyberspace. I had to scroll through about fifty links to news stories about his death before I even got to the personal stuff.

Unfortunately, none of that seemed particularly useful. Pretty much every one of the hits was related to some old football game that he'd either coached or played in.

Then, just when I was about to give up, a truncated, choppy blurb caught my attention.

Hank Killdare . . . Volunteer of the Year . . . Mason Treadwell Military Academy . . . Football . . .

I recognized the reference to the award I'd seen back in Mr. Killdare's den and clicked on the link, curious about Hollerin' Hank's connection to a school for hardcore delinquents, about fifty miles from Honeywell. I knew all about Mason Treadwell, because my dad used to threaten to send me there when I started skipping classes in favor of lurking in the public library. The prospect had genuinely worried me—until I'd learned that Treadwell accepted only boys.

Even after that, though, I'd taken note of the academy when it earned mention in the news, which happened a lot. There was always some kid defecting—and about two years before, one boy had *stabbed* a "classmate."

"Come on," I muttered, getting impatient with a little hourglass draining digital sand on my screen. "This might be big."

What if Hollerin' Hank hollered at the wrong kid when he was volunteer coaching? Namely, a DELINQUENT, STABBING KILLER who got out of Treadwell and came after him for revenge?

I wasn't going to learn anything this evening, though, because the link was obviously dead, and after a few minutes, I returned to Google and typed in "Chase Albright" just to see what might come up.

And what I found definitely intrigued me even more. Because if Coach Killdare was a prominent presence in cyberspace, it was as if the Chase Albright who went to my school didn't exist *at all*.

Chapter 19

W hat do you mean there was nothing about Chase on the *entire Internet?*" Laura whispered, as French class was starting—and the subject of our discussion was sitting less than ten feet behind us. "Everyone's somewhere in cyberspace!"

"Well, there are stories about him playing football here," I conceded, glancing over my shoulder to see that Chase had his nose buried in his textbook. *Studious suck-up! Teacher's pet!* I turned back to Laura. "But it's like he didn't exist before he came to Honeywell. All the other Chase Albrights are, like, accountants, doctors—and a preschool soccer prodigy in England."

Laura smiled archly. "Why'd you Google him, anyway?"

I knew what she was thinking—that just like every other girl at Honeywell, I was attracted to Chase. However, before I could remind her that I had legitimate reasons to check him out—*suspicions* about him and his key to Coach Killdare's house—Mademoiselle Beamish snapped at both of us in her overblown fake French accent, *"Mee-leh-CENT! Loh-RA! Tai-sez-vous!"*

I was terrible at French, and for a second I thought our somewhat burly instructor—she was an assistant wrestling coach, for crying out loud—was going to *tase us* for talking during class. Honestly, the way Laura—who could actually speak the language—jumped, it seemed possible. Then I realized she was reacting—or overreacting—the way she always did when I got her in trouble.

I must've looked pretty alarmed, too, though. Both Viv and Mike were cracking up at me, even though I doubted Mike had understood our teacher, either.

I started to stick out my tongue at them, then judged that to be too childish even for me, who was wearing a Snoopy T-shirt that day, and faced forward as Ms. Beamish said, *"Choisissez un partenaire et discuter de ce que vous voulez."*

Needless to say, I didn't understand *that* long diatribe until Laura suggested, "I guess we'll partner up to talk, huh?"

I wanted to do our semiweekly "free form" dialogue with my best friend, but all at once, I had an idea and turned slowly in my seat, thinking, *If I want answers about Chase Albright, why don't I just ask him questions?*

Unfortunately, Ms. Beamish, as usual, had similar designs on her star pupil.

Chapter 20

*E*xcusez-moi? Mademoiselle?"

"*Oui?*" Ms. Beamish was just about to sit down with Chase, with whom she always "dialogued" because we had an odd number of students in class—and everyone else had *friends*—when she stopped her derriere in mid-descent, looking confused. "*Que voulez-vous, Mee-leh-CENT?*"

"*Je* would like to *parler avec* Chase, if *vous* don't mind," I requested.

Ms. Beamish's square jaw dropped, and I wondered again if she didn't harbor a small, sick crush on Chase, who was watching me and his teacher debate over him with his usual cool detachment, as if he didn't care who the heck he *parler-*ed with.

"*Avons-nous un nombre pair d'etudiants aujourd'hui?*" Mademoiselle asked. She looked past me, appearing to do a head count, so I figured she was asking if we had an even number of students that day.

"*Non,*" I informed her. Then, although I knew Laura was going to hate me, I said, "*LOH-ra* needs a partner. *Mais* I think

I would benefit from *travailler avec* Chase, *parce qu'il est* the best student in class."

I glanced at Chase again, and saw, for the first time ever, this tiny, tiny hint of laughter in his eyes. Then I addressed Ms. Beamish again. *"S'il vous plait?"*

There was basically no way she could argue that I needed help, and Ms. Beamish, with *très, très* obvious reluctance, yielded. *"D'accord. Mets-toi avec Chase."*

"Gracias," I said, watching her thread her blocky body through the desks, toward Laura, who mouthed, in very plain English, "I will kill you later."

Then I slid into the desk next to Chase's, so we were really face-to-face—without a thick pane of ticket-window glass between us—for the first time ever. Well, not counting the time I messed up his shoes. And the first thing he said to me . . . It didn't exactly get us off on the right foot.

Chapter **21**

"I f you don't mind, I'm going to keep my feet under my
desk," Chase informed me, without so much as a *bonjour.*

"I told you I was sorry about that," I reminded him.

He seemed skeptical. *"Non, au contraire, tu ne me l'as pas
dit."*

I was pretty sure he'd just disagreed, but I didn't want to
argue with him. Especially since, now that I thought about it,
I wasn't sure I *had* apologized. "Look." I leaned forward and
spoke more quietly. "I don't really speak French—"

"I figured that out when you said '*gracias*,'" Chase interrupted.

I ignored the dig. "And I'm not particularly interested in
learning how." I really thought the school should offer Man-
darin, if anything, and had started learning a few characters
on my own, in my spare time. "I actually wanted to talk with
you about Coach Killdare—"

"Whose house you broke into," Chase cut in again, so
suddenly *I* was under scrutiny. I'd sort of forgotten that he

probably knew that. He cocked his head, a swoop of flawless hair falling over his forehead. "Why? What were you doing there?"

I felt my face getting red. Still, I managed to ask, with reasonable composure, "If somebody broke into his house—and I'm not saying anyone did—what would make you think it was me?"

"Your hair is distinctive, even in the dark," he pointed out. "And I heard you and your partner squealing each other's names when you ran away."

"Oh." I hadn't realized we'd done that. "That is kind of damning."

He arched his eyebrows, and for the second time in one day, I saw that he was very close to smiling. "You think so?"

His amusement was, of course, at my expense, but it served to ease some of the tension between us—tension that I couldn't explain—and I confessed, with a quick peek over my shoulder, to make sure Viv didn't overhear, "I'm investigating Coach Killdare's murder for the school paper. That's why I broke in—and why I wanted to talk with you. You must've known him pretty well, if you watch his dog."

That brief, tentative connection we'd made broke as quickly as it had formed, and he seemed to get incredibly guarded. Still, I forged ahead. "Is there anything you can tell me? Anything you've noticed when you were with Mr. Killdare on the football field, or when you take care of Chumley?"

He seemed confused. "Who is Chumley?"

"Baxter," I corrected myself, feeling my cheeks get warm again. "I kind of named him."

Chase didn't respond—except to give me a weird look—so I added, "Seriously, is there anything you can share? Especially about a woman named BeeBee? Or Mr. Killdare's health?"

"No."

The answer wasn't exactly rude, but it was remarkably flat, leaving no room for follow-up, and so we found ourselves staring at each other as if neither one of us knew what to say in any language. Or maybe we were finally really sizing each other up, something we didn't have time to do in the few seconds it took to transact a movie-ticket sale.

Was it weird that neither of us was acknowledging that we had a tiny, preexisting relationship and saw each other on a fairly regular basis?

And what was that expression on his face right then? Was he finding me lacking in more than just French vocabulary? It seemed that way, judging from how he frowned as his gaze roved over my pale, round cheeks, my bulldog nose, and my greenish eyes.

While I . . . I was examining his straight aristocratic nose, his strong jaw, and full lower lip.

Darn it! Focus, Millie!

Getting ahold of myself, I suddenly remembered the football game I'd witnessed the previous fall in which Chase had stopped Coach Killdare from giving my father a bloody nose or black eye, and for some reason I said, "Tell me, at least, what you said to Coach Killdare, about a year ago, during the football game when he kicked Buzz. You grabbed his arm and stopped him from hitting my dad. Can you at least tell me *that*?"

"You want to know what I said *a year ago*?" Chase asked, his expression unreadable. "Seriously? And you honestly want to hear *everything* I know about Mr. Killdare?"

"Yes," I said, thinking we were finally getting somewhere. "Yes, I do."

He leaned forward, looking me straight in the eye. "Okay. Here goes."

Then Chase Albright proceeded to unburden himself — in about three straight minutes of rapid-fire French, of which I understood not a word. It was just a big blur of *"nous"* and *"vous"* and *"voulez-s,"* and it all flew totally over my head.

"Does that help?" he asked, sitting back when he was done.

"You are an *el jerko*," I informed him, standing up, even though dialogue time hadn't ended. Ms. Beamish was staring at me, clearly not happy, while I could feel my cheeks getting *angry* red. "And if *you* don't know what *that* means, it's Spanish for 'jerk.'"

Then I turned on my heel — only to feel someone grab my wrist. I wheeled around, so surprised that I didn't even pull free, but Chase quickly let go, like he realized he shouldn't have done that. But it wasn't so much the fact that he'd touched me — again — that sent me off balance. It was the expression on his face. The sincere apology that I could see clearly in his eyes.

"Je suis très désolé," he said. It was still French, but somehow not rude, like before. Maybe because he was talking softer and slower. *"Je te souhaite bonne chance, mais il ne faut pas que je sois impliqué dans cette enquête."*

I might've sucked at French, but my memory really was almost photographic, and I made a point of listening carefully to every word Chase said, locking each one away in my brain. And when I finally got a chance to translate later that night, I got even more interested in the mystery of Mr. Killdare's death—and, I had to admit, more intrigued by an *el jerko* who, it seemed, had both wished me luck with my investigation and advised me that he couldn't be "implicated."

Wasn't that a word people used when they'd done something *bad?*

Chapter **22**

I thought you were investigating Coach Killdare's murder," Ryan noted as he did me the favor of driving me to my shift at the theater in his beat-up Honda. "For the paper. Or to make Viv crazy. Or maybe because you're just morbidly and relentlessly curious."

"I am all of the above," I said, a little confused given that I'd been bending his ear about that very topic for the last ten minutes.

"Then why do you keep talking about *Chase?*"

I nearly broke my neck, I swiveled my head so fast. "What?"

"You say you're looking into Mr. Killdare's death—but you keep bringing up Chase," he repeated.

"In a negative way!" I reminded him. "Because Chase knows stuff he's not telling!"

Ryan turned the corner onto Market Street and parked in front of the Lassiter Bijou. Shifting to face me, he said gently, "Millie . . . I, of all people, know what it's like to be into guys who are out of reach, living here, where almost nobody else is gay, or out, at least."

That reminder didn't exactly catch me off-guard—of course, everyone knew Ryan was gay—but I sometimes forgot his orientation. He certainly didn't act the way most movies and TV shows would lead one to expect. For one thing, he loved sports—the more violent, the better—and I was pretty sure he couldn't hum a Broadway show tune to save his life. Moreover, Ry sucked at fashion, maybe worse than I did, and had a whole wardrobe built upon a foundation of Faded Glory T-shirts from Walmart.

"I think you'd be smart not to get too interested in Chase," he continued, ignoring the way I was opening my mouth to protest. "He doesn't talk about himself much. Well, almost never. But he did mention having a girlfriend, once. And it sounded serious."

"How did *that* come up?" I asked, suddenly recalling that Laura had mentioned a picture Chase kept in his locker. A photo of a girl. "If he's so private . . ."

"The guys were talking about the cheerleaders, joking that Chase could have his pick, but he shut it down pretty fast. Told them he couldn't even look because of some girl named Allison." Ryan shrugged. "I guess she's pretty jealous."

Allison . . .

I was considering that name, thinking how it sounded like it would belong to a girl with delicate features, long dark hair, and wide, wide eyes—a popular girl, but nice and well-mannered, "from a good family"—when I saw Ryan look past me, out the passenger side window. And just as I turned to see what was up, someone scared the bejeepers out of me by rapping on the window, hard, with his knuckles, and saying, loudly and rudely, "Millie Ostermeyer! Get out of the car! I'm tired of waiting for you!"

Chapter **23**

I can't—and won't—tell you anything," I informed Detective Lohser, who was standing too close to me, breathing down my neck while I fumbled to unlock the theater. I was trying to speak with authority, but my shaky fingers no doubt revealed how nervous I was. "I thought you said I didn't know anything useful, anyhow!"

"That was before we determined—almost to the minute —the time of Coach Killdare's death," he said, following me as I entered the theater and began turning on lights, both because he was creeping me out and, as usual, I was running late and needed to get ready for the seven-thirty show. "I need you to confirm your father's whereabouts on Sunday, September first, at nine p.m.," he demanded.

I moved behind the candy counter, putting that barrier between us, and powered up the popcorn machine with fingers that were still unsure—just like my voice. "Where . . . where does Dad say he was?"

"I want you to confirm, not corroborate," Detective Lohser clarified, like he thought my father and I were part of some grand conspiracy. Which he probably did believe. "So where do *you* say he was?"

I started stacking soda cups, which I'd never done before. I just needed a moment to think. He was badgering me, and I didn't want to say the wrong thing. Then I realized I *couldn't* say the wrong thing—because how the heck would I know where my father had been on a certain day weeks before? I didn't know where *I'd* been on September first. "I don't keep track of my dad's schedule," I said. "I have no idea where he was!"

Detective Lohser leaned against the counter, right over the Lemonheads, his expression more sour than the candy. "Sunday night is pretty quiet around here," he pointed out. "Most people"—he made that sound like "most *decent* people"—"spend it at home." He cocked his head, feigning confusion. "So wouldn't it have been unusual if your father was out somewhere at nine p.m.? Shouldn't you at least be able to say, with relative certainty, that he was *home?* Maybe watching *60 Minutes?*"

"Is that still on?" I asked with genuine curiosity. "Really?"

"Focus, Ms. Ostermeyer." Detective Lohser managed to say that without moving his lips. And he enunciated each word very slowly when he repeated, "Where. Was. Your. Father?"

I paused my pointless stacking exercise. Was it weird that I hardly ever knew where my dad was anymore? I didn't believe for a second that he'd commit murder. I mean, Dad felt guilty if he accidentally came home with a municipal-issue ballpoint pen in his pocket and would remind me, "Taxpayers bought that for *official use,* Millicent! It has to go back!" A guy like that, who wouldn't take a ten-cent office supply, certainly wouldn't take a *life*. But lately he was always out, and seldom told me what he was up to, sometimes seeming almost evasive.

"Well, Millicent?" Detective Lohser pressed, clearly sensing—and misunderstanding—my uncertainty. "Surely you remember something. It was just a few weeks ago!"

His practically yelling at me wasn't helping my memory, and I snapped. "I have no idea where he was!"

"Interesting." Detective Lohser's eyes glittered. "Because your father has no idea either."

What? But that wasn't possible. My dad kept a planner for his planner . . .

The badge-wielding badger on the other side of the counter obviously saw my increasing bewilderment. "You seem surprised, Millicent. As if you also think that's strange."

I wanted to be like Chase and tell him to get lost, but— maybe because I could tell that Blaine Lohser really did have it in for my father, as I'd suspected from day one—my usual disregard for authority again failed me, and I heard myself babbling, "Can't you please just leave my dad alone? He didn't hurt anybody. I can name ten other people who would've loved to see Mr. Killdare dead!"

Detective Lohser straightened, seeming intrigued. "Really? You can, now?"

"Yes," I admitted, mainly to distract him. "I made this list once . . ." I tucked some of my hair nervously behind my ear. "A list of people who might want to murder Coach Killdare."

That was definitely the wrong thing to say. Detective Lohser scowled. "What kind of twisted person makes a list like *that?*"

I knew I was still saying the wrong stuff, but I blurted, "It was just for fun!"

He leaned close again. "Does murder amuse you? Does that run in your family?"

"No!" I cried. *Calm down, Millie! He's bad copping you into oblivion!* Yet I couldn't seem to get a grip. "I just saw Mr. Kill-dare on the sidelines at a football game." I did have the presence of mind to omit the part about him fighting with my father. "And I realized that a lot of people *really* hated him."

Detective Lohser crossed his arms, challenging me. "Like who?"

Principal Woolsey. Mike Price—and his parents. The family of a kid named Roy Boyles, who'd gotten dehydrated—and disappeared. Buzz the Bee, who got kicked in the butt. Viv . . .

I could've provided all those names and more, but all at once, I pulled myself together enough to comprehend that the big *loser* across the counter was trying to con and browbeat me into doing his job for him—and make me sell out people who were most likely innocent. People who—even if I didn't like some of them—didn't deserve to be hounded, any more than my dad did. And when I got a grip, I got really angry, and, true to my sometimes overly impetuous nature, I stepped from behind the counter and got right up in his mustache, telling him, "You know, you are nothing but a bully. And I do not think harassing a teenager at her place of work is proper procedure. I should call your superiors!"

It was an idle threat—one that seemed to amuse him, more than anything—but it was enough to make someone intervene. Someone I hadn't even seen come into the theater, but who stepped between me and Detective Lohser, just as he'd stepped between Mr. Killdare and my dad a year before. And while I still didn't know what Chase had said to defuse his coach's anger, I heard him very clearly when he echoed my recent sentiments, only more calmly, telling my tormentor, "Millie's right. You are harassing her. And you should leave, now, before I really do call the cops on *you.*"

Chapter **24**

"Y ou didn't have to do that," I said gruffly. I wasn't sure if I should thank Chase for getting rid of Detective Lohser or kick him out of the lobby for the way he'd treated me in French class. "I could've handled it."

"Yeah, I'm sure you could've." Chase surprised me by concurring. "But I've dealt with guys like him before. I'm used to them."

"Guys like what?" I asked, because I thought Detective Lohser was pretty unique. "How many dweeby yet drunk-with-power men in bad suits do you know?"

But, of course, Chase wasn't going to elaborate. Those sluice gates he called eyes slammed shut again, and he changed the subject. "I came to tell you I'm sorry about speaking French to you today in class. Although I don't exactly know why I have to apologize. It *is* an upper-level course, and you should have a reasonable degree of fluency."

"Is this still part of the apology?" I asked, walking toward my ticket booth, in case *somebody* was waiting to watch a silent comedy called *The Gold Rush*. "And if you're going to stay for the movie," I added over my shoulder, "you need to buy a ticket."

"No, I'm not interested in Chaplin," he informed me.

I turned to face him. "What? Afraid you might laugh?"

It was a joke—admittedly sarcastic—but Chase didn't crack a smile. "I just like dramas."

"Yeah, I've noted your grim tastes."

He arched his eyebrows. "Really?"

"Don't get all full of yourself," I advised him. He was looking at me like I was a stalker. "This theater only has, like, six customers. I can predict who will show up for any film." Then I turned my back on him and started to climb into my monkey cage, because I had tickets—probably four—to sell.

"Millie . . ."

The tone of Chase's voice stopped me, and I turned around again. "What?"

"I really am sorry that I was rude to you," he repeated, seeming more sincere. "I just don't like people prying into my life."

That seemed to be the understatement of the year. "I wasn't prying into your life," I reminded him. "I'm interested in Coach Killdare."

Chase shifted on his feet, appearing uncomfortable. "Yeah, well . . . Just remember that I'm not part of whatever happened to him. I want justice for his murder, too, for reasons you can't understand." His lightly tanned face got the slightest bit pale. "But anything you run across, related to me, as you snoop around . . . Just leave it alone, okay?"

The great Chase Albright, big-shot football player and

shunner of all attempts at friendship by lowly Honeywellians, was asking me for a favor. Actually humbling himself before me. And intriguing the heck out of me, too, so all I could do was look him square in the eyes and say, "We'll see. I guess that depends on what I find, doesn't it?"

He obviously had something on the line, but he didn't beg or grovel more for the protection of his privacy, which I sort of respected. "Just remember that you want to write about Coach Killdare, Millie," he said again evenly. "Not me. My life is not a story that you, or anyone else, needs to read."

I wasn't so certain about that. Or, at the very least, if nobody *needed* to read the tale of Chase Albright, I was pretty sure that a lot of people—especially girls at my school— would *kill* to dive into that mysterious narrative.

I didn't tell him that, though. I just crawled into my booth, and Chase left without another word.

Watching him cross the street to his car, I started to get this strange feeling in the pit of my stomach. It was still hard for me to imagine a teenager getting mixed up in murder, and yet this small part of me couldn't help wondering if *Chase* would kill to protect whatever secrets he harbored.

After all, somebody in Honeywell—somebody strong enough to bash in a skull, and who was familiar with the football stadium—had committed murder for some reason. And secrets deep enough to compel a guy to beg me for protection might, I reasoned, provide a pretty big motive if a certain coach had discovered, and threatened to spill, them.

As Chase opened the door of his expensive BMW, I also

wondered why a guy whose family provided him with *that* would do odd jobs for Mr. Killdare.

Maybe because Mr. Killdare had been *blackmailing* him? Holding Chase's secrets over his head, in exchange for watching his house and dog sitting?

Then I pictured a chicken-themed key holder by Mr. Killdare's door, too. One with a single empty peg.

Chase also had access to all his coach's keys. Maybe including the ones that unlock school property, like storage spaces in the stadium . . .

It was late September and still stifling in the glass booth, but I couldn't help shuddering a little, thinking, *Ryan is wrong about me obsessing over Chase because of some unrequited crush.* Because clearly, any investigation of Coach Killdare's death would necessarily involve a look at Chase Albright's past — and his present — too.

But how could I research a guy who wouldn't talk and didn't seem to *exist?*

Chase's car pulled away, and I watched until it was out of sight. And when the street was quiet again, I also wondered why in the world my father couldn't account for his whereabouts on September first — especially since, in retrospect, I was pretty sure he hadn't been home watching *60 Minutes.*

Chapter **25**

S o, Millie, how is your investigation going?" Ms. Parkins inquired, accepting the books about psychos and detecting that I was returning. "Have you cracked the case —and written that award-winning story yet?"

"Umm . . . It's only been a few days," I reminded her. "And no—I haven't gotten anywhere. So far all I've done is break into Mr. Killdare's house—"

This news caused her to stop scanning my books just long enough to give me a curious look over her cat eyes, but then she resumed the intake process and let me continue.

"—where I took some envelopes that seem to indicate he was sick, and a postcard from a woman named BeeBee." I hesitated, thinking. "I also asked this guy in my class—a football player who takes care of Mr. Killdare's dog—if he knows anything. But he's a bigger mystery than the murder."

Anybody other than Ms. Parkins—any other adults, at least—probably would've given me a lecture about my sleuthing methods, but my librarian merely asked, "How so? What makes your classmate so mysterious? Because—no

offense to them—but most teenage boys are far from enig-
mas."

"Oh, this guy's a total puzzle," I said. "He's incredibly
good-looking, and obviously smart, not to mention the Stingers' quarterback—"

"Chase Albright?"

Ms. Parkins's interruption surprised me. I'd never considered her a sports fan.

"How do you know him?"

For the first time since I'd met her, Isabel Parkins seemed
uncertain. Maybe even . . . cagey? She didn't quite meet my
eyes as she said, "He's in the newspapers, of course. Quite the
star, from what I understand."

"Yeah," I agreed, not entirely buying her explanation. I
skimmed the local paper every day, too—but never bothered
with the sports section. Was she a closet Stingers follower?
"Anyhow," I continued, "he doesn't ever talk about himself
—and he doesn't have any presence on the Internet. When
you Google him—nothing, except football articles."

"Interesting," Ms. Parkins conceded. Then she changed
the subject, asking, "Where are the Nancy Drew books?"

Why did I keep them when I'd nearly choked just to read
one sentence?

"I guess I forgot them." I fibbed for some reason. Then I
frowned. "Do you think Nancy ever verbally attacked a detective?"

Ms. Parkins's bright red lips twitched with amusement.
"I don't think she had that much spunk." She leaned on the
counter. "So what's next? What's your plan?"

"I have no idea," I admitted. "I'm sort of winging it here."

"Maybe I can help." Ms. Parkins was reaching under the counter, and I was pretty sure she was going to offer me some investigating how-to book I'd missed. But to my surprise, she pulled out a newspaper, spreading it open and pointing to an article.

I looked closer.

Well, not an article, exactly, but an obituary.

"If you want to unearth Mr. Killdare's secrets, they might just surface here," she advised me. "At least, that's been my experience."

I thought she was telling me to read Coach Killdare's obit, and I was about to remind her that those things were sanitized to cover both overt flaws and hidden faults. But when I bent closer, I realized that she wasn't pointing to the brief account of his life. Rather, she was directing me to the announcement for his memorial service, since apparently his body had finally been autopsied long enough and yielded all the clues it was going to yield.

"Oh, gosh . . ." I straightened. "I don't know . . ."

I hadn't been to a funeral since my mother's and wasn't incredibly eager to get back in the swing of things. I wasn't much for standing graveside.

I knew that Ms. Parkins understood my hesitation—she'd been right there with me, all through my mom's illness—and she gave me a sympathetic look. "I'll admit, Millie. I don't think Nancy Drew ever had to face a funeral." She smiled. "Then again, she never chewed out a detective, and she never won a national award for journalism."

I didn't make any promises, but I did take the paper and tuck it under my arm. Just in case I got the guts to go — which, of course, I did.

And boy, was I glad about that. Because, as usual, Ms. Parkins was right.

People's secrets did get revealed at funerals.

And not just those of the person getting buried.

Chapter **26**

D on't you think it's going to be weird, us showing up at a teacher's funeral?" Laura asked as she, Ryan, and I trudged through Wildacre Cemetery on a day that was awful for a graveside memorial—or maybe just right. It was chilly and rainy, the dirt path through the graves filled with puddles that we had to navigate on our way toward a distant white tent.

I could vividly recall the tent at my mother's funeral and was glad that she was buried in a different cemetery. One that I didn't visit as often as I should.

Okay, one that I hadn't visited in five years, in spite of my dad urging me to do it. I just . . . couldn't.

"What if we're the only students?" Laura's voice broke into my guilty thoughts. "The only mourners at all?"

"We might be," Ryan noted, ducking his umbrella under some low branches. "I don't know if any other guys from the team are going, even."

Although I'd known that most players hadn't exactly liked

Mr. Killdare, I was surprised by that. At the very least, he'd won them championships. "Really?"

Ryan bent down again because this part of the cemetery didn't seem very well maintained. "Yeah. Mike told—more like *warned*—everybody to stay away. He's still so pissed about losing his quarterback spot that he wants the whole team to boycott the service."

I stopped walking for a second. *Interesting. Mike is furious enough to threaten his teammates. Was he perhaps angry enough to KILL?*

"Somebody'll show up," I said with confidence. But in truth, I hadn't heard anybody talk about attending, even though you could miss half a day of school without any penalty. What did *that* say about Mr. Killdare? "And I have to go," I reminded my friends. "Ms. Parkins says secrets come out at funerals. I don't want to miss anything."

Laura jumped over a puddle. "Do you think BeeBee will show up?"

I tried to jump, too—and fell short, so my right foot got soaked. "I hope so. Not that we'll necessarily know who she is."

All at once, I felt Ryan's hand clasp my arm, and I looked up from under my umbrella to see the funeral tent just a few yards away.

My first thought was, *Okay, maybe Laura is right. It is weird for us to be here.* Because not only was the service already underway, but only about thirty people had turned out.

I took a moment to scan the mourners—or the obligated,

as seemed more likely in Mr. Killdare's case—searching for familiar faces or someone who might call herself BeeBee. And there was a woman in a plainly cut maroon suit who looked to be about Mr. Killdare's age, and who stood alone with her head bowed.

Does she look like a world traveler? Somebody who'd . . . er, "be with" Mr. Killdare? Send him postcards signed "Love"?

It was hard to tell, so I kept searching the gathering, identifying Principal Woolsey, who stood next to my father, and Ms. Beamish, and a few other teachers. And at the very edge of the tent was another person from school. Chase Albright, who'd ignored Mike's "warning" and stood alone, looking very mature in a dark suit that somehow came across as more expensive than my, Laura's, and Ryan's cobbled-together outfits, all combined.

Feeling eyes on me, I found that Detective Lohser was, of course, there, too—and staring in my direction.

Pretending to ignore him, I resumed surveying the crowd —only to stop short at the sight of long blond hair cascading from under a very chic funereal black hat. Although her face was partly obscured, I would've recognized my archnemesis anywhere. Especially since, unlike me, she'd had the presence of mind to bring a reporter's notebook, which she held discreetly in her left hand.

Darn you, Vivienne Fitch!

Chapter 27

I'd mentally prepped to face the memorial service, but standing at the edge of Coach Killdare's grave, my chest tightened as a minister in a black suit intoned a prayer and memories came flooding back.

My mother's casket being lowered . . .

I glanced at my father, who also seemed unnerved—but mainly by my presence. He kept giving me curious looks, as if to ask, "Why are *you* here?"

I averted my gaze, hardly able to bear seeing my dad in a sober suit beside an open grave. The scene was too familiar, almost like Mom had died yesterday, instead of about eight years in the past.

Both Ryan and Laura seemed to understand what was happening to me, and Ry clasped my arm, whispering, "Are you okay?"

"I'm fine," I said softly as the minister wrapped up the world's longest prayer. Then I shrugged free, knowing I had to pull myself together, if only because I couldn't let Viv see me looking weak. She kept peeking at me from under the brim of that little hat, no doubt sensing I was struggling and hoping I'd fall apart.

I glanced over at Chase and found that he was watching me, too, but with something that looked like sympathy. For a moment, I was not only surprised to see that expression in his eyes, but unsure how he'd have any clue as to what I was going through.

Then I realized that even if I didn't know much about Chase, my story was common knowledge. For a long time, I'd been poor, motherless Millie Ostermeyer—a label that still sort of stuck.

Don't be that pathetic kid, Millie. You're on an investigative mission, not throwing a pity party.

Squaring my shoulders, I forced myself to face the casket —just as the minister addressed all of us, asking, as if he'd run out of stuff to say, "Would anyone like to come forward and offer a few words about the man whose life we celebrate today?"

Funerals are pretty quiet to begin with, but that invitation caused a phenomenally profound hush to descend upon that cemetery. The kind of silence that I imagined existed in outer space. Even the birds seemed to shut up, and while I could see that Principal Woolsey was clearing his throat in his nervous way, he was managing to do it soundlessly, like he didn't want to be singled out to speak on behalf of a man who—let's face it—he'd probably loathed.

I sneaked a hopeful look at the woman in the maroon suit, but she was hanging back, too.

And although my dad certainly wasn't shy, he didn't jump

into the spotlight, either—though for once I wished he would. *Go up there and say great stuff about Mr. Killdare, because Detective Lohser's listening and Viv is taking notes!*

I was pretty sure Dad waited because he was a stickler for protocol and would let family—or at least somebody *not* best known for fighting with Hollerin' Hank—go first. Still, I tried to psychically will him to step up to the plate—until somebody finally broke that horrible, awkward silence by saying, in a calm, cool baritone, "I'd like to say a few words."

It probably wasn't appropriate behavior, but it seemed like Laura couldn't keep herself from hopping up and down. "Chase!" she kind of gasped. "Chase is going to talk!"

Chapter **28**

It wasn't anything Chase said during his brief tribute to Coach Killdare that served as the key to unlock a big door to my puzzling, ultraprivate classmate's past.

No, it was something that passed between Chase and the woman I'd potentially—and, I was pretty sure, mistakenly—identified as BeeBee, as he stepped away from the grave and she stepped forward to speak, that caused a light bulb to go on over my head.

It was just a simple gesture—a woman resting her matronly hand on a boy's shoulder and giving it a squeeze, as if to say, "Well done, son." But once I found out exactly who that woman was—when she gave *her* eulogy—that touch, and the way they'd locked eyes, spoke volumes.

I fully intended to confront Chase with my suspicions—huge as they were—but first I had an even bigger fish to fry.

"You guys go on back to school," I told Laura and Ryan after the minister officially dismissed us all. "I've gotta talk to Vivienne."

Chapter **29**

Though not too many people had turned out for Mr.
Killdare's funeral, those who did were, unlike me, obviously not squeamish about sticking around a wet cemetery,
chewing the fat during a break in the rain. Even Chase was
talking for a change, with the woman who'd patted his shoulder, while my dad—after finally stepping up to laud his former
colleague—was in politician mode, glad-handing everybody,
with the exception of Detective Lohser, who hovered alone
near a grave, like a ghost that had slithered up to ruin what
was quickly becoming a pretty decent party. Viv, meanwhile,
had Principal Woolsey cornered, interviewing him in a way
that I knew was too aggressive to get results.

Psychopath! I thought, watching Viv jab her pen at our
poor, flinching principal, practically stabbing him. Honestly,
it was like I was witnessing the shower scene out of—well,
Psycho. He'll never talk if you threaten him!

And, sure enough, when I got within earshot, I heard Mr.
Woolsey say, hands raised to ward off the near blows, "I don't

know what more to tell you, Vivienne. When I said, in my eulogy, that he was an effective coach, that's what I meant!"

"Viv, for crying out loud, leave Mr. Woolsey alone," I urged as soon as I was close enough to intervene. "You're scaring him!"

Mr. Woolsey probably should've been offended, but—as I'd predicted—he was mainly relieved. "What can I do for you, Millicent?" he asked, eyes still darting nervously in Viv's direction. "Hmm?" He dug into the pocket of his suit jacket. "Do you need a pass to return to class?"

"No, thanks."

I actually had plenty of passes, some presigned "Bertram B. Woolsey" in a distinctive florid script, having "borrowed" a pad full of them when I'd been in his office for a halfhearted lecture about missing French *trois* the previous year.

"Millie, what do you want?" Viv snapped while Mr. Woolsey continued to pat himself down. "I'm trying to work here."

"That's what I wanted to talk about, Viv," I said. "I want you to back off this story, because I *did* find the body, and I'm fully capable of covering the murder—starting with an article about this service. That's why I'm here."

I really wanted the chance to summarize the eulogy my father had delivered, because while he hadn't gone first, he'd eventually said some pretty nice stuff about Mr. Killdare and had even gotten a little misty—if only over a victory they'd shared in 2010.

But Viv crossed her arms, challenging me. "Where's your notebook? Huh?"

Of course, I should've brought a pad and pen, but I pointed to my head. "I have more up here, saved away, than you can ever dream of having in your precious notebook."

"All you've got up there is a tangled rats' nest," Viv sniped.

Ignoring her, I appealed to Mr. Woolsey on the grounds that I'd just rescued him, and he was, if only technically, in charge of the school. "Please, Mr. Woolsey. I am *finally* trying to do something academic here—trying to 'achieve my potential,' as defined by the American education establishment —the way you're always telling me to do," I reminded him. "Please . . . Tell Viv that I'm on the murder story now. That, at the very least, I'm covering the service."

Bertram Woolsey looked like he might pee his suit pants to be put on the spot like that, but then a light seemed to dawn in his eyes, and to my utter shock, he turned to Viv and said, "I believe Millicent is correct, Vivienne. Let her cover the service." He addressed both of us. "And then, honestly, I think the *Gazette* will have said enough."

"I'll decide when we've said enough," Viv snapped. She narrowed her eyes at me. "And this had better be one heck of an article, Ostermeyer. I want every detail you've got 'in your head' on paper. And believe me—I'll know if you mess up, because *I* actually took notes."

Then she stalked away, headed down the path toward school, and I turned to thank Mr. Woolsey for his support. But he was gone, too, walking toward my father, who was talking to a couple I didn't recognize, so I just stood there for a moment, reveling in my small victory. Only gradually did it dawn on me that Mr. Woolsey had no doubt backed me up because he was sure I'd *fail*. Maybe even blow off the whole thing.

He really wants this murder swept under the rug. And who better to screw it up than Millie Ostermeyer, who might read Plato, but who skips classes and eschews all organized activities?

"You are wrong this time, Bertram B. Woolsey," I grumbled. "So wrong . . ."

"Are you talking to yourself?"

At the sound of a familiar — but totally unexpected — voice, I turned slowly, refusing to be embarrassed. But I couldn't hide my surprise when the person who'd come up behind me suggested, "Do you want to walk back to school together?"

I didn't answer Chase right away. Instead, I blinked at him about five times, considering that offer. Then I blurted out something that had been bugging me for most of the memorial service, thinking I was most likely to get an honest answer if I caught him off-guard.

"So," I inquired, point-blank. "What the heck did you do to get locked up in a boarding school for *criminals?*"

Chapter 30

I knew you'd figured it out, as soon as Mrs. Blackmoor stepped up to speak," Chase said, opening his umbrella and holding it over both of us. The rain had started again, and I'd left my umbrella back at the service. It was inappropriately cheerful, covered with yellow smiley faces and the admonition "Rain, Rain, Go Away" in a curly font, so I'd stashed it behind a headstone and promptly forgotten it. "I saw you looking between the two of us, the wheels turning in your head," Chase added. "I knew you got it."

He sounded grim, even for a guy who'd just been at a funeral. But he smelled FANTASTIC jammed in next to me under that umbrella.

Enough, Millie! He's a juvenile delinquent!

"So what did you do to end up in prison school?" I asked, returning to the big question. After all, we both knew most of the story. It had started clicking together when the woman in the maroon suit, Mrs. Claire Blackmoor, had introduced herself as the "president"—meaning "warden"—of

Mason Treadwell Military Academy, the place my dad used to threaten to send me. The school where that kid had gotten *stabbed* a few years before.

And as Mrs. Blackmoor had talked about what a great influence Coach Killdare had been on the guys at Treadwell, I'd seen her glance again at Chase, and all the pieces had fallen into place.

Chase *had* attended a boarding school, as the rumors at Honeywell claimed. And it had been "exclusive"—in the sense that it was open only to *kids adjudicated by the courts.*

The only thing I didn't know for certain was whether Chase had watched Coach Killdare's dog as the price for keeping that secret under wraps, or if Mr. Killdare had been a sort of mentor, helping to rehabilitate him.

I glanced up at Chase, bumping into him, and thought, delinquency or no delinquency, Laura would've given her right eye to be in my place. Or maybe her left, because I was walking on Chase's left, and she would've wanted to see him in that suit and tie, and take in his eyes, more blue-gray right then, like they were mirroring the cloudy sky . . .

"So, Chase," I prompted, realizing that I was getting off-track again. "What did you do? How'd you end up at Treadwell?"

"Millie . . ." He put his free hand on my arm, stopping us in the middle of the cemetery. There was nobody else around—nobody aboveground—and as we turned to face each other, I realized that, discounting the times I hung out with Ryan and one terrible school dance that I'd attended with a forgettable boy named Nolan Durkin, I'd never been squeezed that close to a guy my age. And I hardly knew Chase. *Nobody* knew him.

Weird.

"Yeah?" I asked when he let go of my arm. "What's wrong?"

"I'm sorry if I came off heavy-handed when I asked you not to nose around in my life," he said. "And—again—I was kind of a jerk to you when you tried to talk in French class. But I like my privacy—like to just be left alone—and I'm going to ask you again . . . Please don't tell anybody what you know about me."

Chase Albright was hot. He was mature and well-spoken, not to mention charismatic and enigmatic, which was a fairly lethally attractive and hard-to-resist combination. I had a feeling that he got pretty much everything he wanted from girls, whether that meant promises to keep his secrets or . . . other stuff. But I still wasn't sure that I owed him anything, and I refused to commit. If he was prone to, say, taking guns into schools and going on shooting sprees, I was going to warn my friends. "Just tell me what you did," I suggested. "Then we'll talk discretion."

Chase didn't seem happy with that. I could see that his jaw was tense, but he nodded. "Okay. Fair enough." We started walking again, but he didn't spill his guts right away, saying instead, "You're a tough girl, aren't you? Terrible at French, but tough."

Although I was pretty sure I heard grudging admiration in his voice, I wasn't certain if that was a compliment. When I looked up at him, though, I realized that he was as close to smiling as I'd ever seen him. "Thanks . . . I guess," I said. "Now start talking already."

That faint smile vanished, and he suddenly looked miserable — and lost in some past that he obviously didn't like to revisit. Then he sighed and said quietly, "Okay . . . Here goes."

Chapter **31**

How was it that everything Chase confessed to me confirmed my earliest suspicions about him—that he was a rich, privileged, arrogant snob—and worse things than I'd imagined, too . . . And yet, as he told his story, I mainly felt *compassion?* Not for the kid Chase was describing in the past tense, but for the tortured guy who was walking next to me then, being very careful to keep the umbrella over my head, even if it meant he got wet.

"God, I partied every night," he muttered, dragging one hand through his damp hair. It wasn't a boast like some kids made about getting drunk or high. He sounded appalled. "Me and my friends . . . We had enough money and connections to get anything we wanted. We didn't even bother with our parents' liquor cabinets. We did harder stuff."

He didn't seem to want to elaborate, and I didn't press him. I was pretty naive about that sort of thing, but I wasn't cloistered. I saw TV shows about rich teenagers and the powders they snorted and the liquids they injected. I supposed poor and middle-class kids did that stuff, too, but there weren't as many shows about them.

"Is that what you got in trouble for?" I asked, looking up at Chase. We were out of the cemetery by then, walking down a quiet street toward school. "For doing—or dealing—drugs?"

Chase seemed to remember that I was there, and he glanced down at me. "No. Not directly." He also seemed to realize it had stopped raining, and he stepped apart from me to put down the umbrella. It had felt strange to be squeezed so close to him, but suddenly it felt weird to be separated, as if he'd broken down the walls of a confessional. For a second, I thought he wasn't going to finish the story, but he met my eyes and said, "One Friday night, I was hanging out at my house, doing a little pre-party . . . preparation." His jaw got *really* tense and his blue eyes looked almost black. "I left for my friend's house—the real party—around ten, but I was already way too messed up to drive—illegally, too. On a learner's permit." He hesitated, seemingly unwilling to give me details and choosing his next words carefully. "There were . . . injuries. Charges against me. And pressure, by influential people, to make me *really* pay."

He wasn't telling me everything, and I could tell from the way he avoided my eyes that whatever he was holding back was *big*. Like somebody had wound up in a wheelchair or a coma. But he'd revealed a lot and certainly didn't owe me more. I wasn't even his friend.

What he just told me . . . It's terrible. Heinous.

So why did I find myself putting *my* hand on *his* arm and saying, "I'm really sorry, Chase."

He stared down the street, his mouth a white line. "Don't be sorry for me. I don't deserve sympathy. I was a reckless idiot."

"But you obviously served your time—"

"I'll never do enough time," he interrupted, still not looking at me. "A few months in a real detention center and some time in a boarding school . . . That's not enough."

For the first time since I'd seen him at school, I had some serious insight into who Chase Albright was. That big question mark had been at least partly erased. And while I'd been right about some things, I'd been incredibly wrong about others.

He doesn't keep apart from other kids because he thinks he's better than us.

He thinks he's worse. *Maybe that he doesn't deserve friends.*

And even though his story was even more disturbing than I'd ever suspected, I still couldn't help *liking* him.

"Chase . . . Where were your parents while you were getting so out of control?" I asked, in part to draw his thoughts away from where I knew they were stuck. On a dark road that smelled of spilled gasoline and burned rubber, and where people might be crying in pain—or too quiet. "How come nobody was watching you? My dad would ground me for life the first time he caught me stumbling or smelled anything weird on my breath."

Chase seemed to relax, just slightly. "My parents split up

when I was fourteen. I was already hard to control, and my mother gave up custody. She stayed in California, while my dad moved us to Pennsylvania." He finally looked directly at me again. "Dad hoped to get me away from the people I partied with, back in LA."

I could imagine him hanging out with celebrities, but it wasn't the right time to ask if he could name-drop, so I stayed quiet.

"But I found new friends in Philadelphia," he continued. "And as a heart surgeon, my father was too busy to really look after me. For the most part, I was just on my own, living in a huge house with too much time and money at my disposal." He raised one hand, adding, "It's not my dad's fault, though. In fact, he took a lower-paying, less prestigious position here to be close to me when I got sent to Treadwell and then came here."

We'd almost reached the high school, but neither one of us seemed in any hurry to go inside. I was pretty sure that, much as Chase wanted to protect his secrets, he was glad to be unburdening himself to at least one person.

"So where does Mr. Killdare fit in?" I asked, although I was pretty sure I'd figured that out, too.

"I got kind of . . . catatonic at Treadwell," Chase admitted. "I didn't want to talk to anyone or do anything." The corners of his mouth turned up with the faintest hint of a grim smile. "One day, Coach Killdare came by my room, saw me lying on my bed, barged in, and grabbed me by the shoulder, yelling, 'What the hell's wrong with you? You sick or something?' He actually hauled me to my feet, looked me up and down, and said, 'Get your ass out to practice! *Now!*'" Chase continued to grin, just slightly. "I didn't even know what I was going to practice, but I went where he told me to go. And from then on, I wasn't just a guy who'd made terrible mistakes. I was at least a football player, too. And a pretty good one."

"Wow." I was getting a different picture of Chase—and, gradually, a new image of Hollerin' Hank, too. Maybe, just maybe, there had been times and places where his abrasive personality had served a purpose. Maybe even had saved at least one kid.

Chase finally gave me a genuine smile. It changed his whole face in a good way, and I wished he felt he could do it more. "I know everybody at Honeywell thinks Mr. Killdare was just a blowhard," he said. "But he was practically a softie, by Treadwell standards. We were used to getting yelled at, all the time. Hank Killdare didn't really stand out at a boarding school for delinquents."

"So how'd you end up here?" I gestured toward the school that we still weren't approaching.

"Coach Killdare spoke on my behalf at one of my 'progress' hearings, telling the court I was ready to go back into society. Then, from what I understand, he strong-armed Woolsey into not only letting me come here, but allowing me to start over under my middle name."

I jabbed a finger at him. "So that's why I couldn't find you on Google! You had a different name!"

Did I really just say that?

Chase was clearly amused. And maybe slightly concerned. "You Googled me?"

"I don't know . . ." I shrugged, turning away to hide my embarrassment. "Maybe." Forcing myself to look at him again, I asked, "What's your real name, anyhow?"

"*Colton* Chase Albright."

We were having a pretty serious talk, but I snorted. "Jeez, did your parents pick your names from *The Fifty Most Pretentious Names for Boys* book? Because that is a doozy!"

"Is it now, *Millicent?*" he shot back, kind of smiling again.

Okay, he had a point. My name was a mouthful. "Anyway, I guess you owe Coach Killdare a lot for springing you from the pen and helping you start over fresh — with a better name," I couldn't help adding, because, really . . . *Colton?*

"Well, Mr. Killdare wanted me here to play quarterback, too," Chase reminded me. "He had selfish reasons for getting me transferred. Mike is a great player — could probably still go far as a running back if he could get that chip off his shoulder about me taking his place. But Mike didn't lead the team. Hollerin' Hank knew I could do that." It wasn't a boast. Chase almost sounded self-deprecating when he pointed out, "Leaders aren't always liked, and I don't need anybody's approval or friendship."

I didn't really believe that. "Maybe you needed Mr. Killdare's approval?" I ventured. "His friendship?"

Chase didn't buy my attempt at pop psychology. "No, Millie. Not really. But like you said, I do owe Mr. Killdare. A lot. That's why I helped out around his house. Watching Baxter, mowing the lawn . . . It was my pathetic way of saying thanks."

"You could *really* thank him by helping me investigate

his murder," I said. "You seem to know him better than just about anybody. So help me."

That all came tumbling out before I'd thought it through, and I expected Chase to flat out turn me down—or laugh at the ridiculous idea of a teenage girl trying to solve a crime.

Therefore, I was shocked when a moment later he agreed, saying, "Okay. I'll do it. And I think I may have a lead for us to follow."

"What?" My heart started to race—half to know that we had a "lead," which sounded very official, and half, I had to admit, at the prospect of hanging out with Chase again.

Don't be stupid, Millie. He's a delinquent with secrets that he didn't fully divulge. Not to mention still a rich snob—with a girl-friend!

I knew all that, but I still felt pretty excited when he confided, "I noticed two people at the memorial service. A couple I definitely didn't expect to be there—and who I think we should check out."

Chapter **32**

This is not a date!" I told Laura for the millionth time—which didn't stop her from digging in my closet, looking for a different outfit for me. For some reason, she didn't think an Old Navy T-shirt was nice enough for a ride in a BMW with a hot guy, even if we were only going to track down a former classmate who'd disappeared after collapsing at football practice—and whose parents had shown up at Hollerin' Hank's memorial. Chase had recognized Roy Boyles's folks and wondered why they'd pay tribute to a coach who'd driven their son hard enough to maybe damage his brain. "We're going to New Holland to investigate a murder," I added. "That's all."

"Millie's right," Ryan agreed without looking up from his chemistry book, because even though he'd skipped the break-in adventure to study, he'd still bombed his test. "I really think Chase has a girlfriend."

"Nobody knows that for sure," Laura countered as she pulled down a bright green shirt—one of my favorites, with a big owl and the phrase "Whooo Loves You?" on the chest.

Scowling, she put it back, reminding us, "Nobody's ever seen her in person. Where is she?"

Maybe California? I almost said that. But for some reason, I wasn't telling even my best friends everything I'd learned about Chase, not even the mundane stuff, and I shrugged. "Who knows? And Chase isn't into me, anyway. I'm telling you, this outing is strictly business."

Laura would not be dissuaded. "Well, it never hurts to look good." She stopped ransacking my wardrobe long enough to point to my desk, where *The Hidden Staircase* was on top of the pile of Nancy Drew books. "Look at Nancy, climbing around a filthy old house in a pencil skirt. You could at least wear something that isn't *stained.*"

The book did, indeed, feature Nancy in an outfit that I would've considered too fancy for a job interview, let alone exploring what looked like a dirty dungeon. Meanwhile, my T-shirt might've had a *tiny* mark, courtesy of a Fudgsicle.

"This shirt is fine," I said, rubbing the stain. "And I wish you guys would come, too. If we're invoking Nancy Drew here—she always took her friends sleuthing."

Ryan closed his book. "Sorry, but I'm out. I gotta solve 'The Riddle of the Intermolecular Forces,' or my parents are going to kill *me.*"

"And three's a crowd in a BMW," Laura said. "Have you seen the back seat in those things?" She pulled down another shirt and tossed it to the floor. Before I could protest, she added, sort of glumly, "Besides, Chase didn't invite *us.*"

Ryan and I shared a look, as if to say, "Is she jealous?"

"Umm, Laura?" I asked uncertainly.

She twisted to see me at my desk. "What?"

"You don't really care if I hang out with Chase, do you? I mean, it's *not* a date—but . . ."

"It sucks when you like somebody, and your friend gets his attention." Ryan finished my thought. "Even if it's just platonic."

Laura finally abandoned Project Millie Makeover and plopped down on my bed. "No, honestly, you guys. I think Chase is really good-looking, but I don't even know him. Me drooling all over him . . . It's mainly a joke, you know?"

I was glad to hear that she really wasn't jealous, but I was also struck by what she'd just said about not knowing Chase.

Did *I* know him after one admittedly deep talk? And was I doing the right thing, keeping his secrets just that—secret?

I glanced at *The Hidden Staircase* again.

Would sensible Nancy have told her friends Bess and George everything she knew about a boy who'd confessed to wrecking a car before she hopped into his "keen" vehicle?

Jeez, Millie . . . Nance wouldn't go at all. In a way, Chase is worse than most of the villains she confronted. And he hasn't even told you the whole *story. You know he hasn't!*

All at once, I wondered if I was being stupid disappearing into the countryside with a guy I still barely knew, who probably did have a girlfriend, and whose hair might look sun kissed, but who obviously had a very dark aspect to his psyche.

But it was too late to back out—or to change my shirt, which I was suddenly regretting—because the doorbell rang, making me jump.

Chapter **33**

T here were probably dozens of things Chase and I could've talked about as we sat next to each other in quite possibly the nicest car I'd ever been inside. Chase could even set an exact numerical temperature for the interior, while most of the vehicles I was familiar with offered "blue" for cold air and "red" for hot—or, in the case of Ryan's car, windows up or down. I probably could've commented on that.

And, of course, we could've developed a strategy for what exactly we'd do when we reached the address Chase had found for Leonard Boyles, Roy's father, using a simple white-pages.com search.

What do we intend to do there? Peer in the windows, looking for a "vegetative" boy in a hospital bed? Hunt for evidence that Roy doesn't exist at all anymore?

For, like Chase Albright, Roy didn't show up on any of the usual Internet places. I couldn't find a single social media account for him anywhere.

Chase and I probably should've been discussing that stuff.

But all I seemed able to do was stare straight ahead, sweating, even though the fancy temperature readout registered a very comfortable seventy-two degrees. Well, I stared, sweated, and *sniffed,* taking in that wonderful cologne I'd smelled on Chase before, which mingled with the scent of luxurious leather and a more general "new car" smell that a mayor's salary didn't let us Ostermeyers ever enjoy. And where were the fast food containers—the half-empty cups from Wendy's and the stray French fries on the floor?

I stole the tiniest glance at Chase's profile, which belonged on a big screen, not in a small sports car. Hair couldn't be that beautiful in real life. It just couldn't . . .

You are out of your league, Millie! In so many ways! Just like Viv told you!

I was thinking all that, when Chase slowed the car and met my eyes for a second, asking softly but point-blank, "You're nervous to be with me, aren't you, Millie?"

Chapter 34

W hat?" I squeaked. "Don't be ridiculous! Do you think I'm like every other girl who falls apart and gets all tongue-tied in your presence? And I know this isn't a date. I'm well aware of that." I picked up the hem of my shirt, showing him the stain. "Would I have worn this on a date? Of course not! It's covered with Fudgsicle! Who would do that? So why would I be nervous? Huh?"

Chase slowed the car to a crawl and then, much to my surprise, pulled off the side of the road, even though we were still miles from New Holland.

"Why are we stopping here?" I demanded, spinning around in my seat, eyes darting everywhere and still talking too quickly. "Why here?"

And when I turned back to Chase, I saw that his arms were crossed on the steering wheel and his head was resting against them, while his shoulders were shaking. For a second, I thought I'd somehow made the hardened, delinquent quarterback of Honeywell High *cry*. Like maybe my failure to immediately fall for his charms had devastated him. I almost reached out to touch his shoulder and comfort him, when all of a sudden he sat back and I realized that he wasn't upset.

Something, or maybe everything, I'd just said had made Chase Albright—he of the stone face and anguished psyche —*laugh*. Hysterically.

Chapter 35

"I am so sorry, Millie." Chase apologized yet again, swiping one finger under his eyes because I had, indeed, eventually made him cry—from laughing too hard. "It's just that when you showed me the stain on your shirt, talking a mile a minute . . . It just struck me as really funny."

I slouched down in the world's cushiest seat, arms crossed —yet not feeling very comfortable.

Okay, maybe my body felt comfortable, but my pride was stinging because, from Chase's response, it was abundantly clear that I was the only one of us who'd even *thought* of the word "date" in relation to what we were doing. Which was probably Laura's fault.

"I really don't know what's so funny," I grumbled. "And can we go? It's getting late."

Chase didn't put the car in gear, though. "Millie?"

He seemed more composed, and I reluctantly met his eyes. "What?"

"It's been a long time since I laughed like that," he said, no longer laughing at all. "A *long* time. So please don't be angry with me." He hesitated, studying my face and getting even more serious. "And I would never really expect you to get tongue-tied in the presence of any guy. Let alone around an *el jerko* like me. You seem way too self-possessed for that."

His faith in me was somewhat misdirected, but I liked that he believed I was too cool to get flustered by a guy. "Yeah, you're right," I agreed.

He moved to twist the key, but before he started the engine, he admitted softly, "I was afraid you were quiet because you're in a car with a guy who wrecked one. I was worried that you were terrified."

That had crossed my mind, but I told him, "No, Chase. I trust you. You actually seem like a really good driver."

We both knew there was an unspoken "when you're not high as a kite" at the end of that sentence, so there was no need to say it.

Chase put the BMW in gear and pulled back onto the road. "Thanks."

He honestly did seem competent, and I finally relaxed, glad, in a way, that the ice had been broken, even if I'd made an idiot of myself.

"I was really just preoccupied before, wondering how we'll figure out what happened to Roy," I noted. "I was thinking that, when we get to town, we could look for a long-term care place and see if he lives there. If he's really in bad shape, he might need constant care. Then, if that doesn't pan out, we could look for places where kids hang out and ask them if they've ever heard of Roy. Find out if he's enrolled in school and stuff like that."

Chase shifted up to fifth gear and—forgetting the climate control—opened the sunroof, so his hair did that "riffling" thing—while mine flailed about like the snakes on Medusa's head, until I snared it in one of the ponytail holders I usually kept wrapped around my wrist. As we gained speed, he glanced at me again. "Why don't we just go to his house, knock on the door, and ask if Roy's home?"

Well, there was that approach, too. It wasn't very original, but it might get the job done.

"Yeah, maybe," I conceded, tilting my head back so I could enjoy the breeze on my face. Maybe I was still out of my league, but now that the tension was gone, I planned to enjoy life in the majors for a while. And as my eyes closed, I heard Chase tell me, "Millie . . . Thanks for trusting me. And for the laugh."

It sounded as if—and I *felt* as if—I'd done him a real favor.

"My pleasure," I said. "Thanks for doing this with me."

He didn't answer, and we rode along in a silence—an okay silence, me nearly dozing off—until the car stopped and Chase shook me gently, saying, "We're here, Millie. Wake up."

And when I opened my eyes . . . I kind of chickened out. And maybe threw up a little, in my mouth.

Chapter **36**

"W hat is *this* smell?" I demanded, covering my mouth with my hand. "It's worse than when I found Mr. Killdare!" *Does sleuthing* always *have to be rank?* I surveyed the property, not moving from my seat. "And this place is . . . disturbing!"

"Millie, you broke into Coach Killdare's house," Chase reminded me. He had politely opened my door and was leaning down, trying to persuade me to get out into the almost-dark front yard of a dilapidated farmhouse, which was surrounded by hulking, rusty farm equipment. Pointy stuff. Some of which looked like it could easily crush the back of someone's head. And the smell . . . the terrible poopy smell . . . It was making me gag again, and I didn't take the hand Chase offered. "Why won't you do this?" he asked. "We're just going to knock."

"We could do one of my plans," I suggested. "Go back into town . . ."

Chase kept holding out his hand. "Millie, we're parked in someone's yard. If they're home, they've probably noticed and are wondering what we're doing here." He bent lower, so I could see his blue eyes, which were both challenging and laughing at me again. "You're not afraid, are you, Millie Ostermeyer? Do you want to wait in the car?"

All at once, I flashed back to every Nancy Drew book Mom and I had read. *Nancy* had never waited in the car for Ned Nickerson or any of her other "beaus" to do the dirty work. She'd *driven* the car—and led Ned around by the nose.

Pull it together, Millie.

"Step aside," I advised Chase, getting out of my seat— without any help. "And let me do the talking," I added over my shoulder as he trailed me to the door. "You just chime in when you feel like you have to, okay? Because this is *my* investigation."

"Of course, Millie," he promised. "I'm just here for backup."

Then we both stepped onto the creakiest, saggiest porch I'd ever seen, and I raised my hand to knock on the door—but first turned to Chase, asking in a whisper, "Speaking of Mr. Killdare's house and bad smells. Has anybody stepped up to adopt the dog yet? Because I really like him."

Chase didn't answer me. Instead, he grabbed my shoulders and faced me toward the door, where, lo and behold, somebody was standing and in imminent danger of having my knuckles rap right on his somewhat familiar face.

Chapter **37**

R oy, you're alive!"
I probably shouldn't have blurted that out to a former classmate who was, indeed, looking quite hale and healthy. Maybe even more buff than he'd looked back at Honeywell.

"Jeez, do I get sick of hearing *that*, Ostermeyer," he complained, leaning against the door frame and crossing his big arms. He nodded to Chase. "What's up, Albright?" Then he looked between both of us, as if we were two numbers that would never add up. "And what the hell are you guys doing here . . . together?"

I refused to assume that Roy was judging me in the same way Viv did in relation to Chase, and preferred to think that Roy considered me too smart to hang out with a standoffish jock.

I also might've gotten so mired in the question's subtext that I completely forgot to answer it, and was grateful when the boy I'd advised to stay quiet piped up. At least I was grateful until I heard the words that came out of his mouth, which were, "Millie's looking into Coach Killdare's murder for the

school paper. She's hoping to win a national award for investigative coverage."

If Roy was impressed, he didn't show it.

And why was Chase telling so much, right upfront? Where
was the subterfuge? The cover story that would keep us from
getting killed and ground up in what looked like a woodchip-
per at the edge of the property by a guy who might not have
had brain damage, but who definitely seemed bigger and
scarier than I remembered?

I tugged on Chase's sleeve, trying to get him to stop talking, but he ignored me, adding, "I saw your parents at Mr.
Killdare's memorial. We thought you—or they—might be
able to help us."

Roy Boyles didn't jump at the chance to be of assistance.
He stared at us for a long time, then said, softly and sort of
menacingly, "I don't care if that whole thing is ever solved,
and I don't know if my parents care, either. Hollerin' Hank is
the whole reason we're stuck out here, and people think I'm
dead." His voice dropped to almost a growl. "If it weren't for
him . . ."

I got even more nervous—but excited, too, because the
brawny, angry guy who stood before me seemed about to say
something important. Like maybe that he'd hated Mr. Killdare enough to want him dead. Chase tensed at my side, too.
I didn't even dare to pull out my notebook for fear of ruining
the moment, but I was taking careful mental note of every
word, which was why I'd never forget what was uttered next
—and I quote:

"So? Who wants pie?"

Chapter **38**

M om, nobody wants pie," Roy whined as we all followed his mother into a bright, cheerful room that
smelled even better than Chase Albright, leather seats, and
new car combined. A scent that completely banished the hideous reek that enveloped the outside of the house.

In fact, the whole vibe changed when Mrs. Boyles threw
open the door, turned on some lights, and shooed us into
her kitchen, which was ramshackle, like the rest of the house
—but like a dilapidated annex of paradise.

I sucked in a deep and grateful breath while my eyes explored a long counter that was nearly covered by dough and
fresh berries and the blessed union of those two things: Pie.
After pie. After pie.

Forget Hell's Kitchen. This was Heaven's Bakery.

"Mom, seriously, enough with the pie," Roy groaned,
trailing behind all of us—and definitely not speaking for me
when he advised her, "Nobody wants any!"

Moments ago, I'd suspected that I was in the presence of
a cold-blooded killer and had half wanted to run away, but all

that was forgotten as Mrs. Boyles began to search overstuffed drawers for what I hoped was a serving utensil.

"Don't be ridiculous, Roy." She waved a sharp, wedge-shaped silver thing in the air. "Our guests might be hungry."

"Yeah, I might like pie," I agreed hopefully, raising one hand. "I could go for that."

I glanced at Chase for support, and he looked as if he was close to laughing for the second time that day.

"Sure." He addressed our hostess. "That'd be great, thanks."

"Oh, for crying out loud," Roy complained, dropping down into a wooden chair that seemed way too rickety for a guy his size. "Go ahead, Mom. Get it over with."

I got the sense that a lot of people were force-fed pastry in his house and stayed around longer than he wanted them to. Still, he made a weak attempt at being polite, pointing at me and Chase. "This is Millie and Chase. You might remember Chase from when we both played football at my old school. Honeywell." He hesitated, for effect. "You know, the one where everybody thinks I'm *dead*."

Was Roy mad at his mother for the mix-up, too?

It seemed that way.

"I do recall you, Chase." Mrs. Boyles set down a plate and gestured for him to take a seat at a huge farmhouse table. "It's nice to see you again." She placed another plate on the table, adding, "And it's lovely to meet you, Millie."

"Thanks, you too," I said, mainly addressing the pie, whose acquaintance I was very, *very* glad to make. "Seriously, thank you."

I heard a third plate clunk down and saw that Roy had also been served and, in spite of his final sulky protest—"I thought you made boysenberry today"—was digging his fork into the crust.

"So, what brings you all the way out here?" Mrs. Boyles asked, making a half-hearted effort to straighten up the chaos in her kitchen.

If my mouth hadn't been so full, I would've told her not to worry about the mess because I would've eaten her creations in the middle of a sewage-filled dump. And fortunately, Chase once again spoke on our behalf, because, in retrospect, that probably would've been an awkward thing to say.

"We're actually here because Millie is writing about Mr. Killdare for the school paper," he said, slightly amending the explanation he'd given on the porch so that it sounded less like I was investigating and more like I was doing a tribute. I thought that was a smart touch. "I saw you at the memorial service," Chase added. "And since not too many people were there . . . Well, we thought we'd track down as many mourners as possible and get their thoughts on the coach."

Mrs. Boyle stopped wiping the counter and peered more closely at me and Chase, nodding slowly. "Yes . . . I recall seeing you two at the service now. You were the young man who spoke." She gave her son a quizzical look. "Roy, why didn't you tell me they were here to ask about your Uncle Hank?"

I would never have intentionally wasted a bite of that pie, but I'll admit, a few crumbs tumbled out of my slack mouth when she dropped *that* bombshell.

Chapter **39**

Why hadn't I seen the resemblance the moment I'd laid eyes on Mrs. Boyles?

Because you were blinded by blueberries, Millie!

But as Roy's mom joined us at the table, I realized that the similarity between her and Hollerin' Hank was unmistakable. They had the same ruddy skin, the same bulbous nose, the same large ears and wide waistline.

Poor Mrs. Boyles!

"What did you guys wanna ask?" Roy prompted, so I realized I'd been staring at his mother a little too long. "What do you wanna know about Uncle Hank?"

I'd told Chase to stay quiet, but once again, he opened his . . . well, piehole. "Before we even ask about Mr. Killdare . . . Why'd you just disappear, Roy?" he asked. "The whole team thought you had brain damage—or worse. Why didn't you just tell everybody you were moving?"

Roy gave his mother a dark look, then informed us, "My dad took a job here selling organic manure. Would you be bragging about it? I just kept hoping it wouldn't happen." He turned slightly pink—the same shade as his mother and his deceased uncle. "Then I was out for two weeks after I collapsed. I got pretty sick. And there was no sense in going back to school because we moved as soon as I was okay to go."

I was glad that Roy was alive and functional, but the whole story was a little anticlimactic—although it did explain the smell outside. Then I remembered something Roy had said on the porch. "But why'd you say Mr. Killdare is responsible for you being here?" I shot Mrs. Boyles a quick glance and, although I kind of agreed with Roy that living on a rundown manure farm wasn't the greatest, added, "In this lovely place!"

Roy was talking to us, but shooting daggers at his mom again. "Uncle Hank found this 'opportunity' for my dad, and the next thing I knew, we're moving to this hellhole."

"Roy . . ." Mrs. Boyles shook her head as if to say, "We've been through all this!" Then she addressed me and Chase with a smile. "We are all very grateful to Hank for helping us relocate. My husband, Len, had been out of a job for a year. Hank helped us finance this place, and now we're doing very well." She beamed with pride. "I make quite a nice living selling pies to local markets and restaurants, too."

So much for the Boyleses wanting to kill Mr. Killdare. And once again, he was turning out to be someone different from what I'd thought—in a good way. Although Roy clearly disagreed.

"Roy, why didn't you ever tell us that Coach Killdare was your uncle?" Chase asked. "I didn't even know you two knew each other off the field."

I was just about to pick up my plate and lick it clean when I noticed that my partner had pushed his empty plate away and was sitting back.

I reluctantly followed suit, noting, "Yeah, Roy. Why the big secret about your uncle?"

Chase had initiated the question, but of course Roy looked at me like I was an idiot. "Same reason I didn't go bragging about the manure!"

"Roy!" Mrs. Boyles spoke sharply, but her son ignored her.

"Would you go out of your way to tell people you were related to a guy everybody hated?" he continued. He gave his mom a warning look. "And don't act like you two were close or anything. Most of the time you avoided him, too."

That must've been true because Mrs. Boyles squirmed and looked down at her feet. And the fact that neither she nor the missing Len had stepped up at the service probably spoke volumes, too.

"Besides," Roy concluded, "Uncle Hank didn't want any-body knowing I was his nephew, either. He didn't want the guys thinking I got special treatment."

"I definitely never thought that," Chase said. "You caught as much hell as anybody else." He turned to Mrs. Boyles, seeming to catch himself. "Sorry . . ."

Roy's mom smiled and got ruddier, almost blushing—not unlike Ms. Beamish when she interacted with *Monsieur Albright.* "Oh, Chase . . ." She waved her hand. "That's hardly a terrible curse word."

Roy finally smiled, too, and seemed to warm to us, now that the topic of football had come up. "Yeah," he said with a laugh. "Uncle Hank was pretty rough on all of us. I didn't hate that about him, though. He was just trying to get the best out of us."

All at once I realized that I had a secret weapon in Chase when it came to investigating the death of a coach.

He can talk football. And he's charming when he wants to be.

"Hey, Roy." I risked interrupting our bonding moment. "If you want kids to know you're still alive, how come you're not on Facebook or anything?"

"I hate that online social crap," he said. "I have avatars on *World of Warcraft* and places like that. I don't care about updating my status for people." He grinned again. "I'd rather kill 'em."

I met Chase's eyes, and we both shrugged like we agreed that the statement — though creepy — didn't make Roy a murderer. I mean, if everybody who enjoyed killing people online did it in real life, there'd be nobody left to buy manure, right?

As if on cue, we both stood to leave — Chase pulling out my chair, which nobody had ever done, except maybe my dad when we'd gone to a fancy restaurant once. "I guess we'll be going," he said, putting his hand on the small of my back, too, to guide me to the door. Nobody'd ever done that either, and I wasn't sure what to make of it, even though it lasted only a second. "Thanks for the great dessert, Mrs. Boyles," he added. "And you should stop by practice sometime, Roy. This year's blockers could definitely use some tips."

"Yeah, maybe." Roy followed us to the front door, with his mom trailing along. "That might be okay."

When we reached the exit, just as I was about to hold my breath, Chase stopped and turned to Mrs. Boyles. "Umm . . . You wouldn't happen to be in charge of Mr. Killdare's estate, would you?"

For a split second, I didn't know where he was headed with that out-of-the-blue question. Did he want those knick-knacks shaped like foreign landmarks or something?

Roy's mom seemed surprised, too, but answered, "Why, yes . . . I am. Why?"

"Did you know that Coach has—had—a dog?"

My heart almost stopped as I realized where the conversation was headed. *He's giving away Baxter! My dog!*

Mrs. Boyles was also clearly upset, but for a different reason. She pressed her hand to her chest, eyes wide. "Goodness . . . We haven't been to the house . . . It must be dead by now!"

"Way to go, Mom," Roy grunted. "Told ya we shoulda cleaned out Uncle Hank's place."

My heart sank lower because I *really* hated the thought of poor Bax being stuck on a manure farm with a guy who wasn't very nice to his mother and apparently wanted to grab his dead uncle's stuff, too.

"No, it's okay," Chase reassured Mrs. Boyles. "I've been taking care of Baxter since Mr. Killdare stopped showing up at school. I used to do chores for him, so it was no big deal for me to stop by and make sure the dog was okay." He hesitated, then asked the question I'd dreaded. "Do you . . . want Baxter?"

Roy's mom frowned. "I'm sorry, Chase, but my kitchen is state licensed as a commercial bakery. I really can't have a dog running around, getting hair in the pies."

"No, you can't!" I agreed too eagerly. I toned it down. "I mean, of course not."

"If you could keep watching him," Mrs. Boyles added, "I could pay you until I have time to figure out a permanent home."

I wanted to jump in and stake my claim, but I hadn't exactly asked my father yet, so I kept silent.

"I'm happy to dog sit," Chase said. "But I won't take any money for it." Mrs. Boyles was obviously about to protest, but he explained, "I kind of owe Mr. Killdare a debt. I wouldn't feel right taking money from you."

"Sucker," Roy joked. At least I thought he was joking.

"Well, thank you." Mrs. Boyles opened the door for us. "I'll be in touch soon about a more permanent solution. I promise."

The odor of manure was starting to overcome the smell of pie, and I was ready to get out of there, but I realized I'd almost forgotten something important. "By the way," I asked. "Did Mr. Killdare have a girlfriend? Because we'd really like to talk to her if he did . . ."

I let that question trail off because Roy was giving me a weird, suspicious look again. "Did you say this article was, like, a tribute? Because on the porch, I thought Chase said something about an 'investigation.'"

I wasn't sure why I got nervous, especially since I didn't

think Roy was the killer, but I found myself mumbling, "Oh, gosh . . . Investigation, tribute—tomato, to-mah-to —"

"It's a little of both," Chase cut in. He looked at Mrs. Boyles. "So, do you know if your brother was seeing anybody?"

"Hmm . . ." Roy's mother tapped her chin, giving that question serious consideration, and a few moments later, Chase and I walked away with something I'd desperately hoped for but hadn't really expected to get.

Chapter **40**

Millie, you are way too excited about that pie," Chase observed, glancing at me as we rode back to Honey-well. "You've eaten half of it — with your hands."

"I've never heard of peach rhubarb," I said, cradling on my lap the gift that Mrs. Boyles had bestowed upon us. She hadn't been able to tell us anything about her brother's love life, so she'd given us a consolation prize instead. One that was at least as good as information. "You should try this," I told Chase, who — let's face it — probably wasn't going to get more than a few bites. "It's amazing!"

"Do you want me to stop and get you a fork?" he offered, like maybe he was nervous about my sticky fingers meeting his upholstery and astronaut-worthy sleek instrument panel. "I think I noticed a diner about a half-mile back."

I considered that suggestion, then reluctantly pulled some crumpled plastic wrap over the carnage, licked my fingers, and tried to surreptitiously wipe them on my shorts. "Thanks, but I guess I'm good for now."

Chase stole one more look at the semi-demolished dessert. "I guess your mom doesn't bake, huh?"

He was teasing me, but I didn't feel like laughing—or, suddenly, eating. "No, she doesn't bake," I said. *Or do anything anymore.*

Chase must've caught my change in mood and quickly figured out what had gone wrong. "Hey, Millie." He sounded miserable. "I'm really sorry. I forgot about your mother for a second. That was a stupid thing to say."

I shrugged, watching cars pass us in the opposite lane. "It's okay. It's been about eight years."

"Yeah, like that helps."

At first I didn't understand why he sounded so bitter. Then I remembered that his mother was gone, too, in a different way. "Do you talk to your mom much?" I asked, twisting slightly in the seat. "See her on holidays and stuff?"

His fingers flexed around the steering wheel. "No. She *really* disowned me after the accident. And I can't blame her."

Wow. He carried a ton of guilt. Enough that he didn't think he deserved *his own mom's love.* Everybody deserved *that.* But before I could tell him that, Chase again asked about my family.

"What was your mom like? Like you?" He smiled. "Would she have eaten that whole pie with her hands?"

Normally, on the few occasions people mentioned my mother, they did their best to come across as suitably solemn. It felt nice to have somebody smile about her, because she'd been a happy person. "Yeah," I confirmed. "She would've finished the pie—then made you drive back for another one."

I saw, in profile, that Chase was close to laughing again.

How had he gone so long without smiling, which seemed to be coming pretty naturally to him that evening?

Then he glanced at me again. "How about looks? Did she look like you? Have the same red hair?"

"Yes. Her hair was exactly like mine." I smiled, too, remembering me and my mother standing in front of a mirror together on a humid day, our crazy red curls like frizzy halos around our heads. "We both used to complain about it."

"I bet you like it now," Chase guessed softly and more seriously. "I bet you feel lucky to share that with her." He met my eyes briefly, one more time. "Especially since it really is pretty, Millie."

I didn't always feel fortunate about the mess on my head. Some days I hated my hair because it was a pain in the butt and way too bright. And some days, I hated it precisely because it was so much like my mother's. It was like a living, growing reminder of everything I'd lost when she'd died. But that compliment . . . I did appreciate that. In fact, it gave me a strange feeling in my stomach that I couldn't attribute to just overeating, and I was glad the car was dark, because my cheeks felt a little warm, too. "Thanks, Chase."

Before I could decide if I should tell him that I thought his hair was *phenomenal,* he asked a question that I didn't understand at first.

"So . . . why did you ask Roy and his mom if Mr. Killdare had a *girlfriend?*"

Chapter 41

I kind of stole something from Mr. Killdare's house," I admitted. "A postcard signed 'Love, BeeBee.'" I watched Chase's face as I asked him a question that suddenly seemed way overdue, given that he had keys to Coach Killdare's house. "Do *you* know anything about him having a girlfriend?"

And how about you? Some girl back in your home state, maybe? Or Philly?

"Not really," Chase answered the spoken question. "Although I sort of suspected that, because—"

"Of the chicken clock?" I interrupted. "And the knick-knacks on the shelf in his den? The foreign ones that don't seem like they'd belong to a guy who didn't decorate anywhere else? Except with old football awards?"

We were almost back to Honeywell and stopped at a traffic light, so Chase could really look at me. "No. I never noticed any knickknacks, probably because I'm a guy, too. I never noticed anything but the big screen—which was pretty nice."

Guys and their stupid TVs!

"Then what . . . ?"

"I was going to say that one time, when I gave Baxter a bath—which Mr. Killdare didn't do often enough," Chase noted in an aside, "I noticed a can of hair spray next to the sink." The light changed and he put the car back in gear. "Not exactly something he needed."

"No, I guess not." Mr. Killdare had been as bald as the pro-verbial cue ball.

Chase seemed to hesitate, then added, "There were some . . . um . . . other things in the bathroom, too. Stuff that *no* guy needs."

For a second, I didn't get what he was talking about or why he wasn't being direct. Did he not want to say "mascara"? Or "lipstick"? Then I realized that he was using the same tone —and halting delivery—that my dad used when he wanted to know if he should add tampons to his weekly shopping list.

"I getcha," I said, holding up my hand. "Say no more." Then I quickly changed the subject. "So why do you think Mr. Killdare kept BeeBee under wraps?" I paused, peering closely at Chase. "Why would *any* guy do that?"

Chase didn't seem to realize that I was asking about him, too. He shrugged. "I have no idea."

I sat back, muttering, "I think she might be a key to this mystery. We need to find her identity. Assuming, of course, that Viv and Mike didn't kill Mr. Killdare."

"What?" Chase sounded very surprised.

I realized I'd said more than I'd intended. "Can you keep a secret?"

Chase gave me a strange look. "Uh . . . yes. I can," he re-minded me. "I believe that I've proven that beyond question."

Gosh, he had a nice vocabulary and way of speaking. Most jocks would've said, "Der, yeah!"

"So why'd you say that about Viv and Mike?" he prompted.

"The night I found Mr. Killdare's body, I overheard Viv threatening Mike to keep his mouth shut about something they both knew," I confided. "It sounded serious. Plus, I can imagine Mike blowing up at Coach about the whole quarterback thing and just going ballistic."

We'd pulled up in front of my house, and Chase stopped the car. "And Viv?"

I gave him an incredulous look. "You seriously can't imagine her committing murder? Killing the guy who was responsible for humiliating her on the entire Internet—and ESPN?"

"Yeah, that *BuzzKill* video was pretty bad," Chase agreed. "And Viv does seem somewhat . . . intense."

I rolled my eyes. "*That's* the understatement of the year. I mean, Vivienne Fitch meets all the criteria for a complete psychopath, as described in the book *The Psycho Killer Next Door*."

Chase gave me another funny look. "Which you read because . . . ?"

"I needed to get inside the mind of my nemesis. I can't always hope to one-up Viv out of sheer luck." I picked at the plastic-wrapped pie on my lap. "It's not like some kid will drown and latch on to me every day. I need to *actively* combat Vivienne . . ."

I'd started rambling and looked up to see Chase scrutinizing me with a *really* strange expression. "You're a very interesting person, Millie." He offered me yet another slightly ambiguous compliment. "Very . . . unique."

Talk about adjectives that could cut both ways. "Anyhow
. . . I'm still trying to pursue the BeeBee angle, too," I said.
"Just in case Mike is innocent, and Viv hasn't killed anyone,
either . . . yet."

It seemed that we'd reached the end of our adventure, because Chase didn't say anything more. But before I could hop
out of the car, he surprised me by yanking the keys out of the
ignition and dangling them in front of my face.

"What are you doing?"

"Inviting you to look through Mr. Killdare's house again,"
he said. "And this time, you won't have to go in through a
window. Which you left wide open."

I finally got that he was reminding me that he still had a
key to the back door. But before I could take him up on that
offer, I was distracted by a movement I saw over his shoulder,
out the driver's side window. Someone was darting out of my
house and going quickly—furtively, I thought—to a vehicle I
hadn't noticed, parked around the corner. A moment later, I
saw red taillights, and the car was gone.

Dad, what are you up to?

Chapter 42

"Dad, who was just here?" I demanded, entering our house to find him watching CNN, his feet on the coffee table and the tie that he was still wearing askew. "Who just ran off?"

"Oh, hey, Millie," he greeted me—too innocently, I thought. Reaching for the remote, he turned off the set, but didn't answer my question. "Where were you?"

"I was hanging out with Chase Albright. We took a ride. Got a snack. Sniffed some manure."

I knew in my gut that it wasn't the part about the poop that put the look of disbelief on my father's face. I was pretty sure he'd tuned out everything after "I" and "Chase."

Seriously, did everybody—even my own father—have to seem so shocked by the prospect of me spending time with a hot quarterback? Was Laura the only human being who found the pairing plausible in any way, shape, or form?

"I didn't know you two were friends," Dad said when he'd recovered enough to speak.

Are Chase and I becoming friends?

"We're French dialogue buddies," I fibbed, rather than try to explain whatever was developing between me and my dad's star player. Maybe I was also worried that my father would forbid me from hanging out with Chase again—on the grounds that *I* might corrupt *him*. Lure Chase into my vaguely antiestablishment, antiauthoritarian ways and ruin him as a "team player." "We just *parler*-ed together. It was no big deal." I plopped down on the couch, too. "So . . . Who was here?"

My father, who had a mind like a steel trap, suddenly exhibited classic signs of dementia. It was as if this simple question didn't even register with him. "What? What do you mean?"

I nudged a bowl of Chex Mix across the coffee table with the toe of my sneaker. "Our go-to, 'company' snack is in the 'nice' bowl. *Somebody* was here."

"Oh, yes." Dad seemed to regain his faculties. "Municipal business. Nothing for you to worry about."

"Who said I was worried?"

All at once, my father and I locked eyes, really looking at each other for the first time in a long time. And the weird thing was, I saw that he was the worried one. My dad never looked worried. Not even when my mother had been sick. He'd just "soldiered on," to the degree that sometimes I'd wanted to slug him and tell him that he should cry or something, if only to let Mom know that he was upset. But part of me suspected that he did that, in private, and that if I made him do it in public, he'd never stop.

That hidden, tiny, vulnerable part of Dad that I was pretty

sure existed—that's what I was glimpsing in his eyes right then. And as we sat there studying each other, I also knew that he'd just lied to me.

Whoever'd gotten the Chex Mix treatment hadn't just been some municipal crony.

Something important had gone down, like maybe Detective Lohser had come around with a search warrant, looking for a weapon or evidence that would answer the question about where Dad had been a few Sundays ago.

I was still certain that my father'd had nothing to do with Mr. Killdare's murder. Would never doubt that. Yet he wasn't telling me everything, either.

"Dad," I said softly, still searching his face. "What's going on with you? Are you really in trouble about Mr. Killdare? Because Detective Lohser asked me where you were on September first—and told me *you* didn't know."

In the last few days, I'd gotten Chase Albright to open up to me. But I had the opposite effect on my father. He snapped shut, repeating, "There's nothing to worry about, Millie. Except your grades in French. I hope Chase can help you." Then, although I was pretty sure my father knew about Chase's delinquent background—Mr. Killdare must've said *something* when he'd recruited a new quarterback—Dad basically confirmed my suspicions that he considered me a potentially bad influence. "And don't you fill Chase's head with ideas about how structured education is a bad thing, because if he starts skipping classes, he'll be ineligible to play. And we're facing the Bulldogs next week."

"Too late." I stood up, grabbing the bowl. "I've already

convinced Chase that not only is public education a diabolical plot to shackle young minds, so we all become unthinking
grist for the military-industrial complex, but that organized
sports are the modern equivalent of gladiator tournaments.
He now understands that you're exploiting his body to enter-
tain the masses, and he'll be quitting tomorrow."

"Millicent Ostermeyer, you had better be joking," I heard
my father growling as I went up the stairs, taking them two
at a time. "Seriously, if you've said anything to Chase . . ."

I closed my bedroom door, shutting him out, because
while I might've honestly believed, to a large degree, that
stuff about structured curricula stifling the mind, I had an
article due for my school's paper. A story about Coach Killdare's memorial service—and a sidebar about a mysterious
football player who couldn't expect to fly completely under
the radar forever.

But before I powered up my laptop, I reached for those
envelopes I'd swiped from Mr. Killdare's house. I'd sort of
forgotten about them, as I'd started to believe that BeeBee
and her postcard were bigger keys to the mystery, but it
seemed like I should at least follow Laura's hunch about the
medical letters being clues, too. Tearing open three at once, I
scanned the contents, which consisted of incredibly dull stuff
about insurance and deductibles. However, before I gave up
and tossed them on the floor with my other trash, I ripped
into the one with the return address "Cavenaugh-Beecham
Clinic."

And when I read the letter inside—a private message from
a doctor—I sucked in a sharp breath and felt my heart sort of

stop. Seriously, for a second, I thought *I* might need medical attention, and when I could finally breathe again, I muttered out loud, hearing confusion in my voice.

"Dad, did you keep *this* a secret from me, too? Did you know Coach Killdare had *cancer?*"

Chapter **43**

Nice articles," Ryan said, joining me and Laura at my locker. He held up the latest copy of the *Gazette* so I could see my byline atop two stories: "Hollerin' Hank Honored at Memorial Service" and "Former Stinger Resurfaces on Manure Farm: Boyles Related to Deceased Coach." "I always wondered what happened to Roy."

"Yeah, he's not gonna like the way manure got played up in the headline." I grabbed my books for the morning. "But I think he's glad to have kids know he's alive."

At least Roy hadn't balked when I'd called him about revealing his whereabouts. Maybe because he'd been distracted by a video game. I'd heard stuff blowing up as he'd agreed, with a grunt, "Whatever, Ostermeyer. What do I care anymore?"

"You actually made it seem like people really miss Mr. Killdare," Laura noted. "Those quotes from his eulogies . . . He seemed almost *popular.*"

Taking the paper from Ryan, I tossed it into my locker.

"Yeah, well, it's all stuff I remembered people saying. I mean, Hollerin' Hank did have *some* good points."

It struck me that I was developing a soft spot for Mr. Killdare, postmortem. He'd helped Chase, secured Roy Boyles's father solid, if hideous, employment, and nurtured my destined dog to maturity.

"At least I was able to make my dad look like he didn't want to kill Mr. Killdare," I added, slipping my backpack over my shoulder. "I'm sure if Viv had written the article, it would've been headlined 'Assistant Coach Hesitates at Service, Offers Lukewarm Tribute.' With the subhead 'Ostermeyer Still under Investigation.'"

All of a sudden, I got a pang of guilt because if I'd been a truly unbiased reporter, I'd have been digging deeper into Mr. Killdare's cancer diagnosis. Even if that meant reopening an old, potentially mayoral-career-killing rumor about Honeywell High being located on tainted ground.

And if Detective Lohser finds out, will it be another black mark against my father, who definitely wouldn't like to see that gossip start up again?

"So, how was it, hanging out with Chase?" Laura interrupted my thoughts. She dropped her voice, even though Chase was about forty feet down the crowded hallway, opening his own locker. "Did you guys have fun?"

"Yeah, we did," I said, shaking off concerns about my dad—and perhaps answering with too much enthusiasm. Maybe, just maybe, I'd relived aspects of that evening a few times. Such as the way Chase had put his hand on the small of my back and pulled out my chair. Then I glanced down the corridor and saw something taped to the inside of Chase's locker door. The photo Laura'd told me about. It was too small to make out the face, but it looked like a formal school portrait, stuck right in the middle of the otherwise gray, empty space. It was hard for me to imagine Chase Albright doing something as frivolous as adorning his locker in any way, which almost certainly meant whoever was in that picture really meant something to him. I turned back to Laura and Ryan, changing my tune just slightly. "It was okay. No big deal."

"If you're talking about your stupid stories, you're right —they're no big deal. The article I'm going to write, based on my *exclusive interview* with Detective *Loser,* is going to blow them away."

I hadn't even heard Vivienne Fitch slither up behind me like a cobra in a tight sweater, and apparently Ryan and Laura were caught off-guard, too. We all spun around in unison, clunking into each other like the Three Stooges. Viv wasn't laughing at our routine, though—and I wasn't amused, either. Just confused.

"What exclusive interview?"

Viv smiled smugly. "The one I got by just visiting his office, after school, and persuading him to give an *earnest, ambitious* student journalist information that I don't think any other reporter has yet."

I knew what Viv meant by "visiting" and "persuading." They were code for "barging in" and "bullying." Well, bullying no doubt combined with intermittent hair tossing, eye batting, and pouts that said, *Poor helpless me, just trying to get a story from big, strong you!*

All at once, I started to get nervous, because a guy like Detective Lohser wouldn't be able to handle those one-two punches, which would have exploited his incompetence *and* preyed upon his obvious, if completely unwarranted, vanity.

"What did you learn?" I asked, trying to act as if I hardly cared. "Nothing, probably."

"Wrong, as usual, Ostermeyer," Viv said. "I got him to admit that he thinks that alibi your father concocted out of the blue is going to crack and stink like a rotten egg."

I swallowed thickly because, while my armpits were getting damp, my throat was suddenly bone-dry. "What did you just say?"

"That Detective Lohser doesn't believe your dad's alibi for a minute—and neither do I." She snorted, deigning to appear unattractive, if only to demonstrate her disgust for a man we apparently mutually disliked. "What a wuss that cop is, though, and if he blows this case—"

"What are you talking about?" I demanded. I looked at Ryan and Laura, but they seemed as baffled as I was, and I turned back to Viv. "What the . . . ?"

My nemesis rolled her eyes. "I'm talking about your dad suddenly 'remembering' that he was alone with his *girlfriend* when Mr. Killdare got murdered. Like *that* holds water. Like his *lover* wouldn't lie for him!"

All of a sudden, the hallway seemed to constrict. Or maybe that was my chest. I definitely had trouble breathing, and barely got out, "Umm . . . *girlfriend?*"

"Jeez Louise!" Viv seemed to realize—much to her obvious delight—that I really had no idea what she was talking about. Her lips curled into a vile smile as she said, finally really sticking it to me, the way she'd wanted to do for years, "Please don't tell me that you had no idea your father is seeing some dweeby librarian named Isabel Parkins!"

Chapter **44**

"I will not be needing this anymore," I told my *former* librarian, keeping my chin high and defiant, so it wouldn't quiver as I handed in my library card for good. "You can cut it up, or run it through a shredder . . . whatever you do with cards that *won't be used again.*"

"Millie . . ." Ms. Parkins didn't accept the plastic rectangle that had represented the bond between us, and she sounded incredibly sorry—which was not going to soften me up—when she said, "Your father told me how upset you are, and I understand. But believe me, we kept our relationship a secret—even when it cast suspicion on your dad—for you. Until it became *impossible* not to tell Detective Lohser, we stayed quiet for *you*—"

"You did *nothing* for me," I snapped, slapping the card on the counter. "Except *betray* me."

Ms. Parkins reeled back, as if I'd slapped her hard enough to make her big, dangly earrings swing. But she didn't dispute the charge, saying only, "Oh, Millie . . . Your father and I . . ."

I hated that she was talking like they were a real team. One that had formed behind my back.

". . . It just happened gradually between us," she explained, echoing stuff my dad had said when I'd confronted him, too. Had they rehearsed their big rationale during one of their clandestine meetings? "And you were always at the forefront of our minds when we began to realize how we felt for each other." Ms. Parkins kept trying to justify her lies—in vain. "We tried to fight it, for you. Your father . . . He was worried that you wouldn't like him dating. We talked about waiting until you went to college, at least, so you'd have your own life and wouldn't feel like I was intruding in your home." Two round, pink spots formed on her cheeks. "But we love each other, Millie. I'm sorry, but we do."

There was so much to swallow in what she'd just said that it all ended up sticking in my throat. I didn't know how I felt about my father dating again. I wasn't all right with it, but part of me understood that *Dad* wasn't dead. I even thought my mother would want him to be happy . . . if not necessarily *in love* with another woman, even if that woman was great. Or used to be great. Maybe too great . . .

I read a lot of philosophy books, but I couldn't seem to put any of my knowledge to practical use right then—couldn't be stoic or understanding, let alone sort out what I was feeling —and what ultimately came out of my mouth was "But . . . but you're all wrong for each other!"

Ms. Parkins seemed confused. "That . . . that's your main concern?"

I had no idea if that was my "main concern." I'd just blurted it out, and it was true. My dad was sensible and stern and mayoral, while Ms. Parkins was whimsical and funny and quirky and compassionate . . . like my mom had been, only with more rhinestones and chunky rings and crazier shoes . . .

This is all too confusing.

And because I couldn't explain what I'd meant, I pushed the card toward Ms. Parkins again, along with a bunch of long-overdue books that I'd found scattered around my room —the fines on which I had no intention of paying—and summed up my emotions with the bitter reminder, "You were my librarian!"

I knew that Ms. Parkins would understand exactly what that meant. She, of all people, knew the sacred trust that word—"librarian"—implied. Because a librarian was *supposed to be* a spiritual, intellectual mentor who kept your secrets and didn't give you a funny look when you checked out a book about the care and feeding of pythons because you might've borrowed one from your junior high science lab, just to give it a weekend of freedom from a cage. A librarian could've answered questions that you had about a certain guy whom you used consider an insufferable snob but who was turning out to be confusing and maybe likable. Perhaps too likable for a girl with a pug-dog nose and no table manners. A librarian opened up new doors for you, intellectually, too, without shoving you through them.

A librarian was *important.* And now I didn't have one anymore.

No mother. And no librarian.

"You were MY LIBRARIAN" I repeated, too loudly, even for a laid-back library. "Don't you get it?"

Ms. Parkins didn't say anything right away. Probably, I realized, because her eyes were watery and her throat was tight, like mine. "Please, Millie," she finally said softly. "Don't stop reading because of this. Even if you can't forgive me, don't give up books."

"Oh, I'm not giving up books," I informed her, jutting my chin again. "From now on, I'll be using the *school* library."

I'd hurt Ms. Parkins with my accusation of betrayal, but I nearly crushed her when I said that, because we both knew that confining me to the Honeywell High library was the equivalent of putting a lion used to roaming a vast plain and feasting on wild game in a zoo with a few scraps of gray, grocery-store meat. Like confining a majestic Burmese python in a fish tank. It wasn't the school librarians' fault, but they had a limited budget and even more restrictions on what they could buy. I'd never find Alain de Botton's *The Architecture of Happiness* at school, because they needed five copies of *Huckleberry Finn* for all the ninth graders who wanted it for book reports every year. It was a sad economic reality—and my reality for the rest of the year.

"Oh, Millie . . . Please keep your card," Ms. Parkins begged, shoving it back across the desk. "You can come when I'm not here."

But we both knew that when she wasn't with my father, apparently, she was *always* there. Librarian-ing was a labor of love for Isabel Parkins. Which wasn't going to make me like her again, either. Besides, the public library just wasn't the same for me anymore. I didn't want to go there, ever again.

"I guess I'll be seeing you around," I said, turning to go. "Since your affair is out in the open now."

She didn't say anything. She just let me walk out the door, and I hoped, in this mean, hurt little part of my heart, that she was crying, too.

Chapter 45

When I got home, I went to my bedroom, only to realize that I hadn't taken back every book I owed the library. Somehow, I'd overlooked the Nancy Drews that were right on my desk.

My mood even darker, if that was possible, I picked up *The Hidden Staircase* and *The Clue in the Crumbling Wall*, thinking I should march right back and return them, so I could consider my ties with the Honeywell Public Library officially severed . . . at least until I got another notice about my outstanding fines. Those would probably keep coming forever.

But as I stood there holding the books, I changed my mind. Not only didn't I want to see Ms. Parkins again—it definitely would've undercut the impact of my dramatic, final departure if I came crawling back fifteen minutes later—but all at once, I was angry with myself, too.

You didn't handle that very well, Millie. Nancy Drew wouldn't have fallen apart if some lady had started dating her suave, widower father, Carson Drew . . .

"But I'm *not* Nancy Drew," I muttered, staring at the teen sleuth on the cover of *The Hidden Staircase*. A girl who did everything rationally, and with class and manners. Mom and I used to laugh about how Nancy was so prissy and perfect, with her "titian, bobbed" hair always in place, even when she drove around in her spotless convertible with her dorky, do-gooder boyfriend, Ned Nickerson.

That night, I wasn't remotely amused, though.

Why can't you be that pulled-together girl, Millie? Why is everything about you, from your wardrobe to your feelings to the way you learn, messy?

I didn't know. And even though I was, by then, well aware that I'd been childish, veering too close to throwing a genuine tantrum at the library, I wasn't sure if I wanted to fix things with Ms. Parkins, either.

She lied to me.

And just when I finally started to let loose in a different way, by crying, the other last person I wanted to see came knocking on my bedroom door. When I didn't answer, Dad opened it anyhow, and for once he didn't complain about the trash on the floor or the half-empty bowl of Chex Mix or the way my collection of stretched-out bras refused to be fully contained in my underwear drawer. He just stood there, looking uncharacteristically uncertain.

"If you're here to apologize again . . ." I said, turning my back on him because it hurt to see his face. In part because I was furious with him, but in part because he looked miserable, too. Still, I finished my thought. "Don't bother."

I half expected him to ignore my curt dismissal and attempt, one more time, to reach out to me. But Dad didn't
do that. Instead, he just softly reminded me of plans I'd completely forgotten as I tried to sort out my pain and anger.

"Chase is here to pick you up, Millie. He's waiting downstairs."

Chapter 46

I knelt before Mr. Killdare's bookshelf, this time not hiding, since Chase, of course, had let us both into the house and was helping me explore. I could hear him upstairs, presumably in Coach Killdare's bedroom, opening and closing drawers, because he was a lot less squeamish than Laura about intruding.

"Mr. Killdare's gone, Millie," Chase had reminded me when I'd gotten slightly cold feet. "And we're trying to help find his killer."

"And getting nowhere," I muttered, staring blankly at that shelf of knickknacks that I'd thought were so important when I'd first seen them.

I was having trouble focusing because my mind was still on my dad and Ms. Parkins, and how I'd said everything I'd wanted to say right to their faces—yet nothing had come out right.

And my bad mood was compounded by the fact that Baxter had followed Chase upstairs, picking his part-time caretaker over the person who'd clearly been most excited to see him when we'd opened the door. I'd held out my arms, and Baxter had bounded right past me, tail wagging as he'd hurled himself at Chase.

Suck it up, Millie. He was never really *your dog.*

"Okay, let's see," I mumbled, forcing myself to inventory the items on the shelf. There was a porcelain copy of the Acropolis in Athens, a working clock shaped like Big Ben, and a foot-high plaster Leaning Tower of Pisa next to what looked like a brass replica of the Little Mermaid statue in Copenhagen, Denmark, if I remembered correctly.

In all, there were about eight cities represented there.

I peered more closely.

But something was missing.

Something that would've sat at the end of the row, and that had a perfectly square base. I could see the shape, even though dust was starting to accumulate over the spot.

I was very curious about that missing landmark, because who brought back souvenirs?

People who travel and send postcards, that's who.

People like BeeBee—

"Hey, I found some old yearbooks—and something weird in one of Mr. Killdare's drawers." Chase's voice broke into my reverie, as did a cold nose, nudging my hand.

"Get lost, mutt," I grumbled, pushing Baxter away, even though I really wanted to hug him. "Too little, too late."

"Millie, did you hear me, about Mr. Killdare's drawers?"

I turned around and plunked down on my butt, looking up at Chase—and grudgingly accepting a wrinkled head in my lap. "Yeah," I said, still refusing to scratch behind a waiting ear. "And the last thing I want to do is check out something 'weird' in Coach Killdare's 'drawers.' That sounds repulsive —and borderline wrong—to me."

"I'm not talking about his underwear . . ." Chase seemed to catch himself. "Well, I'm kind of talking about that."

My hand, of its own accord, began to stroke that silky canine ear. "There is obviously way too much familiarity in male locker rooms," I noted. "You guys need boundaries."

Chase opened his mouth, and I could tell that he was about to bite on my invitation to start some kind of argument. Then he seemed to change his mind and asked, for at least the tenth time, "Are you sure there's nothing wrong, Millie? Because you have been bad company all night. Where's the girl who cracked me up, eating pie with her bare hands and showing me the fudge stain on her shirt?"

Sure, sure . . . I was great—to laugh at. But *he* had another priority, too. A better, no doubt prettier, girl, with a locker-worthy face. Just like my father had a librarian he couldn't stop loving, even if it hurt me, and Baxter had a better master. I was never quite enough for anybody, was I?

"Nothing's wrong," I repeated, pushing aside Baxter's head, standing up, and brushing off my butt. "What'd you find?"

"Like I said, these old yearbooks." Chase held up a stack of annuals. "Which might give us some clues to friends—or enemies—from Mr. Killdare's past. Or present. There are high school and college books here. Including some recent ones from Honeywell."

"Yeah, I can't tell you how many times I've signed 'Hate

your guts enough to kill you someday. Have a great summer. Stay cool for-evah!'" I drew the numeral four in the air with my finger. "With a 'four' in 'for-evah.'"

I could tell the sarcasm got under Chase's skin. He tossed the books onto the La-Z-Boy. "I didn't say these held all the answers."

Stop taking your bad mood out on Chase, Millie. It's not his fault you're unlovable.

"So, what's so interesting in Mr. Killdare's drawers?" I asked, forcing myself to be minutely less grouchy. "What's up there?"

Please don't say "stains."

"The top drawer in his dresser—where pretty much every guy keeps socks and underwear—is, like I'd expect, a mess," Chase informed me. "Except for about a third of it. There's an empty space, like somebody else kept stuff there, then took it. Maybe after Mr. Killdare died, because it seems like he would've spread his clothes out if he'd still been using the drawer. You know, while rooting around for matching socks, because they definitely aren't paired up."

That was kind of interesting. Better than finding stains, at least.

"And I checked the bathroom again," he added. "There's no sign of the hair spray or . . . you know . . ."

His voice trailed off, and I started to finish the sentence, thinking that we were two practically adults who ought to be able to say the word "tampons"—a word that girls in TV ads said all the time while holding a box to their heads, for crying out loud. But when push came to shove, I couldn't do it.

"Yeah, I know what you mean," I said. "I get it."

"How weird that I never saw a woman here," Chase mused. "I mean, I used to be here a lot."

"Yeah. Weird."

Then Chase and I stood staring at each other, as if neither of us knew what to do with the clues we'd found, even though it was pretty clear that somebody had "bugged out" —which seemed like guilty behavior, if you asked me.

I was also mildly irritated to think that even Mr. Killdare —he of the armpit stains and belly hair—seemed to have had a serious, if secret, girlfriend. Maybe one who'd been passionate enough about him to kill him. Not that I wanted *that*, but still, to be the single-most important person in somebody else's universe . . . That was kind of enviable.

My expression must've given away my further deteriorating mood, because all at once, Chase abandoned investigating and said quietly, "Hey, Millie, I know something that might cheer you up." And before I could insist that I didn't need or want cheering up, he slapped his hand against his thigh and said, "Baxter, get over here."

Maybe whatever was going to happen would make me happier, but that poor basset hound looked downright dismayed as Chase reached down and hoisted him up, grunting, "Come on, buddy. You know the drill!"

Chapter 47

L ook how cute he is!" I cried, piling more bubbles onto Baxter's head, so it looked like he was wearing a little hat. "I wish I'd brought my cell phone."

Chase reached for a cup on the edge of the tub. "I don't think Bax wants this moment to be captured forever. Look at his face."

The wet dog, already clearly miserable at the indignity of being bathed, did seem even more despondent about the insult I'd added to injury. His eyes pleaded for rescue, while Chase's requested permission. He held the cup aloft. "May I?"

"Oh, all right," I agreed reluctantly. "But you have to admit, he looks adorable."

Covering Baxter's eyes with his hand, Chase dumped water over the dog's head, noting, "I never thought you'd use the word 'adorable.' That doesn't seem like something that would be in Millie Ostermeyer's vocabulary."

The dog bath seemed to be ending and I sat back on my heels. "Well, what sort of words would you expect me to use?"

"Definitely nothing in French," Chase joked. "And your Spanish seems sketchy, too—"

"Hey!"

Chase ignored me, reaching past me to pull the drain plug. His arm brushed my shoulder, and even though the touch was slight, I could feel rock-hard muscle. I could also smell that soap or cologne that I was starting to associate with him. But any momentary flutter I felt in my stomach was squashed when he said, "But 'adorable'—that just seems way too 'girly' for somebody who wears Adidas, eats like a linebacker, and likes something as ugly as this mutt." He dropped the towel over the dripping dog in question and lifted him out of the tub. "Don't most girls like Chihuahuas? Dogs they can tuck into their purses?"

I honestly hadn't been drawn to Chase back when Laura'd teased me about watching him in the gym, but the more I was around him, the more I had to admit to finding him attractive. Still, I wasn't about to pretend to be anybody except who I was, even if I didn't fit his feminine stereotype. Heck, how could I do that, even if I'd wanted to, when I was wearing a black "Nihilists for Nothing" T-shirt?

"I don't like purses, let alone dogs that can fit into them," I advised him. "But I'm not a guy, either."

Shaking off the towel, Baxter took off for the hallway, while Chase sank down on the floor at my side, resting back against the tub and grinning. "I didn't say that you were, Millie. I definitely didn't say *that*."

I shifted, too, so we were sitting shoulder to shoulder. "Yeah, you kinda did."

"Sorry." He leaned forward to meet my eyes, as if he wanted me to see that he was sincere. "I didn't mean to do that. And I don't *think* that."

Yeah, but you don't think I'm feminine, either.

The mood—at least my mood—had lightened during Baxter's bath, but as Chase and I sat side by side, studying each other the way we'd done in French class, we both got solemn again. And quiet. A silence that lasted for what seemed like a long time, until Chase ventured, "What do you think of me, Millie? Huh? Because I used to get this feeling that you hated me—and maybe everybody else in school, too."

"What?" I wasn't sure I'd heard right. *Me? A hater?*

"Well, you always act like school is beneath you," Chase said. "I see you in French class, reading anything but the textbook, like you don't *want* to learn the language—maybe just because you're supposed to." He gestured to my shirt. "And then there are the T-shirts with the ironic cartoons and the philosophy jokes that seem designed to go over most people's heads."

Forcing myself not to get that flutter in my stomach again—this time over his correct use of "ironic"—I started to protest, because first of all, the cartoons weren't really meant to be viewed that way. Couldn't a girl genuinely like Schopenhauer *and* Snoopy? And as for learning French . . . Well, maybe he had a small point about that. Regardless, Chase wasn't done yet.

"Plus I never see you with anybody but Laura or Ryan." He shrugged. "I just thought you were a snob."

I nearly laughed. "I thought the same about you because you never hung out with *anybody*. And talk about being superior. I know the movies you like!"

We kept searching each other's faces, as if looking for evidence of lingering pretentiousness, until I said, "Maybe we were both wrong, though."

Chase continued watching me, to the point that I almost started to squirm. "Yeah, maybe," he finally agreed.

Then I asked quietly, almost like I didn't want to scare him off with the question, "Why do you talk to me, Chase? I mean, you must feel like hanging out with the guys on the team sometimes. But you've kept aloof for more than a year. Why talk to *me*?"

He seemed almost as confused as I was. "I don't know, Millie. There's just something about you . . ." He paused, watching me blush just a little. Then, his gaze shifting to my cheeks, he asked, even more softly, "Why were you crying tonight?"

"I wasn't—"

"Millie . . . I can still see the tear stains on your face." For a second, I thought he was going to touch my cheek. He lifted his hand—then dropped it. "So why?"

Oh, gosh. Maybe Chase wasn't sure why he talked to me, but I was pretty sure why I opened up to him. Because when he really unlocked those eyes, they weren't just magazine-picture pretty. They were really beautiful in a different way. That stuff he'd gone through had obviously given him a capacity for empathy that I didn't think my other classmates had yet. Even Laura and Ryan, who understood me pretty well, didn't quite get pain the way I thought Chase did.

I wanted to spill my guts right then and there, but I didn't exactly answer him. Instead, I asked my own question. "Chase . . . Does your dad ever date?"

He shook his head. "No, he's too busy."

I picked at my shoelaces, avoiding his gaze. "Would you hate it if he did?"

"No." But he quickly added, "I think it's different for me, though. My parents fought all the time. I'd be okay if either one of them found somebody who made them happier." I felt him shrug again, his shoulder brushing mine. "Maybe my mom already has."

"Why can't I feel that way?" I muttered. "Why can't I be happy that my dad is dating my librarian?"

Chase bent to try to see my face again. "You 'have' a librarian?" He frowned. "That's different."

"Yeah. I do have one," I confirmed, still avoiding his eyes. "And she's been seeing my father."

"So . . . What's wrong with that?" Chase nudged me with his shoulder, trying to cajole me back into a better mood. "Does she shush you too much outside the library?"

I finally looked at him again, and the expression on my face wiped the smile off his. "No," I said. "Ms. Parkins is wonderful, actually. Perfect. A lot like my mom. And she and my dad are *in love.*"

"Hey, Millie . . . It's okay." I hadn't even realized that a tear had spilled out until Chase really did brush one finger across my cheek. "It's okay."

"Why can't I just be good with it?" I asked, my voice catching. "Why did I have to be a jerk to both of them?"

And how did it feel to be comforted—touched on the face—by a guy my age who wasn't Ryan? How strange was it to feel Chase put his arm around my shoulder, even tentatively? Although he sounded pretty confident when he said, "The whole thing is probably worse because this Ms. Parkins is 'perfect.' If I were you, and had been close to my mom, I'd be terrified that she'd replace her. Maybe, if I were you, I'd push your librarian away and act like I *hated* her. Because some people . . . You just never want them to be replaced. Or *erased*."

Oh, he totally understood the whole dilemma, had articulated exactly what I was feeling. And I was pretty sure I knew why he was able to do that and could get how scary it was to think that someone might be "erased." *That person he hurt in the accident—the part of the story he held back . . . He can't let that go.* But I didn't bring that up. It wasn't the right time. And I didn't want to break the moment between us. I didn't want Chase to pull away because—even though I'd hardly cried since my mother had died—my stupid eyes were betraying me again and really welling up. Forcing myself to smile, I raised my face to Chase's and ventured a joke. "Jeez, Albright. I guess you've really learned something from watching all those old, gloomy movies. You definitely understand pathos."

This time, Chase was the one not laughing. On the contrary, he seemed almost haunted, informing me in a tight voice, "Yeah, well, it's not just from watching movies, Millie."

Then we got quiet again, while I continued to compose myself, with the comforting weight of Chase's arm around me.

Well, it was comforting—and something more.

Gradually, as we sat there, my sadness and anger started to be replaced by a new set of equally confusing emotions. And I saw something change in Chase's eyes, too. The slow emergence of an expression I'd never seen in a boy's eyes, and certainly never expected to see in his. Especially not after the stuff he'd just said about me.

Millie . . . What are you two doing?

Something I really wanted to do—but didn't want at all. Not with Chase.

He'd basically just told me that I wasn't his type. Had enumerated all my flaws. What kind of girl wanted that? Let alone to get a first kiss in a *dead coach's bathroom?* In sight of a toilet, for crying out loud.

And yet . . .

Chase seemed uncharacteristically uncertain, too, as he continued to study my eyes. My muddy-green eyes, which weren't model-icious, like his. "Millie . . ."

He *sounded* unsure, but I definitely felt his arm tighten, just slightly, around me, and I rested more heavily against him— then pulled right back, because, of course, he felt amazing. Too amazing, probably, for a girl who wasn't even sure she was wearing a clean shirt, which she'd plucked off a pile on her bedroom floor.

All at once, I could hear Chase's critique echoing in my head.

"... *Somebody who wears Adidas, eats like a linebacker*..."

Not to mention *"There were injuries ... Charges against me..."*

And that picture in his locker . . .

But the *feel* of Chase pulling me even closer. His reassuring muscle. And those eyes. Those incredible empathic eyes, and the way he was shifting to face me more fully, maybe unsure right then, but obviously experienced, his hand moving to rest under my chin so he could tilt my face upward, his voice even lower and more throaty as he whispered, "Millie . . ."

Forget the setting, Millicent! Forget everything! Just go for it!

Before Baxter comes bounding in!

Only that noise that I was hearing in the hallway . . . It wasn't a dog.

No, of course the sound that was just barely registering in my muddled brain was a *person*. One who interrupted me and Chase's almost kiss with a supercilious "Well, well, well . . . What have we here?"

Chapter **48**

The realization that I'd almost had my first kiss on a bathroom floor next to a tub that needed to be wiped clean of dog hair was bad.

And the fact that said near kiss had been interrupted by a smirking Detective Blaine Lohser—even worse.

But the look on Chase's face—the regret mingled with near horror that I saw in his eyes as he disentangled us, pulling his arm from around my shoulders . . . *that* was the worst part of the whole farce.

"What the hell did we almost do?" he seemed to silently ask me. Standing, he helped me to my feet, his grip hard around my hand and his mouth in a grim line. *"Me . . . with YOU?"*

Before I could try to convey something similar so he wouldn't think I'd actually wanted that kiss, either, he turned to Detective Lohser, who stood in the doorway, and asked, not rudely, but not exactly politely, either, "What are you doing here?"

"I'm investigating a murder," the cop in an off-duty, off-brand polo shirt reminded us, no longer grinning. He moved farther into the small room, so I ended up wedged against the vanity and medicine chest. Catching a glimpse of myself in the mirror, I noticed that I looked guilty. Maybe not of murder, but of being a teenager caught with another teenager of the opposite sex, about to do teenager stuff that adults like Blaine Lohser clearly disapproved of. "I saw a car outside the house, and lights on, and . . ." He took a step closer, getting right in Chase's face. "I recalled how criminals often return to the scene of the crime, and thought I'd investigate."

Really? He had to "recall" something I knew from a million television shows?

How had I ever been intimidated by this man?

Chase didn't seem impressed, either. Moreover, he didn't step back, so the two guys stood practically chest to chest, which gave Chase a height advantage. "I've never heard anything about the murder taking place here," he pointed out.

Detective Lohser seemed to realize he'd misspoken, and he backtracked, stammering. "Well, er . . . This is still a place of interest . . ."

Chase wasn't listening. "We're here to take care of the dog—at the request of Mr. Killdare's family. I have a key and every right to be here."

"Looks like you were taking care of other business, too," Detective Lohser countered. "Maybe the same 'business' you two were addressing under the bleachers the night a *body turned up?*"

Okay, it was starting to get creepy for an adult to keep referencing kids making out. Especially since Chase and I hadn't really been doing anything. *God forbid!* But Detective Lohser wasn't quite done, and he narrowed his eyes at Chase. "It must be nice to have the keys to an *empty* house, huh, Romeo?"

Chase took another step forward, and for a second, I almost felt sorry for Detective Lohser. I doubted he had any idea that he was up against somebody who'd dealt with authority figures who made Hollerin' Hank Killdare look like a teddy bear. There was no way a guy who'd probably been voted "most likely to shoot his own foot" at the police academy was going to bully a Mason Treadwell alum. "What, exactly, are you implying?" Chase asked. "Huh?"

Detective Lohser had no choice but to step back, but he remained on the verbal offensive. "Maybe that you wanted Hank Killdare out of the way so you'd have *unfettered access to your love nest.*"

That was the worst "bad cop" line I'd ever heard, and I nearly burst out laughing. I also finally understood why my father had once said jokingly, "I think the county made Lohser a detective because around here it keeps him behind a desk, away from the real criminals!"

"Come on," I interjected. "You can't really think that. I mean, we might just be kids, but even we know the house will be sold—and probably soon. My dad says real estate moves like lightning in Honeywell. Who would kill for a few weeks of . . . ?"

I wasn't sure how I wanted to end that sentence. Maybe with "privacy"?

Detective Lohser didn't need me to finish my thought, anyhow. "People have killed for less," he said evenly. "Much less."

"I don't really think so." Chase agreed with me. "And if we honestly *took a life* to get access to this house—even for a few weeks . . ." He finally looked at me again. "If Millie really was my girlfriend, would we be *sitting on the bathroom floor?* Would we go to all that trouble for *that?*"

He was supporting me, but that sort of stung, too. A "girl-friend" would've gotten better treatment. That girl in his locker—Allison—wouldn't have had to stare at plumbing fix-tures as he'd put his arm around *her.*

All at once, I started to get frustrated with guys in general —ones who almost kissed you, then looked mortified, and ones who abused their authority. I also happened to think of something else that was irking me about Detective Lohser. "Yeah," I said. "And why did you tell Vivienne Fitch—a stupid student reporter—about my dad's alibi? Are you supposed to tell the press stuff like that? Whatever happened to 'I can't comment on an ongoing investigation'?"

"I know how to handle the press," Lohser grunted, but evasively, in a way that told me Viv had—as I'd suspected— manipulated him into saying more than he'd wanted. "I did everything by the book."

Yeah. The "Big Book of Bad Detecting." The "Idiot's Guide to Being an Idiot."

I really didn't know what would be worse. Having a com-petent detective investigate Mr. Killdare's death, because there was circumstantial evidence against my father, or to have a completely incompetent blabbermouth with a ven-detta on the case. Maybe I—and my dad—couldn't have won either way.

"You'd better stop talking about my father in public," I warned him. "We'll sue you."

It was my second threat of litigation in less than a month, and I had no idea if we'd have a leg to stand on. But Detective Lohser didn't seem to care, anyhow. In fact, he suddenly seemed distracted, his eyebrows scrunching together as he frowned at something behind me.

"Step aside," he muttered, pushing me with his arm. "I want to see something again in the medicine cabinet."

I edged over, and Chase and I looked at each other, both shrugging, as if to say, *Oh, well. At least he's off our case.*

Well, I thought I was glad that Detective Lohser had shifted his attention—until he opened the cabinet and plucked a bottle of pills from the top shelf. I wasn't sure why, but something about the way he stared at that container— like he'd found the Holy Grail—made me nervous, and since I was standing right next to him, I did my best to read the label.

And when I did, I got a little sick to my stomach—although the product in his hand, dexamethasone, was, ironically, meant to ease nausea.

I knew that because my mom had taken it to counter the effects of chemotherapy. I'd brought it to her dozens of times during her treatment.

And I really hated the look in Detective Lohser's eyes—the hostile little gleam—as he met mine, saying, like he knew what he held, too, "Interesting, huh?"

Maybe, just maybe, he wasn't as much of an idiot as I'd thought.

Chapter 49

W hat was that all about, with the medicine?" Chase asked when we were outside, standing next to his car on Mr. Killdare's dark driveway. Detective Lohser was still spooking around inside. I saw a light go on in the kitchen and seriously hoped he wouldn't kick Baxter, which seemed like something he might do, just for laughs.

I waited too long for the right moment to ask for a dog. Now Dad and I aren't even speaking—

"Did I miss something there?" Chase interrupted my thoughts, tossing the yearbooks he'd managed to swipe into his BMW. "Why'd you both get strange about that pill bottle?"

I hesitated, then realized there was probably no reason not to tell Chase about the drug. Still, I lowered my voice, in case Detective Lohser came outside, on the off chance that he didn't really know what he'd discovered. "It was a bottle of dexamethasone—"

Chase raised a hand. "Slow down, Millie. It's like you're talking French."

I ignored the joke. Especially since I wasn't sure he should be mocking me right then. I was pretty sure we'd discussed my flaws enough for one night. "It's a drug that relieves nausea in chemotherapy patients," I explained, leaning against his car, forgetting that he probably cared about the paint job. "My mom took it, too."

Chase raised an eyebrow. "So . . . Mr. Killdare had *cancer?*"

"Yeah. I also know that from a letter I found. He had acute myelogenous leukemia. AML, for short."

"French again, Millie."

"It's pretty common, actually," I said. "In fact, some people think it's *too* common for anybody who works or goes to school at Honeywell."

"Still not quite following," Chase admitted.

"A few years ago," I whispered, "there was talk about the school giving people cancer because it's located on an old industrial site. A place that used benzene, which has been linked to AML." I dropped my voice even lower. "My dad almost lost an election before you moved here because he fought to have the school built there. The soil and groundwater have always tested safe, but when two custodians and a teacher got sick, these rumors started. There's no way there was a connection—the school had only been open about a year, for crying out loud—but people freaked out about the coincidence."

Even if he wasn't familiar with antiemetic drugs or myeloid leukemias, Chase was a smart guy, and he quickly put the rest of the story together. He fell back against his car, too, exhaling with a whoosh. "Wow, Millie . . . So your dad possibly had several reasons to want Mr. Killdare dead. The big fights. The head-coaching job. Wanting to keep the cancer thing silent if your dad knew about it . . ." He bent to look at me. "You're not just investigating this murder because you want some journalism award. You're worried about your father."

I shrugged. "Maybe."

"Millie . . ." Chase seemed genuinely confused. "Why didn't you tell me this earlier?"

"I don't know," I told him. "I guess I keep stuff to myself, too."

"So did Mr. Killdare," Chase noted, looking impressed. "He must've been pretty sick. But he never let it show at practice or school."

Once again, Hollerin' Hank was turning out to have had some good points. He'd obviously sucked up some pretty serious misery, continuing to coach without burdening his squad or letting his students know he was suffering.

I bit my nail, staring blankly down at the driveway.

But had my father known? Could Mr. Killdare really have kept something so big from his right-hand man?

Would I ask Dad, if I ever talked to him again?

"Millie?"

Chase's voice, softer than before, again broke into my thoughts.

I looked up to see that his mood seemed to have shifted. "Yeah?"

"I'm sorry . . . about almost kissing you."

"What?"

Somehow I'd thought we'd never mention what had almost happened by the tub. I'd thought we'd both just pretend that nothing had occurred.

"I shouldn't have done that," Chase continued. "I really shouldn't have —"

"Okay, Chase," I interrupted. I was starting to get annoyed again. "I get it."

"No, you don't understand." He shifted, so he was leaning on his side, facing me. "I just . . . I just can't, Millie. But you looked so sad, and your big green eyes . . ."

Oh, gosh. He'd nearly kissed me out of *pity?* Because I looked like Baxter during a bath, all droopy eyed and woebegone? That was even worse than, say, "momentary, if ill-advised, lust."

"What?" I asked, hearing an edge of anger in my voice. "You're the universal antidote for female sadness? One kiss from Chase Albright sends every girl into ecstasy? So you thought you'd spare a dose for pathetic, eats-like-a-linebacker me, even if it made you ill?"

Chase shook his head. "No, Millie! It's not like that. You're misunderstanding and putting words in my mouth. I'm trying to say that you just looked . . . It seemed like . . ." He dug his fingers into his too-good-for-me hair, concluding weakly, "But I *really just can't.*"

I knew what he was trying to say without rubbing my nose in it. That he had a girlfriend. And more to the point, I wasn't the type of girl guys like him kissed. I didn't need a PowerPoint presentation, or even completed sentences, to grasp the two main thoughts he was trying to express.

"Chase Albright, if you wrap this up with 'It's not you, it's me,' I am going to break your perfect nose," I informed him. "So I suggest you stop talking now." I started to walk away, even though I really would've liked a ride home. "And don't be in any hurry to contact me in the future, either," I added him over my shoulder. *"El jerko."*

Chase didn't try to persuade me to come back. He didn't say a word.

And when I finally made it home, there was a neat pile of yearbooks waiting for me on the front porch like maybe our brief investigative partnership really was over.

Picking them up, I opened the door and went inside — only to nearly drop the whole stack when my dad, looking pale, informed me, without so much as a hello, "I'm being taken in for official questioning, Millie. Don't wait up for me."

Only then did I realize that Detective Lohser had beaten me to my house, too.

He was standing in the living room.

Needless to say, smirking.

Chapter **50**

D ad, what happened?" I asked, bounding off the couch when he finally got home around midnight. "Are you okay?"

"Of course I'm fine," he said, not exactly meeting my eyes. We hadn't really looked at each other since the whole affair . . . of the affair. He loosened his tie roughly, like it was a noose that he couldn't wait to shake off, and headed for the stairs. "Just go to bed, Millie."

"I . . . I made you a snack," I said, grabbing a plate of cheese and crackers off the coffee table. Okay, maybe I hadn't so much "made" as "assembled" a snack. "Are you hungry?"

He already had one foot on a riser and a hand on the banister. "No. Thanks."

Ditching the plate, I followed him. "Dad . . ."

He finally turned to look down at me, seeming borderline exasperated—and completely exhausted. "What, Millicent?"

"Did you . . . Did you know about Mr. Killdare's cancer?"

He frowned—even more, if that was possible. "How did *you* know?"

"I just . . . did." I studied his face. "But you . . . Did *you* know?"

Dad's lips clamped into a white line, and he shook his head. "No, Millie. This is the first I've heard of it, tonight. I didn't know Mr. Killdare was ill."

He started to head up the stairs again, but I stopped him one more time. "Dad?"

His hand clenched on the rail, and he exhaled with a big sigh. "What?"

"Are you . . . Are you going to be . . . *arrested,* or something?"

Dad didn't exactly answer me. "They don't have a murder weapon."

That was all he said. Then my father trudged upstairs, and I wondered whether he would call Ms. Parkins to tell her everything that had happened. Unburden himself to her. Or had I really ruined all that?

I couldn't ask. He clearly didn't want to talk to *me* that night. Maybe because he was sick of talking, or didn't want to bother me with his problems, or thought my concern was too little too late. Or maybe he was upset with me because Detective Blaine Lohser had snitched about me being on a bathroom floor with Dad's prize quarterback.

Maybe it was a combination of all that stuff.

I stood at the foot of the stairs, listening to my father close the door to his bedroom and thinking that somebody had better find that murder weapon soon.

Because, of course, *that* would exonerate my dad.

I mean, how couldn't it?

Chapter **51**

What's going on with you and you-know-who?" Laura whispered. She looked past me toward Chase's desk, an area of the French classroom that I was studiously avoiding. Actually, I'd never been so studious about anything in my entire life. "I thought you guys were getting kind of . . . friendly."

God love Laura Bugbee. She was the only person who'd ever thought there could be anything, even friendship, between me and Chase Albright, and she continued to cling to her delusion.

"That ship has sailed—and sunk," I informed her quietly as I folded the latest edition of the *Gazette*, which *didn't* feature Viv's interview with Detective Lohser. The story had been pulled at the last minute, because apparently the too-chatty cop had called Mr. Woolsey, admitting that maybe he'd told Viv too much and begging for intervention. Needless to say, Mr. Woolsey—who knew what it was like to be manipulated by Vivienne Fitch, and who wanted the story gone, anyhow —had been more than happy to exercise power for once.

I shouldn't have told Viv that I reminded Detective Lohser he shouldn't comment on an ongoing investigation, but I couldn't resist seeing her throw a massive, hilarious hissy fit—

"Millie?" Laura was lightly smacking my shoulder. "Ships sailing? And sinking?"

I finally dared a glance at Chase, who was busy doing what Laura and I were supposed to be doing: conjugating on a worksheet. He seemed oblivious to me, head bent and pen moving. I turned back to Laura. "Actually, it was kind of like the *Titanic* crashing into one of those boats named after states. The *Arizona*, or the *Maine*." I bashed my fists together and made a sound like a small explosion. "Boom! Luxury liner Chase meets battleship Millie with disastrous results."

Laura clearly wanted to know more, but my maritime-disaster reenactment had drawn Mademoiselle Beamish's attention, and she said sharply from behind her desk, *"Mee-leh-CENT! Taisez-vous!"*

Of course, most kids were amused, as usual, to witness me getting in trouble. But for once, Viv wasn't among them. She was watching me with cold eyes, obviously still enraged about my messing up her "exclusive" story.

I stared back, not intimidated. *What's your big secret, Vivienne? The one that you don't want Mike to EVER reveal?*

Then I looked at Mike Price, who was also studying me—and who wasn't laughing, either. On the contrary, his simian brow was furrowed, like he'd pushed the right buttons but the researchers hadn't given him the banana he'd expected.

He's stupid and full of testosterone. But is he really brainless —and hormonal—enough to commit an impulsive murder? Kill a coach who'd messed up his one shot at playing big-time college ball . . . ?

"Millie? Are we gonna dialogue?" Laura was tapping me again, apparently alerting me to the fact that it was time for Monday's free-form dialogue session.

I didn't answer her, though. I was watching, confused, as Viv *didn't* pair up with Mike.

No, she stood up, and with one more evil glance at me, made her way directly to *Chase* before Ms. Beamish could even hoist herself out of her chair.

But . . .

"Millie? Are we gonna talk?" Laura asked again.

I wanted to spare my friend yet another painful conversation with our instructor, who was already — clearly unhappily — searching for another victim. I really did.

Yet I found myself looking once more at Mike Price, potential killer, alone and baffled with nobody to talk to — a sitting duck, maybe just waiting to make some verbal slip that would implicate him in a murder — and I heard myself saying, "Sorry, Laura. I gotta talk with the *other* worst speaker in class."

Chapter **52**

W hat do *you* want?" Mike asked when I slid into the desk next to his. "Huh?"

"I just thought we should talk," I said, too cheerfully. "You know, we've gone to school together forever. But do we really *know* each other?"

"What the hell are you talking about?" he mumbled. He was addressing me—at least, making semihuman sounds— but staring at Viv and Chase, clearly unhappy that he'd been abandoned in favor of the quarterback who'd also stolen his football glory.

I found myself watching Viv and Chase, too, as they conversed with apparent ease.

Is Viv finally making her move on Chase? And does he like talking to her? Because he might think she's intense, but let's face it, she's got those boobs . . .

I turned back around, forcing myself to focus on Mike, and because we only had a few minutes, I stopped acting like I wanted us to be pals. "First of all," I said quietly, "neither

one of us speaks French, so let's not even pretend to try."
When he didn't respond—didn't even give any sign of having
heard me—I added directly, "How about Coach Killdare getting murdered? Huh? What do you make of *that?*"

Okay, that wasn't exactly brilliant on my part, but at least
Mike grunted a response. "I'd say it sucks. For him."

I was interested in that last prepositional phrase, but I also
kept wondering how Viv could stand spending time with a
guy who spoke in monosyllables, even if he did her bidding.

I shifted once more to see Viv and Chase chattering away,
no doubt in French.

*Sure, they're both smart, good-looking, and can use "dejeuner"
correctly. But* he *would never like HER* . . .

Turning back around, I tried to focus on my own partner
again. "I guess it sucks for you, too," I noted. "I mean, Mr.
Killdare was your coach and mentor. Probably like a father
figure."

Mike gave me a look like I was the dense one. A look I'd
probably earned by pushing it too far with the "father figure"
comment. "Are you nuts?" he asked. "You know he brought
in Albright as a ringer, so I'm not quarterback anymore, right?
I hated that jerk!"

Okay, Mike didn't say "jerk." He used a very nasty epithet
that made me reel back in my seat. "Wow," I said. "You really
did despise him, huh?" Then I leaned forward and narrowed
my eyes. "Maybe enough to wish he was *actually dead?*"

As soon as I said that, I couldn't believe the words had
come out of my mouth, and needless to say, even Mike un-

derstood what I'd done. He cocked his head and said pretty loudly, "Did you just accuse me of *murder?*" He looked around the class, as if for support. "What the hell?"

"Sssh!" I ordered him. Kids were staring at us, and Ms. Beamish was also watching, with a look of displeasure so profound that it seemed to have drained all the color from her face. I couldn't believe she wasn't storming over to insist that we use French. Speaking even more softly, I told Mike, "I didn't accuse you of anything. At most, there was a slight inference . . ." I could tell I'd lost him with that word, and concluded, "Look, you were the one who said you hated Coach Killdare, then got all defensive when I called you on it. You made yourself look guilty." All at once, I realized Mike really had overreacted, and I added, "You're the one who used the word 'accuse.' I never said *that*."

He didn't answer me. He just sat there, watching me with his dim eyes.

Eyes that, I realized, might actually be unfeeling enough to belong to a killer.

I didn't think he was a manipulative psycho, like Viv, but— jokes about monkeys aside—he did have an animalistic quality, and I could imagine him, in a moment of rage, acting on the impulses of his id.

I broke our gaze to look at his hands. And he had big hands, powerful enough to wield a heavy object and perhaps crack bone.

Then I really noticed Mike's arms for the first time, too. He had massive biceps, easily strong enough to drag a body to a storage space that a multisport athlete like him would've been familiar with.

Viv's words again echoed in my head. The stuff she'd said as she and Mike had walked past the theater. *"Look, idiot. You know what happened. I know what happened. But nobody else will ever—and I mean EVER—find out."*

Suddenly, I got sickly warm.

Did I just accuse—er, make an inference about—the honest-to-gosh killer?

Less than two feet away, Mike continued to glare at me, his oversize fingers flexing on his desk.

Holy crow, Millie! What have you done?

And it was too late to fix anything because right then the bell rang, dismissing class. Mike got up slowly, and I stood up, too. It crossed my mind to attempt to patch things up, maybe to say, "Hey, fun talking with you!" But something about the look on Mike's face told me not to bother. Plus, he was already walking away from me, so I spun on my heel, thinking that, no matter what was up with me and Chase, I wanted to tell him what had just happened. I was pretty sure he'd be interested to know that I was placing his teammate near the top of my list of suspects.

However, Chase was already gone.

And so was Viv.

Chapter **53**

I was sitting in my booth in front of the Lassiter Bijou, trying to think of a six-letter word for "despondent," because
I couldn't seem to bring myself to visit the Honeywell High
library for a new book and was reduced to killing time with
the *New York Times* crossword.

I miss the public library. Miss Ms. Parkins.

"Woeful," I said out loud, printing the word in the little
blank squares—and purposely keeping my head down. I
needed to stop looking up every five seconds to see if a distinctive black BMW had pulled into one of the many free
parking spots in front of the theater. We were showing a
dreary movie called *The 400 Blows* by a French director whose
name sounded like a high-priced mushroom—Truffaut—and
I was pretty sure Chase would come.

So why did I nearly jump out of my skin when a hand
came into my line of sight, pushing money into the small
pit designed for ticket exchanges, and a deep, familiar voice
asked, "Can I have *two* tickets, tonight, please, Millie?"

Chapter **54**

I'm really not supposed to do this," I told Chase, even as I sat down on one of the ancient, upholstered theater seats next to his. "And you buying me a ticket and popcorn doesn't make it any better. I'm still supposed to be working. I'm not really a paying customer."

Chase made a show of craning his neck and looking around the theater. "Millie, there's only one other person here. And since when do you care about what you're 'supposed' to do?"

He had a point, but my father would kill me if I lost my job. We still weren't exactly on the best of terms.

"I just don't want to get in trouble at this particular moment," I said. I twisted to look behind me. "And what if she needs a snack or something?"

"Here, scaredy-cat." Chase handed me the popcorn and stood up, calling back about ten rows to a woman who was also a regular. "Mrs. Murphy? Are you going to want anything? Like a drink? Because I invited Millie to watch the movie with me, but she's worried that she's going to get in trouble for abandoning the snack bar."

I spun around again, even more surprised than I'd been when Chase had shown up at my booth asking me to see the movie with him.

Why is he doing this?

And did he just call a customer by name? Do they know *each other?*

Apparently so, because the older woman in the back row was beaming at Chase. "You two don't worry," she said. "I brought a snack from home." She held up a baggie full of food I couldn't identify—but which I should've confiscated, according to theater policy. "Just enjoy your date," she told Chase. "It's nice to see you here with a *young* friend."

"Thanks, Mrs. Murphy." Chase sat down again and tried to reclaim the popcorn, which I did not relinquish. "Can you relax now?"

"How do you know her?" I whispered, ignoring his question—and overlooking Mrs. Murphy's assertion that we were on a date, because Chase hadn't bothered to correct her, either. I was pretty sure we both knew that wasn't the case, though, after our discussion in Mr. Killdare's driveway. "Are you two, like, friends?"

Chase grinned at me in the increasing darkness as Mr. Mordrick lowered the house lights from the projection booth. I probably should've been worried about my elderly coworker tattling on me, but I doubted he could see well enough to know I was even there.

"Mrs. Murphy sits with me sometimes," Chase confided. "I tease her that she's my girlfriend, and she brings me cookies." He dug into the popcorn. "She's been widowed for eight years, but always worries that *I'm* lonely."

That was quite possibly the geekiest, saddest, most embarrassing ritual that I'd ever heard a teenage guy admit to, but the fact that Chase told his story without shame somehow made him seem even hotter, if that was possible. Only a truly confident guy would confess to being fed and fussed over by a grandma figure. And maybe it was genuinely cool, in a way, that he'd befriended a lonely old lady. Or vice versa.

I squirmed in my seat, watching Chase in profile as he tossed some popcorn into his mouth, his eyes trained on the screen, where cartoon penguins invited patrons to visit the currently unattended snack bar.

Is there anything I don't like about this guy—except for the way he DOESN'T like me? How did that happen?

Chase must've seen me observing him out of the corner of his eye. He gestured to the front of the theater, reminding me, "The movie's starting."

I didn't face the screen right away. Instead, I leaned closer to Chase, asking, in a whisper, a question that I couldn't contain for two full hours: "Chase, why are you so dead set on me seeing this? It looks terrible."

He met my eyes in the darkness, and I saw that he was no longer laughing. "I don't really know, Millie." He hesitated. "I . . . I just think you'll get it."

I didn't know if he meant I'd grasp the importance of the movie in and of itself—the artistry and message—or that I'd come away knowing something about him. But as the story of a boy who goes down the wrong path and finds himself incarcerated with hardened criminals began to unfold, I suspected that it was the latter. And by the time the movie ended, with that young man staring ambiguously at the camera, the ocean that represented liberation behind him, so I wasn't quite sure if he really felt free or not . . . I knew that Chase had dragged me along to share something about his soul.

It didn't even seem weird when the lights came up, to realize that I had a lump in my throat—and my hand on Chase's arm, squeezing him to sort of comfort him, and myself, too.

I let go pretty quickly, but we still sat in silence for a minute, even after we heard Mrs. Murphy discreetly remove herself, without saying goodbye, as if she knew better than to intrude.

I had all kinds of questions for Chase and wanted to tell him that whatever had really happened, back on that dark road, he'd served his time and should let it go. That he wasn't some kid in a movie. But Chase spoke first, and I could tell that he wasn't going to elaborate on the film—that we weren't going to talk about "feelings" or his past—when he asked, "So, what the heck did you and Mike talk about in French class that compelled him to blurt out 'murder'?"

Chapter 55

C hase had parked his car at the theater, but he walked me home after the movie because it was a beautiful October night, and we both wanted to stretch our legs after sitting for so long.

Okay, I would've taken a ride—would I *never* get back in that awesome car?—but when Chase suggested a stroll, I could hardly refuse.

"So what do you think about Mike?" I asked after I'd related everything that had happened in class. "Do you think he's capable of murder?"

I sort of hoped Chase would say yes, because I was already composing the headline for my next story: "Brutish Football Player Implicated in Slaying." With the subhead "Jeez, He's Best Pals with Viv! What Did You Expect?"

Okay, maybe that fantasy was a little over the top, but the more I thought about Mike Price, the more my gut said he was capable of, if nothing else, acting on a base impulse, if he and Coach Killdare had ever had it out some late evening after practice . . .

"Millie, are you listening to me?"

"Sorry," I told Chase. "I was imagining Mike bludgeoning things. In the daydream, he's wearing an ape suit."

I was immediately uncertain about the wisdom of adding that last part, but Chase didn't even give me a strange look. Instead he said, "I was basically agreeing that Mike doesn't seem to engage in much higher-level cognitive activity— which is why Mr. Killdare swapped him from quarterback to running back." Chase looked down at me. "Not to sound conceited, but—along with being a leader—a quarterback has to think ahead, and that wasn't Mike's forte."

"So you agree that Mike could've gotten mad and lashed out?" I started to spin a scenario, but could tell that Chase wasn't necessarily buying my theory.

"I don't know, Millie," he said. "I met a lot of offenders when I was in the system."

It was almost impossible to believe that the polished guy who'd just used the phrase "higher-level cognitive activity" had ever been incarcerated. But who would've thought my father and my librarian would have a secret, shared life, either?

"And most of them were surprisingly intelligent," Chase continued. "We didn't get in trouble because we were stupid —in terms of IQ. We did things because we were smart but bored, or angry, or looking for the next adrenaline rush. And then, of course, there were those Hannibal Lecter wannabes who had brains but no conscience."

I nodded. "Psychopaths. Like Viv."

Chase grinned. "I don't know if I'd go *that* far about Viv."

"I disagree." I glanced up, trying to read his expression, and asked, sort of offhandedly, as if I didn't really care, "What did you two talk about? In French class?"

He shrugged. "Football. Cheerleading. Her hatred of you."

I felt my eyes get wide. "No!"

Chase smiled down at me. "No, not really. Just football and cheerleading."

I debated whether to tell him that Viv had set her sights on him, like a big-game hunter aiming to bring down the most majestic elk in the herd, but I was pretty sure he knew what she was up to. I had a feeling he was used to girls hitting on him.

"So what's next?" he asked, turning the conversation back to my investigation. "Are you going to follow up on your suspicions about Mike?"

"I'm not sure," I admitted. We'd reached my house and stopped walking. A light was on inside, like my dad was home. Probably alone. "I mean, I want to, but I don't really know what to do."

Chase took a moment to consider my quandary, then said, "I think there's a place we can go to learn *too much* about Mike. And if he's hiding a murder weapon, it's probably there. Along with a bunch of Coach Killdare's stuff. Things that he wouldn't keep at his house."

I got a little excited. "What? What are you talking about?"

This was obviously a secret that Chase wanted to keep because it amused him, though. "Just meet me tomorrow at school, at about seven-thirty," he said. "Inside the front doors."

"Won't they be locked?" I pointed out.

"No." Chase gave me a funny look. "The football team will have left about a half-hour before, and there's practice for the fall musical that goes on until at least eight-thirty." He paused. "Haven't you *ever* done an extracurricular activity, Millie? Besides working for the paper?"

"I'm founder and president of the Philosophy Club," I said. "But we meet . . . Well, it's just me, and we don't really meet."

He didn't seem to know how to respond, so I added, "I'm saving my energy for adulthood, Chase. I plan to start ramping it up in my twenties and be a huge success by age thirty. I honestly think the rest of you are peaking way too soon."

Chase took a moment to digest that, too. "Have I mentioned that you're . . . unique?" he finally asked.

"Yeah, you have. Let's not beat it into the ground, okay?" I remembered that we'd been making plans. "So what are we gonna do at school after hours?"

He still didn't explain. "Just trust me—and meet me there. Okay?"

"Okay," I agreed. Then, making a split-second decision —voicing something that I hadn't considered before the moment it popped into my head—I blurted, "But in exchange for me not asking questions, you have to do me a favor."

He seemed intrigued. Or on guard. "What?"

I was already regretting opening my mouth, but it was too

late to turn back, so I said, "Come with me to the fall formal next week." I saw the surprise—coupled with dismay—on his face and added, "Just as friends. Not like a date." I held up my hands. "Believe me! I know where you stand on *that* prospect."

Chase looked down the street. "Millie . . . It's not that. It's just . . . I don't usually go to that kind of thing."

"Oh, for crying out loud." I really thought he was going overboard with the self-inflicted penance, and that old Mrs. Murphy was right. He was too isolated—which was why I'd asked him to go in the first place. *I* didn't really want to attend a lame, tropical-themed "gala" in a school gym. "Are you refusing because you'd be embarrassed to go with me?" I challenged him. "Or because you think you should never have fun again, like a 'normal' kid? Because you know I'd make the whole thing fun."

Chase looked me in the eye. "Millie, I would be far from ashamed to go to a dance with you . . ."

Actually, I'd said "embarrassed," not "ashamed." Was one of those words a little harsher?

". . . But I've told you, I try to lie low," he said. "And I really feel strange doing anything related to partying. As you've noticed, I don't socialize much outside of football."

"I think you *are* embarrassed to be seen with me," I countered. "You think I'm going to stick my face in the punch bowl and lap up Hi-C like Baxter or something. Don't you?"

"No. That's not it," he insisted. "I just don't think it's right for me."

"Is it your girlfriend?" I asked bluntly, bringing up a subject I'd never broached before. Maybe because, up until the incident at Mr. Killdare's, this teeny part of me had hoped everybody was wrong, and she didn't really exist. But there was no reason to avoid the subject anymore. "Huh? Is that it?"

Chase gave me a sharp look. "Who told you I have a girlfriend?"

I realized that I probably shouldn't know that. "Ryan said you mentioned it once or something." I tried to play innocent. "I don't even know why we were talking about it."

"Oh." Chase seemed to accept that explanation. In fact, he appeared distracted and even more unhappy. "It's not exactly her," he said softly. "I mean . . . Not the way you think. Not like a jealousy thing." He seemed oddly tongue-tied. "It's just me . . ."

"Well," I said, taking a new tack. "If you're really so dead set on never having fun again, and punishing yourself forever, you should definitely take me up on my offer. Because from where I'm standing, it seems like you think going to a dance with me would be a *terrible ordeal.*"

Something—probably everything—I'd just said finally made Chase laugh again. And although it was at my expense —again—I had to admit that it was a pretty nice sound. A good complement to the smile that he seemed to be using more often lately. Then Chase forced himself to be serious and said, with semi-sincerity, "Millicent Ostermeyer, I would be honored to take you to the Honeywell High School fall formal." He glanced at my feet. "Provided that you agree not to stick your head in the punch—or wear those sneakers, because no offense, but I would be embarrassed if you did either of those things."

I looked down at my shoes, too, suddenly not sure what I intended to wear on my feet—or my body, for that matter. Then I stuck out my hand. "Deal."

It wasn't until Chase had walked away, headed back to his car with a reminder about our meeting the next evening, that what had just happened really sank in.

I, Millie Ostermeyer, who hadn't had a date for a dance since the Nolan Durkin debacle of ninth grade, had just asked the most desirable guy at school to escort me to a formal.

A guy Vivienne Fitch also wanted.

Viv, a possible killer, who would see me with Chase in the gym and maybe misunderstand. Who might just think Chase and I were more than friends, and that I was stealing him from her, just like I'd stolen her thunder at camp—only a thousand times worse.

Seriously . . . What had I just *done?*

Chapter 56

M illie, if we're here to return books, why are we lurking behind a tree?" Laura asked. "Why not just go in
the library? Because this is embarrassing!"

"You're the one who's all about copying Nancy Drew," I
said, shuffling the pile of books I was finally returning until
I found *The Bungalow Mystery.* I pointed to the cover, which
showed Nancy peering out from behind a tree trunk, watching a shack. *"She's* not embarrassed."

"Nancy's also wearing a shirt dress," Laura noted, looking pointedly at my usual T-shirt-and-jeans combo. "So apparently *you're* allowed to pick and choose when she's a role
model."

Sometimes having a perceptive, logical friend could be a
pain in the butt. "Just . . . keep hiding," I said, pressing the
books against my chest and scooching farther behind the tree
because the library door was opening, revealing a glimpse of
a chartreuse sleeve.

Ms. Parkins.

I watched her step into the fading sunlight and thought my

former librarian seemed washed out, too. Sure, her sweater was trademark bright, as were her pink stilettos and her floral tote bag, but her shoulders drooped and there was no spring in her step as she walked to her car.

"You came to see her, didn't you?" Laura asked quietly. "Because you're worried about her."

I didn't answer. I just kept spying on Ms. Parkins, who sat in her little Mazda like she wasn't in any hurry to leave. *Maybe because she has nobody to go home to . . .*

"Millie," Laura said gently. "If you're so concerned about Ms. Parkins and your dad, why don't you give them your blessing? Tell them to go ahead and be happy together?"

I kept observing, avoiding those — also very logical — questions.

How could I tell Laura that I wanted to do those things, but that every time I tried to open my mouth, to my dad at least, my usually uncontrollably flapping tongue froze up?

And how could I explain that my desperate desire to consult with Ms. Parkins about the upcoming dance was turning my tongue to *marble?*

How could Laura ever understand that while I wanted Ms. Parkins's advice about picking a dress, because she had a crazy, but wonderful, sense of fashion, and wanted to ask her what to say to Chase if things got stilted, because she always knew how to keep a conversation going, I just couldn't.

Those are things I would've asked Mom about. I shouldn't crave somebody else's guidance that much.

Ms. Parkins finally started her car, and I withdrew my head, telling Laura, "I guess she's okay."

Fibber! Big, white-lying fibber!

Laura also clearly knew that I wasn't being truthful, but she didn't press the issue. "Can we go in now?"

"Yeah . . ." I came out from behind the tree—then stopped. I *still* didn't want to go inside the library. And maybe I wasn't ready to return the books, either—and not just because Ms. Parkins's replacement at the desk might be stricter about overdue fines. "You know what?" I said. "I think I'll come back later. I've gotta get home, anyhow. Ry's picking me up in a few minutes, giving me a ride back to school."

Laura's eyebrows shot up. "You? *You're* going back to school? After hours?"

I almost told her that I not only was returning to Honeywell High, but meeting Chase. I knew that would make up for dragging her to the library parking lot, and she'd probably squeal for vicarious joy. But—just like I hadn't told her about the dance yet—I hedged. "I'm doing something for the paper. Covering a late meeting."

I wasn't sure why I didn't mention Chase—whom I hadn't exactly mentioned to Ryan, either. But later that evening, when Chase and I were alone in a dark and secluded space, after pretty much everybody else had gone home for the day, I'd sort of wished I'd told *somebody* what I was up to.

Chapter **57**

"Jeez, this is like a shrine to sweat!" I cried as Chase escorted me into the guys' locker room, which was, as he'd promised, empty of athletes by seven forty-five. I kept gawking around, my jaw hanging open. "A freakin' Taj Mahal—discounting the damp towels."

"The girls' locker rooms aren't this nice?" Chase flipped on lights to reveal a corner that housed a metal tub that looked like something livestock would eat from. Yet I instinctively knew that vat was a good thing—and denied to us girls. "You don't have hydrotherapy tubs?" he asked, following my gaze.

"In spite of Laura circulating a petition, sophomore year, we don't even have a *tampon dispenser*," I muttered.

All at once, although still dazzled by the guys'—or, let's be honest, football players'—facilities, I realized that word was finally out there.

I kind of wished it wasn't.

"How come you guys get such great stuff?" I asked, turning to face Chase. "Whatever happened to Title Nine? Equality for the genders, in terms of sports?"

"Don't be naive, Millie." He led us deeper into the room, toward a dark alcove. *There's more?* "Honeywell might be a small town, but its football program is big business. Don't you see the corporate ads in the stadium? Who do you think pays for turf upgrades and things like that? Girls' field hockey doesn't draw crowds—or, by extension, money."

"It doesn't seem fair not to share, though."

Chase disagreed. "Tell that to the guys doing twice-a-day practices, like the one that almost killed Roy, and the players getting pummeled every Friday night." He flipped on one more light, revealing a locker room within a locker room exclusively for the football team. It had special niches to store shoulder pads and assigned lockers. The guys' names were on them. "We earn this stuff."

I crossed my arms. "Have you ever seen girls' field hockey? It's pretty rough."

"I didn't say it wasn't," Chase conceded. "And I didn't say the system was fair. It's just a function of what people want to see and support. Americans are obsessed with football, and Honeywell is the bottom rung on a ladder that sometimes leads to the NFL. Companies like Nike and UnderArmour recognize that."

"It still seems wrong." I followed Chase farther into the high school equivalent of Batman's underground lair. "And you . . . Do *you* want to play in the NFL?"

"I'm expected to be a doctor," Chase said over his shoulder. "And I want that." He shrugged. "I am getting scouted by Big Ten schools, though, and I'd like to go that far. Just to see if I could cut it at that level."

Chase had just described Mike Price's dream—Mike's probably former best shot at televised glory and a free college degree—in a way that came off like, "Eh. Whatever."

No wonder Mike seemed to despise Chase, too. Maybe as much, if not more, than he'd hated Coach Killdare.

All at once, I felt uneasy for Chase, because if Mike really did kill Mr. Killdare, maybe his teammate was next . . .

It wasn't until I bumped into Chase that I realized we'd reached a door while I'd been worrying. One that had a plaque that I assumed used to read Head Coach Hank Killdare. But that name was taped over, and the sign now said, in handwritten letters, Acting Head Coach Jack Ostermeyer.

It wasn't my dad's writing and had probably been put up by Big Pete Lamar, but I still almost tore it down because as Chase led us into the office, I realized that I'd actually *underestimated* Dad's potential motives for killing Mr. Killdare. Looking around the clean, well-appointed space, which was nicer than my father's mayoral digs at the town hall, I fully grasped, much to my dismay, that being head coach of the Honeywell Stingers wasn't just a nice perk in a small town like ours. It really was kind of like being a . . . king.

No wonder Detective Lohser—and other people—might think Dad wanted complete control of this operation—

"Millie?" Chase's voice broke into my thoughts, and I saw that he was tapping the keyboard of the sleek computer on Mr. Killdare's . . . er, my father's? . . . desk. "Don't just stand there," he said. "Help me hack."

Chapter 58

I 've tried every variation on 'Stingers,' 'football,' and even 'Baxter' that I can come up with," Chase muttered, rolling back in the sweet leather chair that my dad now got to enjoy. "He wasn't a very complicated guy. What could his password be?"

"I thought we were here to investigate Mike," I reminded him. "Not hack a school computer."

"I've heard that Coach kept detailed notes on all his players," Chase said, eyes still trained on the screen as he tried another password—only to be rejected. "And we will look at Mike's locker. But we should do this first, in case the cleaning staff comes in. We can probably explain being in the locker area alone together, but not in this office."

I knew what Chase meant. If they discovered us, the cleaning staff would—like Detective Lohser—just assume we'd been making out.

Would I ever get to actually *do* that? Because it seemed like I was starting to get a "reputation"—without any of the benefits.

"Millie?" Chase prompted. "Password ideas?"

"Maybe my dad changed it. Maybe it's 'mylovelydaughter-millie' now."

"I doubt it," Chase said, so for a second I thought he understood me and Dad's relationship, because I didn't really think my dad would call me "lovely," either. Obstreperous, maybe? Then Chase explained, "The system still signs on automatically as 'HKilldare.' And I hardly ever see your dad in here. It would probably look weird, like he couldn't wait until the body was cold . . ." Chase seemed to realize we were talking about my father, and he glanced at me. "Sorry."

"I'm actually glad to know my dad hasn't been a complete office vulture," I reassured him. "It's one of the few things that *don't* make him look guilty."

"Anyhow . . ." Chase returned his attention to the screen. "What could the password be?"

I took a moment to think about all the things I'd learned about Coach Killdare since I'd started to investigate him, and stuff I knew from before that, too. And after dismissing "Bee-Bee" as a possibility—I still couldn't picture him as "cutesy" —I came up with what I thought was a pretty good guess.

"Step aside," I told Chase, pushing his chair, so he didn't so much step as roll.

Then I started typing, and a few seconds later, we both had access to Mr. Killdare's private, supersecret football—and personal—files.

Chapter **59**

How did you come up with SirHank16?" Chase asked, rolling back over to the computer and standing up, ceding the chair to me. He rested against the edge of the desk, crossing his arms over a powder-blue T-shirt that made his eyes look even more intensely azure, if that was possible. That shirt did a pretty nice job of spotlighting his chest, too.

And I seriously thought he'd planned to kiss me once!

"What does that even mean?" Chase added. "'Sir' Hank?"

"It was actually easy," I informed him, taking a seat. "I just thought about Mr. Killdare's interests—and his greatest triumphs—"

"Like . . . seven state championships?" Chase ventured. "But how does that—?"

"Not the stupid football trophies!" I cut him off. "Stuff that really matters. Like—duh—*eating the sixty-ounce porterhouse* at Sir Loin's Steakhouse. Which gets you automatically knighted. They put a picture of you on the wall, holding a sword and shield!"

Chase appeared confused. "Millie, what are you talking about . . . ?"

"Mr. Killdare is on Ye Olde Wall of Fame," I tried to explain. "He's only the sixteenth person ever to complete the challenge. It's *huge!*"

Chase still seemed uncertain. "The steak . . . or the honor?"

"Both!" I said, imagining, as I sometimes did, the day when I'd hold that shield, which featured a mighty griffin, rampant, hoisting aloft a giant slab of meat impaled on a spear. Maybe —because many tried, but few succeeded—I'd be right next to Mr. Killdare on Ye Olde Wall. "Someday, *I* aspire to be Sir Millie," I added wistfully. "Sir Millie, the seventeeth Earl of Porterhouse."

"Uh . . . '*Sir* Millie'?"

I woke up from my fantasy to find Chase giving me a weird look. Weird enough that I kind of wished I hadn't added that last part.

He is DEFINITELY not attracted to you right now, Sir!

With a sinking heart, I remembered some plans we'd made and hazarded, hesitantly, "Umm . . . Are we still going to that dance?"

Chase didn't exactly answer. He just leaned past me and opened Mr. Killdare's email.

I took that for a yes.

And a few minutes later, I forgot all about the formal, anyway, when we found a bunch of emails between Mike Price, Mike's parents, and Mr. Killdare, some of which were filed in a big folder that was surprisingly—or maybe not surprisingly—labeled "Threats."

Unfortunately, there were a lot of messages from other people in there, too.

Including a few irate missives from—heavy sigh—my father.

Chapter **60**

D on't get too excited, Millie," Chase warned me as I skimmed a long exchange between Mike Price's dad and Mr. Killdare. "I'm sure Detective Lohser has seen all this stuff, too, and he's still hounding your father—who also wrote some pretty harsh messages."

I knew Chase was right. My dad and Coach Killdare had apparently bickered electronically, too. But I couldn't help getting a little enthused about the notes that had passed between Mr. Price and Coach Killdare, which I was scanning quickly, because we had to be running out of time. The custodians probably spent half their evenings cleaning this veritable replica of Versailles that Chase had revealed to me, right inside my high school.

"Look at this," I said, reaching back to smack Chase in case he wasn't keeping pace. Then I read a message from Mr. Price dated from the previous September, shortly after Chase had first been brought in as quarterback.

"'*You stupid son of a bitch . . .*'" I glanced up at Chase. "Pardon my French."

The corners of his mouth turned up with amusement. "Millie . . . That's *still* not French."

I shot him a dark look, then resumed reading. *"'Youre killing my sons career he's NFL material and I think he's right to hate your guts. I wont tell him to calm down because he's also right that somebody outta teach you a lesson. I wouldn't blame Mike if he beat the crap out of you.'"*

I spun to face Chase again. "Wow, somebody ought to teach Mr. Price a lesson—in grammar, spelling, and punctuation. No wonder Mike's the way he is. That apple didn't fall far from the tree, huh?"

"It's also not too smart to admit that you've given your son the go-ahead to beat up a coach—and to write that down, for the record," Chase agreed.

I closed out the email and stood up, thinking we'd seen enough on the computer. "Come on. Let's check Mike's locker. Maybe there's, like, a bloody cleat!"

But Chase grabbed my shoulders, gently stopping me. "Millie, I repeat: Don't get too excited." He bent slightly, forcing me to meet his eyes before he released me. "That message is pretty old. And in the meantime, I'd say Mike has calmed down. He's still not happy about playing running back, but most days, he just comes to practice or the game and sucks it up."

"Yeah, but that doesn't mean Mr. Killdare didn't push Mike's buttons one day and piss him off again," I pointed out. "Hollerin' Hank wasn't exactly a master of diplomacy. I can imagine him taunting Mike, telling him after some mistake on the field, 'Hey, bonehead!'" I rapped Chase's skull with my knuckles, illustrating a classic Hank Killdare move, while adding, in my best low, manly voice, "'That's why you're not quarterback anymore, moron!'" I resumed my normal voice. "And the next thing you know, Mike and Mr. Killdare are duking it out, and things go really wrong."

Chase rubbed his head where I'd hit him, maybe a little too hard. "That was a pretty good impression—and, I have to admit, a plausible scenario."

"So let's open the locker," I suggested with a glance at the small room where the football players stored their gear. "Although, I gotta say, you'd have to be *really* stupid to stash anything *that* private in here."

"I don't know," Chase said, leading the way. "These lockers are pretty sacrosanct."

Most girls—okay, including myself—were probably attracted to Chase's appearance. For example, the way his butt looked in the Levi's he was wearing that evening, a sight that was nothing short of perfection. But it was how Chase could toss off a word like "sacrosanct," out of the blue, that really made my tongue hang out as I followed behind him.

A guy with a vocabulary . . . Talk about *hot.*

And taken, Millie!

"So, if these lockers are so sacrosanct"—seriously, what a great word—"how will we 'hack' into Mike's?"

"I'd say we use the same reasoning you just used to figure out Mr. Killdare's password."

"Meaning?"

"We'll take what we know about Mike, such as his—no offense—basic level of intelligence. Then we'll consider the things that are important to him—his 'greatest triumphs,' to use your phrase—only this time, we'll interpret them numerically."

I knew that Chase had a girlfriend, and that he had zero interest in me, but at that moment, I couldn't help thinking that he was almost irresistible. Who *said* stuff like that?

And who could deny that we connected on some mental level, at least, when we both looked at each other and said, simultaneously, "Four to the left, four to the right, four to the left."

Chapter **61**

How did you know Price's old jersey number?" Chase asked, spinning the knob on Mike's locker. "You don't strike me as a sports fan."

"It's on those fake Eagles jerseys he wears every other day," I explained, then admitted, "Actually, I assumed he was still number four."

"No." Chase pulled down on the lock, which did open. Neither one of us even registered surprise. "Running backs have higher numbers. Quarterbacks get the pick of one through nine."

"Lucky you." *By which I mean, "Who cares?"*

The locker was just waiting to be explored, but Chase hesitated. "Um . . . Do you know *my* number? Because I know you've covered games for the paper . . ."

Was he still worried that I was stalking him, or fishing for flattery? If it was the latter, I was about to disappoint him. "No clue. For all I know, you wear a pink unicorn on your jersey. Or a big question mark, like the Riddler."

That was a joking reference to that old doodle I'd drawn of Chase. The one with a question mark where his number would've been.

How much do I know about him now?

That he used to be a hard-partying delinquent, but that he had a good side, too. And a great grasp of the English language. And a nice butt.

But there's still something mysterious about him . . .

"So let's open this, huh?" I urged, remembering we weren't there to investigate Chase. Then I took a few steps back because, while I was eager to see the contents of Mike's locker, I'd been burned a few times, amateur detecting, and wasn't exactly excited to *smell* any dirty laundry, be it literal or figurative.

In fact, just to be on the safe side, I decided to let Chase do the honors of rummaging through Mike's stinky cleats and soiled jock straps while I went to check out that cool hydrotherapy tub.

"Call me if you find anything interesting," I said, stepping up to the tub. "And make it quick, before somebody comes—"

Then I stopped talking because, as it turned out, we already weren't exactly alone.

I stood there for a long time, trying to get my heart to restart and my vocal chords to relax enough to speak again. But it seemed to take forever before I could tell Chase, with what I thought was admirable composure, "Umm . . . Chase? I don't think Mike is the killer anymore."

"No?" It sounded as if his head was in a locker, but I could tell he was surprised. "Why not?"

"Because," I said, swallowing thickly, *"his body* is kind of in your special whirlpool."

Chapter 62

My God, Millie . . ." Dad grabbed me and squeezed me tightly. Not only did he not seem angry with me anymore, but it was the biggest public display of affection he'd ever offered me—even if "public" meant in an isolated locker room, in front of one football player. "It's one thing for you to stumble on a weeks'-old body," he said, seeming close to shaken. "But I just saw Mike." He loosened his grip and glanced at the tub, although he probably couldn't see the corpse. Once we'd determined that Mike really was dead and called my father and 911, Chase and I had backed far away. "This must've just happened . . ."

I hadn't understood why my dad was so freaked out until I got what he was trying to say. Prying myself free, because Chase was watching and I wasn't *five,* I said, "Wow . . . I never thought about that." I looked at Chase. "We could've walked in on a murder."

That realization gave me the chills—and I also felt like a thoughtless, selfish heel when Chase, suddenly pale, said softly, "Maybe we could've stopped it . . . *saved Mike* . . . if we'd come earlier."

Oh, gosh. How many times did he intend to get his passport stamped on his endless guilt trip?

But before I could inform Chase that Mike's death wasn't his fault, my father asked a question that I probably should've prepared for while we'd waited for him to arrive.

"What were you two doing here—alone—in the first place?"

In fact, not only should Chase and I have been ready to answer that for my dad, we should've anticipated that somebody else would be curious about our after-hours exploits in a boys' locker room. Somebody who was, right then, shoving open the door and noting, in a voice rich with twisted glee, "Well, well, well . . . Isn't *this* a cozy reunion?"

Chapter 63

S o, *kids* . . ." Detective Lohser managed to sneer that word. He clearly had issues with teenagers—no doubt rooted in his own not-too-distant youth, which I would've bet my meager life savings had included a fair amount of wedgies and perhaps even a "swirly" or two. "What were you doing here alone?"

"Ease up on Chase and Millie," my father said softly. "They just lost a classmate."

A classmate whose body was still in a nearby tub, being examined by a bunch of police officers and other people who were traipsing in and out of the locker room, carrying official-looking gear and muttering quiet but official-sounding stuff.

"They still need to explain themselves," Detective Lohser told my father. Then he addressed me and Chase again, speaking slowly, like we were preschoolers. "What. Were. You. Doing. Here?"

Chase and I shared a look, silently asking each other, "What should we say? Why didn't we discuss this?" Then I met Detective Lohser's beady eyes and informed him, "We were looking for clues about Coach Killdare's murder."

"You were *what?*"

My dad and Detective Lohser blurted that at the same time. However, my dad sounded genuinely baffled, while the cop he'd fired seemed ready to burst out laughing—which I thought was phenomenally inappropriate on more than one level.

"It's not funny," I said, getting irritated. "I'm investigating the story for the school paper."

"And I'm helping her," Chase added. "I brought her in here."

Detective Lohser's mustache twitched, as if that really amused him, too. "Did you now?"

"Yes, he did," I said, crossing my arms. "And I'm probably going to win a major national award when we *solve the crime.*"

Okay, I had, as usual, taken things a little too far with that boast, but he was really ticking me off, especially given that he didn't seem to have any answers and was wasting all his time sniffing around my dad.

Detective Lohser finally got suitably serious for a murder scene, telling me, "Kid, you"—his gaze flicked to Chase—"and your boyfriend don't know the first thing about solving crime." He spoke directly to me again. "In the future, stick to giggling with your little friends at slumber parties, or whatever teenage girls do. Because in case you didn't notice, this is serious stuff here. *Dangerous* stuff."

I opened my mouth to inform him that I'd never giggled

in my entire life, and that he was the one not being serious enough, when, much to my surprise, I felt my father's hand on my shoulder. "I agree that investigating a murder is too risky for young people," he said. "But don't ever underestimate my daughter, Detective. And don't disrespect her—or Chase. I don't like the way you're addressing them."

Detective Lohser didn't seem to know what to make of that, while I also struggled to grasp what had just happened.

Had my father just *complimented* me?

I turned to meet his eyes, silently thanking him. And to my further surprise, he smiled ever so slightly and squeezed my shoulder before taking away his hand.

But the brief moment we'd shared was messed up as soon as I turned back and saw the look on Detective Lohser's face. A cat-stuffed-with-canary look.

"Fine," he agreed. "I'll treat these young people like adults." He addressed Chase. "So, young man. When was the last time you saw Michael Price alive? Who was he with?"

I'd never seen Chase Albright look anything but confident —well, except for the time he'd nearly kissed me. He'd gotten pretty uncertain then. But when Detective Lohser posed that simple question, Chase seemed completely at a loss for words. And I didn't understand why he kept looking at my dad as he struggled to form an answer, his mouth opening and closing.

I tried to give him an encouraging look, like, "Just say something. It's a pretty simple question!"

But Chase wasn't looking at me. He was still meeting my

238 * BETH FANTASKEY

father's eyes, until my dad gave him some sort of dispensa-
tion I didn't understand, either. "It's all right, son. Tell the
truth."

Chase nodded and took a deep breath, answering Detective Lohser—but looking at me with apology in his eyes.
"Mike was with Coach Ostermeyer," he said. "Here. In the
locker room."

What?

Detective Lohser looked as if he'd hit the jackpot on every
slot machine in Las Vegas, and possibly Atlantic City, too.
"And what, exactly, were they doing?" he asked, not even trying to hide his smarmy grin. "Hmm?"

Wow, did Chase look miserable. But I still couldn't stop
myself from hating him a little when he admitted, "They
were . . . They were *fighting*."

Chapter 64

W hy did you have to tell him about my dad and Mike fighting?" I cried, punching Chase's arm. It wasn't a playful punch, either. I kind of slugged him, enough that he rubbed his bicep. "How could you do that?"

"Millie . . ." Chase looked across the dark school parking lot. At least it was dark except for the flashing lights from a bunch of squad cars and an ambulance that was way too late. Just like Chase's apology was going to be if he didn't offer one soon. Which he didn't exactly do. "Detective Lohser would've found out the truth." He finally met my eyes again. "I wasn't the only person who saw them. Half the guys on the team were still in the locker room, too."

"Maybe Detective Lohser wouldn't have asked the other guys," I pointed out. "He's not the world's brightest detective!"

Chase didn't seem convinced. "He was bright enough to ask the right question. It was almost like he already knew about your dad and Mike."

That was kind of weird, but it also might have been a lucky guess. My dad was a coach, Mike was a player, and it was a weeknight during the season. Duh. They almost certainly would at least have been seen together, at practice.

"What were they fighting about?" I grudgingly asked a question that I was pretty sure Detective Lohser was asking my dad, maybe right then, because my father'd been detained. "Was it bad?"

Chase shook his head. "No. It was just the usual stuff. It sounded like Mike was mad about your dad not reinstating him as quarterback, now that Mr. Killdare is gone. I guess Mike thought your dad—who, let's face it, disagreed with Coach Killdare about everything—would switch him back in, now that your father's in charge."

Oh, this stupid quarterback idiocy! Seriously, WHO CARES?

"I thought you just said, when we read the e-mails, that Mike didn't get all lathered up about that anymore."

"He didn't, usually," Chase agreed. "It was the first time I'd heard him get upset about it in a while. And I didn't know Mike would get . . ." He didn't seem to want to voice something that I knew we were both avoiding. A truth we'd have to deal with later. *Somebody we knew—maybe didn't like, but who was our age—has been murdered.* Instead, he said, "I just didn't think you needed to know about some argument your dad had with a player." He dragged his hand through his hair, his usual gesture when he got uncomfortable. "I didn't think it was that big a deal."

"It was obviously big enough that you had to narc on my father to Detective Lohser."

"Millie, your dad was okay with it. *He* didn't want me to lie."

"You should've anyway!"

Chase wasn't convinced. "And that would've helped things . . . how?" He paused, adding, "It would've come out, Millie. Your father would've admitted to the whole thing if I hadn't. He's always telling us about honor on the field."

I wasn't sure that my father would've told Detective Lohser about fighting with Mike. Honor, schmonor. My dad knew how to keep secrets. I still didn't know exactly how long he and Ms. Parkins had dated. And if Dad was aware of Chase's background, as I suspected, he'd never spilled that story, either.

"Millie," Chase said more softly. The flashing lights kept splashing his face with red, and although I could see his expression clearly only in short bursts, I could tell that he was even more miserable when he reminded me, "I have a record. One that I try to keep quiet. I don't need to be a focus for anyone in law enforcement. And I could get in serious trouble for lying during a murder investigation."

I blinked at Chase, thinking that if he was trying to justify his actions to me, it wasn't working. On the contrary, he'd just made me *furious* with him.

He'd sold out my father to *save himself?*

He *was* a selfish, spoiled brat, just like I'd guessed.

"So ratting on my father . . . That wasn't really about honor at all, huh?" I challenged him. "It was about protecting yourself — at my dad's expense."

"Millie, the stakes are high for me," he tried to defend himself.

I wasn't buying it.

"I'd say the stakes are a lot higher for my father," I said evenly. It was almost like I was too angry to yell at him. Or maybe I was so disappointed that I just . . . couldn't. For once, I understood those times when my father logically should've hollered at me but got silent instead. Still, I managed to add, "You *suck,* Chase Albright."

Chase didn't dispute that. He just looked as if I'd hit him again. Then he pulled his car keys out of his pocket and said softly, "Come on, Millie. I promised your dad I'd give you a ride home. He might be stuck here awhile."

I really, really could've used the comforting embrace of a soft leather seat, but I didn't accept his offer. Without another word, I turned on my heel and stalked away from him, across the lot. He must've watched me for a long time, because I didn't hear the purr of a German-engineered motor, even after I reached the street.

I wasn't sure why, but all at once, when I knew he couldn't hear me or see my shoulders shaking, I started to cry—about all sorts of stuff. Tears of frustration for how the universe was messing with my poor dad. And tears of sadness over the guy I'd started to like too much and who'd let me down—as well as for the guy I hadn't liked at all but who'd been *killed.*

Poor Mike.

I'd read lots of philosophers' views on death and had taken comfort in the optimistic Socrates and the pragmatic Zhuangzi since my mother had passed away. But right then, alone in the dark with thoughts I'd suppressed, I couldn't seem to think rationally.

I didn't really pull myself together until I was practically at my house. But by the time I got inside, I knew that while there was nothing I could do for Mike Price—or about my wrecked friendship with Chase—I could try to fix one big disaster.

Getting out my cell, I searched the Internet for a phone number I'd never used before, but that I was sure my dad knew by heart. Taking a deep breath, I dialed it, and a few seconds later heard a familiar, feminine voice offer an uncertain "Hello?"

"Hey, Ms. Parkins," I said, wiping my wet cheeks with my sleeve and hearing a lingering trace of sniffling in my voice. "Can we talk?"

Chapter **65**

That's a good story about finding Mike," Ryan—grimly —complimented me, resting back in his cafeteria chair while he read the *Gazette*. Everybody was reading the paper for a change. The caf was practically wallpapered with the second special edition of the year. "And a nice tribute to him, too," Ry added. "I didn't think you liked him that much."

I picked glumly at my grilled cheese. "I didn't. But everybody deserves a decent memorial." I thought about Coach Killdare, and how I was learning positive things about him now that he was gone. "Who knows? Maybe I misjudged Mike in life."

"I don't think so," Laura disagreed. "But you're right about the decent memorial thing." She accepted the newspaper from Ryan and skimmed my work, noting, "These *are* good stories, Millie." Then she frowned. "Wow . . . You actually put in here about your dad getting questioned again, and him fighting with Mike."

"I had no choice." I looked across the cafeteria to the table where Chase usually sat alone, nose in a textbook. He was missing in action, though, and I returned my attention to my friends. "*Somebody* spilled the beans. The best I could do was tell my dad's side of the story, about how Mike was fine when Dad left the school." I dropped my sandwich, giving up on lunch. "Besides, writing the article is already a pretty big conflict of interest for me. If this was a real paper—and Mr. Sokowski was a real publisher, instead of a clueless, over-whelmed new teacher—I'd never be allowed to write any-thing. If I want to keep covering the murders, I have to report the facts. Otherwise Viv will take over."

Laura gave a small shudder. "I can't believe you found *two* bodies. Or that two people have been murdered here."

"What were you doing in the locker room, anyhow?" Ryan asked. "*That's* not exactly clear."

I pushed away my tray. "Chase and I were snooping around. We had this idea that Mike was the killer. Until, of course, I found him in the tub . . ."

Dead of "blunt force trauma." That was the official cause of death. I'd used it in my article.

Even though I didn't say that out loud, Laura, Ryan, and I got quiet. Then Laura said softly, "Maybe you and Chase aren't such a great combination, after all. It seems like mur-der follows you two around."

She was joking, in a bleak way, but to me, it was the under-statement of the century.

Chase and I were a terrible combination. Worse than "four to the left, four to the right, four to the left."

I guess we definitely *won't be going to that dance—if they even hold it.*

I was yet again mentally writing off Chase Albright, but I found myself glancing once more toward where he usually sat.

I didn't really expect him to be there, but apparently he'd come into the caf at some point and claimed his spot.

Only this time, he wasn't alone.

In fact, he was—once again—deep in conversation with none other than Vivienne Fitch, who'd pulled up a seat next to his. *Very* next to his. As I watched, Chase handed her a napkin, which she used to dab under her expertly lined eyes, like she was crying—which I doubted. I mean, she and Mike had spent a lot of time together, but I was pretty sure she'd regarded him more as a multifunctioning tool—a human Swiss Army knife—than a friend. Plus Viv was . . . Viv. The unfettered-by-emotion "psychopath next door."

Was it possible that Mike had been about to spill that secret she'd warned him never to share, and she'd silenced him, permanently?

I kept staring at Chase and Vivienne, who managed to pull herself together—probably because she'd never fallen apart. Then Viv stood up, smiling in a way that was no doubt meant to be "brave." And while I was no expert lip reader, I was pretty sure I saw Chase tell her, as she backed away, "Sure. See you then."

Chapter 66

*H*enry *Killdare entertains as Cap'n Andy in Pineville High's spring musical,* Show Boat."

"Wow," I muttered, peering more closely at an image of the man I would come to know as Hollerin' Hank, who was belting it out in a different way on the stage of an Ohio high school, back in the 1980s. "Who knew?"

Then I slammed shut the yearbook that Chase had swiped from Mr. Killdare's place, tossing it onto the coffee table with some others. I was culling each one for clues to the mysterious BeeBee—just in case she was some long-lost love—but so far, the old annuals had proven about as useful as I'd predicted. Although there was one vaguely threatening inscription, which read, "Watch your back, S.O.B.!!" I was almost positive it was a joke, though, because the author had added, "You are RAD TO THE MAX!" I wasn't sure what that meant, exactly, but it was followed by a smiley face, which basically negated any ominous overtones.

"Crud," I grumbled, sinking lower on the couch—and checking the clock on our ancient DVD player.

Nearly seven. The dance is probably starting.

Is that what Viv asked Chase about, in the caf?

I could easily imagine Viv finessing *that* date — actually using Mike's murder to get the guy she *really* wanted. *"I'm chair of the dance committee, and I have to go, Chase. But it'll be so hard to face it alone. I don't suppose you'd do me a favor . . ."*

"Millie, are you okay?" Ms. Parkins came into the living room, seeming worried by my posture and, no doubt, the look on my face. "Maybe it's not such a good idea, all of us eating dinner together." Gesturing toward the door, she offered, "I can leave. Call your father and tell him something came up."

"No, it's okay," I promised her, although I wasn't exactly sure how I felt about all of us sitting around the table like some old sitcom family. I mean, my dad was just getting takeout Thai, so it wasn't like Ms. Parkins was cooking or anything, but even just hearing her rooting around in the kitchen, getting out plates and stuff like she belonged in our house . . . It *was* kind of bothering me. And things were still awkward between us, too. But I'd promised, when I'd called her and apologized for melting down at the library, that I wouldn't be a selfish baby anymore, and I added, "It's not you, or dinner. I'm just having a bad week."

Part of me really wanted to tell Ms. Parkins that I was disappointed — way, way too confusingly disappointed — about missing a stupid school dance, which was going to be somewhat depressing, anyhow, in spite of its island theme, because it would feature a last-minute tribute to Mike Price and Coach

Killdare. But I couldn't quite do that. Couldn't quite let her back into my life to that degree.

"I'm just going up to my room," I finally said, standing up and moving toward the stairs. "And don't worry about calling me for dinner. I've got some stuff to do, and I'll eat later." I forced a smile. "You guys have a nice time."

Somebody ought to have an actual date tonight.

Ms. Parkins seemed to misunderstand, though, and she held out her hands, like she was going to physically stop me. "No, please, Millie . . . We'd like you to eat with us!"

Oh, good grief. Would we never communicate the way we used to?

Had I *really* lost my librarian—by inviting her into my home?

Because Ms. Parkins's cheerful, floral appliqué sweater, which seemed so right at the library, seemed equally out of place in my and Dad's musty house, which—let's face it— hadn't received a lot of love since Mom's death. And I couldn't think of the right thing to say to her. I just knew that, right then, as she watched me with an unfamiliar pleading look in her eyes, I was desperate to retreat.

"I'm seriously fine for now," I promised. "Not really hungry."

Then I bolted up the stairs before she could say anything else.

I hardly even noticed, as I lay on my bed, staring at the ceiling, that the doorbell rang. Or if I did notice, I guess I just assumed that my dad was overburdened with chicken satay and curry and couldn't turn the knob.

Needless to say, I was incredibly surprised when Ms. Parkins knocked softly on my bedroom door, then opened it and whispered uncertainly, "Millie . . . Chase Albright is here. And he says you two have . . . a date?"

Chapter 67

W hy did you tell him to wait?" I demanded after Ms. Parkins came into my room and closed the door, no doubt so Chase wouldn't hear me freaking out. For some reason, although I had no intention of going to the fall formal with a self-interested betrayer of fathers, I was rooting through my closet like a maniac, almost like I was searching for something to wear. "I can't stand him! I'm not going anywhere with him! He threw Dad under the bus! Then drove the bus over him—backed it up, and squashed him again!"

"Millie. Millie." A pair of surprisingly firm hands clasped my shoulders. "Take a deep breath."

"I am breathing!" I insisted, tossing aside my "Whooo Loves You?" owl shirt, which Laura should've ditched when she'd gone through my closet. Why hadn't she done that, over my objections? What kind of friend was she? "I am breathing *too* deeply!" I added. "Hyperventilating! How did he have the nerve to show up here?"

"*Millie!*" Ms. Parkins gave me a sharp verbal slap, enough that I froze in place, clutching an empty hanger. Then she spun me slowly until I was facing her. "Just relax," she urged in a soothing voice. "This is going to be okay. In fact, I'm not sure what's wrong."

"I'm not sure, either," I admitted, shoulders suddenly slumping. I kicked at my purple shag rug. "I'm really not."

"Why . . . why don't you try to explain?" she suggested, releasing me. "Just try."

"It's just . . ." The stuff I wanted to say was hard to share, and I hesitated. Then I raised my face again and confessed, "I don't know why I like a guy who implicated my father in a murder, and who has basically declared that he has no interest in me, except as a 'pal'—and who has a girlfriend, to boot. A no doubt beautiful, perfect girl, who I'm sure doesn't aspire to be dubbed sir for consuming a sixty-ounce steak."

Ms. Parkins probably didn't understand that last part, but she got the gist of what I was trying to say, and asked quietly, "Do you want to know what I think, Millie? And I'll understand if you don't."

She definitely got my conflict. And I did take a moment to consider her offer.

This isn't any different from a conversation you would've had at the library, Millie.

Your relationship hasn't really changed—except for the venue.

And Mom wouldn't want you to go it entirely alone.

"Okay." I nodded. "Yeah. I'd like to know what you think."

Ms. Parkins pursed her lips, as if she took her job seriously, then advised me, "You can't make some boy like you if he doesn't, Millicent. That's just the hard truth. But you can't compare yourself to some girlfriend he has, either. You are a unique, beautiful girl in your own right, and if I were you, I'd put on a dress, and I'd go to that dance, and I'd have a great time as the one-and-only Millie Ostermeyer."

She was right, and I could do that. But . . . "What about how Chase sold out Dad? There's that, too."

"Yes, your father told me what happened," Ms. Parkins said. "And we both agree that Chase did the right thing." All at once, she seemed apologetic, and I knew we weren't just talking about Chase when she added, "Lying—even telling lies of omission—clearly doesn't help anyone. It just makes things worse."

We really met each other's eyes for the first time since my meltdown. "I guess you and Dad *were* trying to do the right thing by keeping your relationship from me," I finally conceded. "I mean, I *did* freak out, and break you up."

Ms. Parkins glanced past me, and I realized she'd noticed the overdue Nancy Drews on my desk. But she didn't bug me about returning them. Instead, she asked a question that at first seemed entirely random. "Did you ever read *The Mystery of the Glowing Eye,* Millie?"

"No." I gave her a confused look. "I stopped reading the books after Mom died. I guess we didn't get to that one."

"Well, it's the only book in which Nancy's widower dad, Carson, has a love interest—"

I plopped down on my bed, finally getting where the conversation was headed. "Yeah," I interrupted glumly. "And Nance handled it perfectly, I'm sure. She probably threw a tea party for them or something, with fine china."

Ms. Parkins sat down next to me. "Actually, it's the only

volume in which I ever recall Nancy being described as 'cross' and 'petulant.' Throughout the whole novel, she's in a jealous, sulky—sometimes rude—funk . . . until she gets her wish and the relationship doesn't work out."

That was a shocker. "Really?"

"Yes, Millie." Ms. Parkins ventured a smile. "You're actually handling your father's dating much better than Nancy Drew did when confronted with the same situation."

I met her eyes again, and doing that seemed more natural. "Thanks, Ms. Parkins."

I still wasn't entirely comfortable with having a new mother figure in my house—and let's face it, I saw the way Ms. Parkins and my dad looked at each other, and she wasn't going anywhere—but right then, I knew we'd ultimately figure it out and make it work.

If only the same could be said for my wardrobe vis-à-vis a formal dance.

What was I going to do? Turn my "Nihilists for Nothing" T-shirt inside out, tug it to my knees, and call it a little black dress?

But, of course, if there was one thing Isabel Parkins knew, beyond books, it was fashion, and it was almost like she read my mind when she squeezed my hand and said, "Come on. Let's get you ready for a dance."

And about twenty minutes later, when I walked—okay, wobbled—down the stairs, Chase and my father both spun on the couch and nearly spat out the satay they were scarfing down, sputtering simultaneously, "Oh . . . wow!"

Chapter 68

Millie, you really do look nice," Chase said, helping me get out of his car. I normally would've found the gesture far too corny, but I was still pretty shaky on my borrowed heels and let him take my arm. "I know you keep telling me to shut up—which dampens the classy effect a little bit—but you really have to believe me when I say you look *amazing.*"

Actually, I'd seen that in Chase's eyes when I'd walked down the stairs—clinging to the banister for dear life, because Ms. Parkins's deep-purple strappy shoes were not only three inches higher than anything I'd ever worn before, but a half-size off, too. She'd also loaned me her plum, satin, sleeveless top, which we'd paired with a black skirt that—thank God—I had, for emergencies. Then, in a burst of courage, I'd gone to my mom's old dresser, which Dad had never cleared out, and found a pretty printed scarf, which Ms. Parkins had fashioned into a belt, like some sort of sartorial MacGyver.

It felt nice to be carrying a reminder of my mom on my first date.

Well, sort of date.

"I don't think this is really a traditional dance outfit," I said, smoothing my skirt. I wasn't sure why I kept apologizing for how I looked. "It's not super formal—like your suit."

Which is . . . unbelievable!

I had to admit, I'd sucked in a breath when I'd seen Chase, too. He wore a dark suit that was even nicer than the one he'd worn to Mr. Killdare's memorial. The jacket fit his broad shoulders perfectly, and he seemed to have a knack for picking shirts and ties that made his eyes look as blue as the Caribbean that was the inspiration for the dance. At least, I assumed his eyes were Caribbean blue. I'd actually never been farther south than Virginia Beach.

Chase and I had started walking toward the school, but I stopped, seeing a bunch of other girls in what looked like serious cocktail dresses heading for the doors, too. No kidding, I would've worn any of their getups to the Oscars if I ever got invited. "I really think I'm underdressed," I said yet again. "Maybe we should just go get a pizza or something."

"Millie, your outfit is perfect," Chase promised. "It fits who you are—and that's a good thing," he added, probably because he saw me opening my mouth to ask if he was being sarcastic. He grinned. "And at least you're not wearing that crazy owl shirt your dad's date had on."

"Uh, yeah." Feeling my cheeks get warm, I went overboard to deny my connection to "Whooo Loves You?" "What was up with *that?*"

All at once, the silence that I'd feared descended upon

us—swooping down like a stealthy owl—and Chase and I looked at each other. Only it didn't seem like we lacked things to say. On the contrary, there was *too much* unspoken stuff between us.

I was the one who broke the spell first, admitting quietly, "I didn't think you'd show up tonight. After how I treated you."

We were standing in the parking lot, not far from where I'd blown up at him. Only this time, there were no flashing lights. Just a street lamp that cast his handsome face in a much more forgiving light. I could see his eyes better, too. See how they'd gotten a little hard toward me, as if maybe, in spite of keeping our date, he still harbored some anger toward me. "I told you that I was going to take you to the dance, Millie," he said. "And regardless of what you think of me, when I make a promise, I keep it."

"I also kind of wondered if you were going with Viv," I confessed.

I didn't think I could've surprised Chase more if I'd said that in perfect French. "What?"

"I saw her talking to you in the caf . . ." I realized that I was saying too much, and concluded with a shrug, "I don't know . . . I just heard this rumor that you were taking her."

"Millie, you had to practically bully me into doing this," he reminded me. Then he frowned. "Plus, Viv . . . No offense to her, but she's kind of terrifying. She tried to muster some tears for Mike, but couldn't quite pull it off, and eventually just gave up. That's pretty cold."

Not just cold. Psychopathic! "So what did she want?"

"A study partner. She wants to do a precollege summer program in France. I'm helping her prepare."

"Oh." Maybe Chase *was* naive. Viv was the president of the Language Club and practically fluent. "Well, good luck with that."

"I know what you're thinking," he said. "But trust me. Even if Viv is into me, I don't have any interest in her." He seemed about to say something else—then stopped himself.

When it became apparent that he definitely wasn't going to add anything more, I said, "Anyhow . . . I'm really sorry for yelling at you." I looked down at my feet. "I'm just so worried about my dad. But you were right that evening. You did the right thing by telling the truth."

"Hey, Millie?"

I raised my face to see that Chase was smiling. "Yeah?"

"I actually think it's great how you defended your father, like a pit bull—even if you did leave a bruise on my arm. And you stood up to Detective Lohser, too. That took guts."

Once again, it was a different kind of boy-to-girl compliment. Not like the ones he'd offered earlier, about my appearance.

Did guys find girls with "guts" attractive?

No. Of course not. They judge them "pit-bull-ish."

Unfortunately for me, guys liked girls with tame hair, sparkly nails, and—in my experience—vapid eyes with fluttering lids and who could walk in heels, just naturally.

For a split second, I started comparing myself with a girl

I'd barely glimpsed in a locker, not to mention a bunch of classmates who'd be in the gym, dancing effortlessly on their stilettos. Then I remembered what Ms. Parkins had told me earlier.

I'm Millie Ostermeyer, dammit. And if that's not what Chase, or any other guy, wants, then screw it. His loss.

"Come on, Chase." I started leading us toward the school again. "The punch and cookies won't last forever."

It was Chase's turn to hang back, and I knew what he was thinking. That he didn't belong at a dance. That he should be home alone watching some dismal, maybe Norwegian, DVD whose bleak landscape and bleaker plot would remind him how awful he used to be.

"Hey, I guess we could also go to my house and get *Kitchen Stories* on Netflix," I suggested, recalling the most depressing foreign film we'd ever screened at the Bijou. From what I'd gathered, it was about two sad old Swedish guys who never left their gray kitchen. I also remembered that Chase had bought a ticket. "You wanna see that again?"

He almost smiled. "I can't believe you know that movie."

"I can't believe you *watched* it." I tugged his sleeve. "Come on, already. If I don't get a cookie because of all this yapping . . ."

"Okay, okay," Chase agreed. Then he took a deep breath and—maybe because he *was* a guy of his word and had promised to take a girl to a dance—said, "Let's go."

We'd only taken a few steps when Chase, no doubt noticing that I was having trouble navigating the parking lot,

260 * BETH FANTASKEY

wordlessly slipped his hand into mine to help hold me up the rest of the way to the gymnasium doors.

Or maybe I was helping Chase—the hottest, most mature, most confident, *self-hating recluse* I'd ever met—face the crowd in the strangest faux tropical paradise I'd ever seen.

One where a good deal of the crepe paper was black.

Chapter 69

"Well, this is cheerfully morbid," Chase observed, ducking as we entered the gym so he wouldn't get hit by a plastic parrot. It hung from an equally fake palm tree, crudely fashioned from cardboard and strips of green Saran Wrap by someone on the decorating committee who'd clearly overestimated his or her abilities with a glue gun. He released my hand as we both stopped in front of two easels, heavily draped with black crepe and placed so everyone entering would have no choice but to pause and pay tribute to Coach Killdare and Mike Price. "I do not know what to make of this," Chase added. "It's a nice gesture, but . . ."

"It's terrible!" I finished the assessment for him, speaking just loudly enough to be heard over the music. "And who chose those pictures?"

It almost seemed as though whoever'd killed Mr. Killdare and/or Mike had subsequently been tapped to create their pictorial memorials. The photo of Coach Killdare, affixed to an oversize posterboard, captured him on the sidelines at a game, red-faced and bellowing, his trademark vein popping in his neck. And the picture of Mike wasn't any better —although it was his official junior year photo. Regardless, he was wearing a too-tight polo shirt, as if he'd grudgingly ditched the Eagles jersey on "picture day," and he was scowling like he wanted to beat the crap out of the photographer.

"Not exactly flattering," Chase muttered. "Coach Killdare, at least, deserved better."

I'd kind of forgotten that Chase had shared a bond with Mr. Killdare, and I tentatively touched his shoulder. "Hey, Chase . . . Sorry this is so crappy."

He met my eyes and shrugged. "It's okay. I know most people didn't get him. *I* didn't always get him." Then he reached for a marker that was dangling by a string tacked to a corner of Mike's poster. "I guess we should sign both of these, though."

That was the first time I noticed that what I'd taken for black squiggles around the edges of the posterboard were actually notes written by kids and chaperones. It was like the most dismal, oversize yearbook ever. Still, I reached for the marker that swung next to Mr. Killdare's picture, agreeing, "Yeah, I guess so." Then, while Chase tried to figure out what to leave on Mike's board, I bent down and wrote, at the very bottom of Mr. Killdare's frame, "Journey safely, Cap'n Andy." And although I wasn't sure I believed in angels—or that Hollerin' Hank would be in their company if they did exist—I added, "May you sing 'Ballyhoo' forever with a heavenly chorus!"

"Millie, what does *that* mean?"

I heard Chase asking me to explain my inscription, which

referenced Mr. Killdare's star turn in *Show Boat,* but I didn't answer him. I was too busy fixating on the note right next to mine. A very brief farewell. In fact, all it said was "Farewell." Without a signature. But something about that writing . . .

All at once, realization dawned on me, and my heart started to race.

"Chase!" I reached behind me and groped blindly for my date, half afraid that if I turned around, that word would disappear. "Get down here!"

"What?" He bent down next to me. "What is wrong with you? Maybe you should just take off those shoes—"

"It's not the shoes!" I finally looked away from that terse sendoff, long enough to meet Chase's eyes as I informed him, my words sounding strangely at odds with the background melody of an incredibly sappy Celine Dion song, "I think the killer's here!"

Chapter **70**

That script didn't look the least bit familiar to you?" I asked after Chase had pulled me away from the memorial. We had started to look like a pair of ghouls, lingering forever near those horrible pictures. We were also no doubt drawing attention because nobody'd expected to see Chase *or* me at a dance, and our arrival together was obviously blowing minds sky-high. I had to keep giving kids my best what-are-you-looking-at glare—while Chase, used to being an object of worship, seemed blissfully oblivious. He took his time getting us a snack, choosing novelty-shaped iced shortbreads from a table decorated with plastic grass skirts and lawn flamingos.

Is this all I've been missing? Is this really how we Honeywellians interpret "tropical paradise"?

And what kind of theme is "Into the Sunset" for a dance that honors two murder victims, anyhow?

Who picks that for ANY dance?

"No, Millie," Chase said, so for a second I thought he was answering my unspoken questions, at least about the decor.

For just a moment, I hoped he was about to tell me that I'd been missing tons of great stuff, and that any minute now, the bleachers would part to reveal a sparkling pool surrounded by real tiki torches and exotic flowers. But, of course, he was still talking about the writing we'd seen on the poster. "It was only one word, and I guess I don't notice handwriting that much to begin with." Chase piled me high with food. "It could belong to any girl."

I bit into a cookie, then covered my mouth before speaking. Even I knew better than to spray a quasi date with crumbs. "You definitely think it's feminine, though."

Chase was not eating any of the—let's face it, putrid— treats. "Yeah . . . I would say that."

I swallowed my cookie and ditched the rest in a garbage can that was also wearing a grass skirt. Then I began to scan the gym again, eyes narrowed, searching for someone who'd give me an "aha" moment. Somebody who'd let me connect the writing on the postcard to the writing on the posterboard and then to a real person.

But it didn't happen. All I saw was a bunch of kids—the girls looking, for the most part, like they were about thirty, in dresses they'd no doubt spent days picking out, and the boys looking almost uniformly thirteen, in ill-fitting suits they'd probably last worn at their confirmations, bar mitzvahs, or whatever "welcome to puberty" traditions their particular families followed. There were also a few chaperones milling around, but nobody who stood out.

"Pardonnez-moi!"

The deep voice cut into my thoughts, and for a second

I thought Chase was giving me a hard time by talking in French again. Or maybe that he was going to suavely ask me to dance. Then I turned around and realized that not only was Chase not talking, but I wasn't the one being asked to partner up on the crowded floor.

As I—and Chase—looked on in horror, *Mademoiselle Beamish* said something to her favorite student that even I understood.

"Voulez-vous danser, Chase?"

Chapter **71**

"I owe you for the rest of my life, Millicent Ostermeyer," Chase whispered directly into my ear, which wasn't hidden by red curls because Ms. Parkins had also given me a two-second updo. Fortunately, my hair was thick enough to conceal a drugstore ponytail holder and some bobby pins, so the effect was pretty nice. "You saved me back there," he added, pulling me closer. I felt his lips turn up against my ear. "*Merci.* Meaning 'thank you.'"

"I know what *'merci'* means—*el jerko,*" I informed him with a quick shove to his shoulder. Just enough to push us apart and send our gentle swaying off rhythm.

In truth, I was trying to keep us almost continually offbeat and to ignore how strong Chase's shoulder felt when I rested against it, like I was doing then, because he'd somehow, without hardly moving, pulled me closer again. "You practically told Ms. Beamish *'Back off! He's mine!'*" he teased.

"Somebody had to save you," I said, suddenly depressed, because the guy holding me . . . He *wasn't* mine. I tried once more to put some distance between us—but couldn't. Not because he was squeezing me too hard. On the contrary, he was applying just the right amount of pressure to the small of my back, and trapping my hand lightly against his shoulder. I just didn't have the will to push him away, it seemed. Still, I said, "It's no big deal. And we probably had to dance at some point, anyhow."

"Millie . . ." Chase pulled back, so I could see his eyes. He seemed surprised by my comment. "I *wanted* to dance with you." He smiled again. "Even before Ms. Beamish made her move, unleashing your inner Doberman."

"Chase?"

"Yes?"

I dropped my voice to the merest whisper, not believing what I was about to say but saying it anyway. "Could you —just for this evening—not refer to me as any kind of dog —especially the vicious, fighting breeds—or compare my eating habits to those of any member of the football team, be it a fullback, a tackle, or a kicker even?"

He started to speak, but I held up one hand, signaling that I wasn't done. "And last but not least, could you just *shut up* for the rest of this dance, because . . ." I hesitated, then forged ahead. "Because some perverse part of me *likes you,* Chase Albright. As more than just a buddy." His blue eyes widened, so I wished I'd stopped earlier. Maybe at my bedroom door, before even walking down the stairs. But what could I do except finish at that point, saying quietly, "I know you don't like me back—but just let me, for a minute, *like you.*"

Of course, it was just my luck that the stupid song ended

at that exact moment, because songs only last three minutes, and my monologue had run at least two-point-five.

But contrary to what I expected, Chase didn't push me away—or run out the door, knocking down the tribute posters and bonking his head on the plastic parrot in his haste to escape.

Instead, he kept holding me and swaying, until I started to feel awkward because other couples were separating. But sure enough, within a few seconds, another song started. Another syrupy, slow song by some retro artist my dad had probably danced to back in his day. Maybe . . . Sinatra?

Not that it really mattered, as Chase did as I'd requested. He didn't say a word, but just kept holding me close, his hand pressed against my back and his head tilted next to mine, so anybody who saw us—and I was sure a lot of kids saw us— could've easily gotten the wrong impression. But I didn't care or worry about what Viv might be thinking, even, if she'd shown up.

I'd never been like that with a guy. Never. And although this small part of me knew that Chase was dancing with me because he owed me for saving him from a worse partner, for some reason that hardly hurt my enjoyment of the moment.

And I got the sense that Chase was maybe okay with what we were doing, too. I had no experience with boys, but as the song continued and we kept swaying, I could've sworn that I felt something change in the way he held me. In the way his heart beat under my hand, which he'd moved to the center of his chest, like we were getting even closer, sort of shutting out the rest of the dance with its cheesy music and even worse decor, and making a really nice space of our own.

I honestly started to believe that, enough that my heart began to race a little when Chase finally spoke, whispering even more softly, his voice rough with that throaty quality I'd heard once before. "Millie . . ."

What was it I heard when he spoke my name?

Desire? For me?

Guilt? Over dancing so close when he has Allison?

A touch of regret, even, that he's taken?

All of that?

I could hardly wait to know what he was thinking. It was almost killing me by the time he repeated, even more quietly, "Millie . . . I . . ."

You what, Chase?

You can?

You can't?

You WANT TO . . . ?

I swore my head was going to explode if he didn't say something soon, and I winced as pressure seemed to build in my ears—only to realize that we were both cringing at the phenomenally abrasive screech of feedback from a microphone, and the even screechier voice of Vivienne Fitch, who stopped the dance dead by commandeering the sound system and practically shouting at the crowd, "*Attention,* Honeywell students! It is time for our tribute to Mr. Hank Killdare and beloved student athlete Michael Price!"

There was nothing that Chase and I could do but pull apart and face the small stage at the far end of the gym, where I saw that someone had moved the posters. But I noticed that Chase didn't separate himself from me entirely. No, he kept one hand lightly on my back, connecting us as we moved with other students to gather around the stage. Even when we found a spot in the crowd, close enough to get a good look at Principal Woolsey taking over the microphone, Chase didn't pull his arm away.

Oh, gosh . . . What is happening?

And if he has a girlfriend, is even this much wrong?

I didn't have a chance to grapple with those questions, though, before another one came to mind. An important one, which had to be voiced, and although a big part of me didn't want to mess up whatever was taking place between us, I turned to Chase and whispered, "Where the heck have I seen that tropical train wreck of a shirt that Mr. Woolsey is wearing?"

Chase didn't answer right away. He seemed to be looking intently at that shirt, too. A T-shirt emblazoned with two big palm trees, which arched in a way that framed Mr. Bertram B. Woolsey's middle-aged paunch, the better to highlight the boast "I Rode the Big Banana at Kona Dreams Outrigger Rental!"

Then, all at once, Chase and I apparently made the same connection—one between Mr. Woolsey's outfit and a photo on Mr. Killdare's refrigerator, in which the coach wore *the exact same shirt*. We met each other's eyes, both of us no doubt registering excitement, shock, and maybe a small degree of discomfort as we muttered, simultaneously, in disbelief, . . .

"*BeeBee?*"

I also couldn't help noticing, out of the corner of my eye, that someone else had become aware of that other connection Chase and I had made. The physical one.

In fact, when I looked at the stage again—this time at Vivienne Fitch—I saw her staring at me and Chase. At the way we were still very close, his body positioned slightly behind mine and his hand now at my waist, so it was very clear that we were together.

And, oh, the look in her eyes.

It was like I'd won Camper of the Year, a pumpkin full of Halloween candy, and at least ten Pacemaker awards, all at the same time, while she'd gotten a bucket of goo dumped on her, *Carrie*-style, in front of the whole school.

Chapter **72**

T his can't be true, right?" I asked hurrying with Chase down the dark corridor, away from the gym—and Viv's deathly stare, thank goodness—and toward Mr. Woolsey's office. For the second time that evening, he was holding my hand, but I was pretty sure it was to again help me stay upright.

Touching Chase is nice—really nice—but ENOUGH, Cinderella. By midnight, you're going to be on the curb with a bunch of rats and a rotten pumpkin, while he goes home to dream of his girlfriend.

"Wait." I pulled free of Chase, then bent down and liberated myself from my purple pumps, too. Straightening, I looped the straps around my wrist. "There." I heard relief in my voice. "Now we can hurry."

Chase glanced at my bare feet. "Okay, let's go."

"We can't actually believe that Mr. Woolsey is BeeBee . . . Can we?" I whispered. Ditching the shoes had the added benefit of making us more stealthy. "I mean, that would mean that he and Mr. Killdare were almost definitely . . ."

We'd arrived at the door to the suite of administrative offices, and Chase reached up and deftly plucked a bobby pin from my hair, so some of my curls leaped free.

"Hey!" I started to protest, then realized he was using the pin to pick the lock. Besides, I was already shoeless and my scarf-belt had gotten askew. Who really cared if my updo was perfect?

Must be nearly midnight, Cinderella!

"I know it seems hard to comprehend," Chase said, using one of those vocab words that made me wish I really did have a fairy godmother who could deliver a prince for more than one night. "But we both saw that picture of Mr. Killdare, wearing the same shirt, at his house . . ."

"And you'll see," I promised, as Chase—athlete, closet geek, and former delinquent—popped the lock and let us into the offices. "Mr. Woolsey—*Bertram B.* Woolsey—is posing against the same backdrop. He has the *exact same* photo on his desk." I accepted the bobby pin Chase was offering back and stuck it in my hair. "What are the odds of *that?* I mean, doesn't it seem like they went on a vacation together? And Mr. Woolsey's initials. B.B. . . ."

Chase opened the door, letting me in first. "I don't know, Millie. It's hard for me to imagine Coach Killdare as gay, but . . . I guess you never know, right?"

I led us past the secretary's desk toward the door to Mr. Woolsey's private chambers. "Yeah, it was almost impossible for me to believe Ryan was gay when he came out."

Chase seemed taken aback. "Ryan is gay? Ryan Ronin?"

I had my hand on the knob, but turned to face Chase. "Yeah."

"Wow. I had no idea."

"You are seriously clueless, aren't you?" I said, opening the second door, which wasn't locked. "Don't you know *anything* but French?"

He didn't answer, probably because he was picking up the photo I'd seen a thousand times on Mr. Woolsey's desk, without ever reading the small print on his shirt about riding a banana-shaped boat. "You're right," Chase said. "This is the exact same image. It's like they photographed each other, trading places between shots."

He looked at me over the picture frame, and I ventured, "Grown men don't take vacations together unless they're . . . *lovers,* right?"

Okay, I wasn't sure I'd ever said the word "lovers" out loud, in any context, and it came out kind of . . . ugh. Not because I was applying it to my principal and a football coach, but just because it seemed . . . *ugh.*

Chase didn't seem to know how to follow up on that, either. He didn't exactly answer, asking instead, "The postcard, from BeeBee. You say it's from Switzerland?"

"Yeah?"

"Do you know if Mr. Woolsey traveled overseas this summer?"

"No idea," I admitted, starting to circle my principal's desk, looking for, say, a mug that said I ♥ Lucerne or a heavy, three-hole punch that might be used for clubbing a . . . lover.

"I pretty much try to forget Mr. Woolsey on my time off."

Chase resumed studying the picture, getting quiet. Pensive.

"Chase?" I finally asked softly, opening a drawer to discover that Mr. Woolsey kept a stash of Devil Dogs. *So, somebody has a sweet tooth — among other secrets.* I considered helping myself to just one, but had a pang of conscience and shut the drawer. "Would it bug you if Mr. Killdare really was gay?"

Chase looked up from the picture, seeming surprised. "I grew up in California, Millie. About five miles from Venice Beach. I am not freaked out by homosexuality." He resumed staring at the picture, though, as if *that* was freaking him out. I was about to tell him that a vacation snapshot probably wasn't going to yield any more answers when he turned it over and peered at it even more closely, saying, "I don't think we should jump to any conclusions, though . . ."

The weird thing was, I was also backing off my theory about our principal killing Coach Killdare during a passionate quarrel because I'd discovered something else on Mr. Woolsey's desk. Not bloodstained office equipment or a damning European mug, but a pad of hall passes, some already presigned.

"There's a sticker on the back of the frame," Chase continued while I picked up the pad — which was not unlike one I'd swiped the previous year. "It says 'PIAA Annual Conference, 2010, Oahu.'" He set down the photo. "Mr. Killdare and Mr. Woolsey probably . . ."

". . . Went to some stupid high school sports conference

together," I said glumly. "And hated each other the whole time. Which is why they aren't in the photo together, palling around." I held up the pad for Chase to see. "And Mr. Woolsey's handwriting . . . It's pretty girly, but it's not the same as BeeBee's." I tossed down the pad, feeling defeated. I guess I'd really thought I'd found a new prime suspect—a boyfriend who might've had a deadly argument with the ever-volatile Coach Killdare. But I'd been wrong.

Had I seriously believed Mr. Woolsey was strong enough —emotionally or physically—to crush a skull? His hands were softer, and finer boned, than mine. I'd forgotten about the feminine-hygiene products at Mr. Killdare's house, too. I could imagine Mr. Woolsey using hair spray to keep his comb-over in place, but he obviously didn't need *those*.

"I should've known Mr. Woolsey's not BeeBee," I grumbled, mentally kicking myself. "I've forged his writing a million times. I know every loop and swirl he makes—and how weak he is."

I was pretty sure Chase was about to ask why I'd faked our principal's signature, but before he could open his mouth, we both heard something in the hallway. Footsteps, coming closer.

"What do we do?" I whispered, because there was no back way out of the office, and whoever was coming would definitely see us if we bolted out the regular way. Especially since the person sounded like she—or probably he, given that I didn't hear the click of heels—was only a few yards away. I came around the desk, snatched the photo from Chase, and returned it to its proper place. "We are so busted if that person comes in here!"

"Millie, calm down," Chase urged, even though the footsteps had halted — *right outside the office door.*

My heart started to race as I then heard *Bertram Woolsey* muttering to himself, "Now where did I put my keys . . . ?"

Freakin' Mr. Woolsey!

"Come on," I told Chase, grabbing his wrist. I could hear the panic in my voice and feel how wide my eyes were. Way, way too wide. I tugged his hand, not understanding why he wasn't nervous. In fact, he seemed close to laughing when I suggested, "We'll hide behind the ficus! And if — when — we get caught, we'll say we were . . . we were checking it for blight, for a botany unit in advanced bio. It looks blighted, right?"

Outside the door, I heard a jangle, as if Mr. Woolsey had at least found his keys, if not the right one yet.

Time's a wastin'!

But Chase didn't budge. Instead, he rested his hands on my shoulders and said, calmly and still with a hint of laughter, "I'm not going to blame my actions on blight, Millie. Just relax, okay? It's *Mr. Woolsey.* We'll think of something."

"Okay," I agreed, taking a deep breath. "You're right."

Why was I getting so worked up? I was the one who skipped classes and flouted authority, and more to the point, we were talking about Bertram Woolsey here. I'd probably be able to convince him that he was intruding on *us.*

Honestly, it was like a repeat of the time I'd hidden from Chase in Mr. Killdare's house. Something about getting

caught sneaking around—it apparently triggered an adrenaline rush in me.

And it was that rush . . . That's what I would blame for
what I did next. Which was put my arms around Chase—just
as the door opened—and kiss my sort-of date right on the
mouth.

Chapter 73

I kissed Chase because Mr. Woolsey—just like Detective Lohser—would almost certainly assume that's what I and a hormonally charged teenage guy would be doing alone in his office after slow dancing, and—unlike if we admitted to snooping through his Devil Dogs—he'd probably just shoo us, awkwardly, back to the dance. And I kissed Chase because I was sick of people thinking we were making out, and me not getting anything out of it but a bad reputation, if only with an authority-drunk cop and now my principal. And, let's face it, I kissed Chase because I was an impulsive person, and I wanted to do it. Had wanted that for quite a while, actually. Just one quick touch of the lips—not his fault, only mine—to see what it would feel like.

And wow, did it feel amazing.

More . . . *powerful* than I'd expected. So powerful that I immediately wished I hadn't done it. Because the second my mouth met his, everything I'd started to feel for Chase—the stuff I'd pushed away, and tamped down, because I knew he didn't feel the same way for me—all overwhelmed me, in a way, and even though we were barely touching, it *hurt*.

Ms. Parkins was wrong. I was wrong. I can't just not care that he doesn't like me.

Stop now, *Millie!*

"Sorry," I muttered, dropping down off my tiptoes, averting my eyes, and wiping my mouth with the back of my hand, although we hadn't gotten sloppy with the whole thing. Chase hadn't even responded. His lips had been hard against mine.

"Um . . . Millie . . . ?" Not surprisingly, he sounded pretty confused.

And Mr. Woolsey seemed shocked, too, as he came into his office—I'd almost forgotten him—and flipped on the bright overhead light, echoing Chase—although in a higher, less appealing voice, "Millie?" Then he turned to the guy I'd just pawed. "And Mr. Albright? What are you two *doing* here?"

Chapter **74**

I feel like such an idiot," I mumbled, walking with Chase
across the dark parking lot toward his car, my strappy
shoes dangling from one hand and a detention slip crumpled
in the other. "Two days' punishment for me — and you have to
sit out a game, which means Dad will kill me, too." I winced.
"Plus my feet hurt. There are little stones everywhere."

Chase stopped and held out his arms, an uncertain look on
his face. "Millie, I could, um . . . It wouldn't be a problem . . ."

Yeah. It would be. For me. The last thing I needed was
Chase *carrying* me with his stupid, wonderful strong arms.

Why did I kiss him?

"No, thanks," I said, continuing to pick my way across the
lot. "I'm not really a mutt like Baxter. You don't have to haul
me around."

We'd made it to Chase's car, and I was grabbing for
the door handle when he reached past me, stopping me. I
thought he was going to be polite and open the door. But all
of a sudden, without saying a word, he took me by the wrist

instead and turned me to face him. Then Chase wrapped both those stupid, wonderful strong arms around me and kissed *me*. And not just some little peck on the cheek or the lips.

A *real* kiss.

Chapter **75**

"Chase," I whispered when we separated for a moment. Long enough for me to realize I'd dropped my shoes, lost my detention slip, and was leaning against his car, both of us breathing hard, because apparently I wasn't the only one who'd kept feelings pent up for a while. The kiss we were sharing—the one that was starting again, his lips brushing against mine, shutting me up, although I had no idea what I'd been about to say—had begun intensely, almost feverishly, both of us clinging to each other and me, embarrassingly, kind of groaning now and then.

But I couldn't help it.

The whole thing was pleasure, but still tinged with a hint of the pain I'd felt back in the principal's office, too.

I knew then that Chase really did want me in the same way that I wanted him, but it was wrong. He was giving in —but trying to stop himself, too. I could feel it in the way he held me, and the way he kept saying my name, "Millie . . ." There was frustration in his voice—and apology—even as we both gave in again, only more slowly and tenderly this time, like we were managing to get control of ourselves, but still couldn't completely part.

Just kiss me, Chase, I thought, slipping my hands up into that thick, amazing hair. But the weird thing was, I wasn't really focused on how Chase looked or how his perfect muscular body felt—although those were definitely things that had first attracted me to him. But as we finally really touched each other, his lips rough but gentle against mine, I knew that what I was truly drawn to was . . . Chase. The guy who cared about a coach everybody else hated, and affectionately babysat an ugly dog, and shared cookies with a lonely old lady, and who beat himself up for some mistake he'd made in the past. A mistake I still didn't know *all* about.

"Chase." I said his name again, more firmly, if still a little breathlessly. "Chase . . . Maybe . . ."

He seemed to understand, and he pulled back so I could see his eyes.

Oh, gosh, I was so crazy about those eyes, and all the things that I could see in them. Even the bad stuff, like the guilt.

"Millie," he whispered, resting his forehead against mine and cradling my face in his hands, his thumbs brushing my cheeks. His breath was a little ragged, too. "I'm . . ."

"Don't say 'sorry,'" I warned him quietly. I'd never held a guy in my life, but I somehow knew that I was supposed to slip my hands around his neck and stroke his hair. How could it feel so right to stand like that? So natural? And yet . . . "Just don't say 'sorry,' okay?"

"I . . . I don't know if I'm sorry," he said softly. "I've wanted this . . ."

"Me, too," I admitted. "But I never thought you would . . . You know, with me . . ."

We weren't managing complete sentences, but we somehow understood each other.

"Millie." He began to whisper the words I'd wanted to hear since I'd first pretended not to be interested in him, right after he'd moved to town. Real compliments. "I think you're the most incredible, unique girl I've ever met. You have this . . . *thing* that other girls don't have." He paused, no doubt trying to figure out how to explain a word that must've sounded wrong to him, too. Then he continued. "You . . . You make me laugh, and you try to act so tough when you're really not." He withdrew slightly and brushed some of my curls— which were in total chaos, my updo demolished by his hands —from my face. "And I can't stop looking at you. You're so pretty, even if you don't believe that."

Everything he was saying was making me feel happy in a way I'd never felt before—even though I knew there was going to be a "but." One that came way too soon. He spoke even more softly, and his blue eyes registered regret—and something like pain that I didn't quite understand. "I just . . . I don't think I'm . . ." We were completely calm then, no longer sucking air, but he still didn't seem able to express himself the way he usually could. "I don't think I should . . ." His frown deepened, and then he said the word I'd been dreading. Her name. "It's like I'm betraying Allison," he finally admitted.

"Moving on . . . Caring about somebody else—more than I did for her, which makes it even worse . . ."

I'd thought I'd understood what he was trying to say—thought I'd been filling in the copious blanks—but all at once, he'd lost me. It was "like" he was betraying her?

"You're . . . You're talking in the past tense," I said, searching his face—hopefully, in spite of the hurt I saw. "Like you two aren't together."

Something about what I said caused a flash of raw agony in his eyes.

"Oh, God, Millie," he groaned, resting his forehead against mine again, but this time bracing his hands on either side of me against the car. Not holding me anymore. "I should've told you before I kissed you . . ."

"Told me what?" I asked. My heart, which had just been—for lack of a less hokey word—soaring, iced over and started its inevitable plummet. Still, I had to ask, my throat tight, "What, Chase?"

The wretched anguish I heard in his voice wasn't enough to keep me from getting sick—physically ill—when he confessed, more loudly, like he needed me to hear and understand, "I *killed my last girlfriend*, Millie."

I didn't even feel the stones under my feet as I ran home, barefoot, without ever looking back.

Talk about the clock striking midnight and everything just exploding. And when I got to my house, bursting through the door, my dad and Ms. Parkins, who were sitting on the couch, jumped apart like they were teenagers caught making out.

But to her credit, even though I'd obviously lost her shoes and was clearly upset, my librarian-slash-father's-girlfriend knew when to back off, and neither she nor my dad followed me to my room, where I lay awake all night, pretty sure that Chase was referring to an accident, but still wondering . . .

Did I just kiss a murderer?

Chapter 76

T his is a pathetic Saturday night, even by our standards," Laura complained to me and Ryan the evening after my disastrous dance. She was sitting cross-legged on my bed, flipping through my latest edition of *Philosophy Now* magazine, a gift subscription from my father, for my seventeenth birthday. I'd been surprised by the thoughtful present, but now strongly suspected that Isabel Parkins might've played a role in its selection. "Do you want to take the 'Am I a Moral Beauty or a Beast' quiz?" Laura asked, sounding less than enthused. "I see the name Schopenhauer in there, so it might be fun for you at least, Millie."

Ryan was stretched out on the floor, tossing a ball he'd formed out of my stray socks toward the ceiling. "Go ahead," he urged Laura. "It couldn't make this night *more* boring."

"Yeah, whatever," I also agreed with indifference, even though I'd just been puzzling over that very theme as I sat at my desk, idly shaking the mouse connected to my laptop.

What is Chase?

Beauty or beast? Or both?

Am I more upset that he lied, at least by omission, or that he TOOK A LIFE?

I shuffled the mouse again.

And why am I afraid to confirm what I suspect? Because I know his true name and could Google the story. At least, I hope I know his real name . . .

"Millie, I was asking you whether you'd lie about your immigrant friend Sonja's employment status if telling the truth meant she'd be deported and maybe imprisoned by a harsh regime," Laura said, snapping me back to reality. She sounded exasperated. "It was a long scenario, and I think you daydreamed through the whole thing!"

Ryan sat up and checked the old Winnie-the-Pooh clock on my nightstand. "And aren't you supposed to be at work? Why are you even here?"

"I called in sick," I told my friends. *Because we're showing Ikiru, a Japanese film about a lonely bureaucrat dying from cancer, and Chase will show up for that.* "I guess I'm a beast," I concluded gloomily. "No need to take a quiz."

"Millie, what is wrong with you?" Laura tossed aside the magazine. "Why won't you tell us what happened at the dance? Was Chase a jerk or something? Did he dance with a bunch of other girls and leave you by the wall?"

I'd finally come clean about going to the formal, if only because by Monday word would be all around school about how the ultimate-outsider quarterback had finally deigned to attend a school function—with Millie Ostermeyer, who'd teetered around on too-big shoes and worn a scarf as a belt.

I cringed at the recollection.

What had I been thinking?

"Hey, Millie." Ryan tapped my leg. I looked down to see that he was deadly serious. "Chase didn't try anything, did he? Because I'd kick his ass if he didn't take no—"

"No!" I said quickly. I was upset with Chase, and confused, but he was no date rapist. What little we'd "done," I'd technically started, and I'd wanted every second of what had followed, right up to the point when he'd confessed to *killing someone.*

"No," I repeated. "Please don't think *that* about him." Then, because I had to tell somebody, and Laura and Ry always kept my secrets, I said, "We did sort of . . . kiss, though."

Ryan didn't seem surprised, but Laura's eyes got huge. "You did *what?*"

"Kissed," I confirmed. "A lot. In the parking lot."

Okay, it sounded borderline sleazy when put that way. But we'd been caught up in a moment . . .

How could I get butterflies again just thinking about how it had felt when Chase had first pulled me to him, and how I'd never wanted to be so close to another human being in my life, and had almost blurted out "I love you."

Not only would that have been about ten years premature, but I couldn't love somebody I didn't even know, right? And I certainly couldn't love somebody who kept a secret *that big.* We'd talked about Allison before. *He should've said something . . .*

"Millie, was it *bad?*" Ry asked. I could tell he was still ready to beat up Chase if necessary. "Because you don't look very happy about it."

"I can't explain it," I told them both. Yet I tried to. "It was too good, in a way." Then, because it wasn't my place to spill Chase's secrets, I just concluded, shoulders slumping, right as the doorbell rang, "Anyway, it's over now."

Or maybe it wasn't, because a few moments later, my father rapped on the door to my room and poked his head in. "Millie? Chase is downstairs. He's returning your—Isabel's—shoes." That clearly displeased him, but he was being uncharacteristically cool about my coming home a mess, without part of my outfit. "He'd like to talk to you."

"Millie!" Only Laura seemed happy about that prospect. She shooed me with her hands, practically bouncing on the bed. "Go! Talk!"

My heart was pounding, too—but I wasn't ready to see Chase. "No," I told Dad firmly. "Tell him thanks for bringing back the shoes. But I don't want to talk."

Dad opened his mouth, as if he finally couldn't stand not knowing what was up. But then he glanced at Laura and Ryan and must've judged that it still wasn't the right time. "Okay," he agreed. "I'll tell him." He started to close the door, but paused. "Millie . . . Do *I* need to talk to Chase?"

I knew he was thinking the same thing Ryan just had. *Did Chase go too far?*

"No. It's okay," I promised. "We just had a . . . fight. That's all. Nothing that requires paternal intervention."

When my father left us without another word, my friends stayed quiet, all of us listening to Dad and Chase confer downstairs. I couldn't make out what they said, but a minute later, I heard the front door close.

Laura turned to me, confused. "Millie, why not *talk* to him? What is really going on?"

I couldn't explain more, though. Instead, I finally turned to my laptop—moving the screen so only I could see it—and typed "Colton Chase Albright fatal accident" into Google, fingers flying so I couldn't back out. Less than thirty seconds later, I found an article from the *Philadelphia Inquirer* about the drug-addled son of a prominent cardiac surgeon who'd walked away from an accident that had left a state lawmaker's daughter dead.

"He murdered my little girl . . . admits she was reluctant to get into that car . . . I'll see Colton Albright in prison, then hell . . ."

The rage and agony of a grieving father were palpable in the quotes, and I quickly clicked off the site, sick to my stomach again.

What if somebody had taken my mom like that? What if a drunk driver, not a disease, had claimed her life? I would never, ever forgive that.

"Millie, are you okay?" Ryan edged closer. "Why are you so pale?"

"Yeah," Laura agreed. "And what are you doing on the computer?"

Before I could answer—even try to explain why I was acting so weird—the doorbell rang again, and as if on cue, we all got up and went to the top of the stairs. Laura seemed excited, while Ry was obviously still in big brother, protective mode.

"Dad, tell Chase I *really* don't want to talk to him now," I hollered down. "Seriously!"

But as my words faded away, I realized Chase hadn't returned. My dad was talking to someone else. Namely, Detective Blaine Lohser, who was informing him, "I have a warrant here, authorizing us to search your property, *Head Coach* Ostermeyer."

"What?" I heard disbelief in my father's voice. "What are you talking about?"

I couldn't see Detective Lohser, but I could easily picture the smarmy smile that was no doubt forming under his dated scrub brush of facial hair when he said, "We have reason to believe the weapon used to murder Henry Killdare is buried behind your house."

Chapter 77

W hat are you doing?" I demanded, tugging on Detective Lohser's arms, which were crossed over his chest. We were standing in Dad's and my dark backyard, and a team of police officers was digging, under lights, in what used to be my mother's veggie garden. "This has gone far enough!" I cried, way too loudly.

"We got a tip, kid." Detective Lohser repeated stuff he'd said earlier when he'd barged into our house, waving papers under our noses. He didn't bother looking at me. He was watching that team of cops intently. "We think it's legit."

"This is crazy," I insisted, hauling on his sleeve again. "Stop it!"

"Millie!" My father spoke sharply, but his arms were gentle as he came up behind me and wrapped them around me, like a paradoxically comforting straitjacket, and walked me back from Detective Lohser before I could pull him to the ground. Then, when we were a few steps away, my father did something he hadn't done since I was a little child. He kissed the top of my head, sort of rocking me and saying softly, "Quiet, Millie. It's going to be okay."

I wanted to believe him, but I hadn't had such a bad year since my mother'd been diagnosed with cancer. My senior year so far was a disaster, and going downhill faster than an Olympic bobsled. I'd had a first kiss and gotten my heart broken on the same night. And if anyone—some pathetic guy pretending to be a detective—separated me from the man who could be distant, but who was, on that chilly October night, continuing to hold me, as if I were six again . . .

That can't happen. I can't lose my dad, too.

Resting against my father's reassuringly broad chest, I also watched the police officers, not understanding.

What did they think they'd find back there? Who was this "tipster"?

"Don't cry, Millie," Dad whispered, kissing my head again. I was cognizant of people gathering in the alley behind our yard, checking out the commotion and lights, and wondered whether Laura and Ryan had hung around for moral support, or if they'd listened to my father and gone home. I hoped they were still close by. "It's going to be fine," Dad promised. "There's nothing here."

I hadn't even realized that my breath had gotten shaky. That I was struggling to bottle up tears of frustration and anger, both for me and for my dad—who was obviously very wrong, because moments after he assured me that there was nothing to be found in our yard, one of the uniformed officers, who was digging like a gopher, announced loudly, "Found it."

My dad was clearly stunned. His arms around me locked up, like he had rigor mortis. Releasing me, he stepped woodenly back, handing me over to Ms. Parkins, who had arrived at some point and must've been waiting in the wings for the proper time to help. She didn't cradle me like my father had, but she did rest a small but strong hand on my shoulder. Meeting her eyes for a second, I saw that she was grim but calm.

At least this, between me and Ms. Parkins . . . This really is going to be okay.

Then I turned back to the disaster unfolding in the garden, just in time to see the gopher cop hand a plastic bag to Detective Lohser, who brandished it like a trophy, holding it up for inspection. Which was kind of bizarre, because—even in that pretty dark yard—it was quite obvious that the object he held was, indeed, a . . . *trophy.* One of those big, weighty ones with a guy holding a victory torch. An object that, if wielded in anger, might be heavy enough to bash in a skull.

"Oh, hell," Dad muttered. He turned to me and Ms. Parkins and, for the first time I could remember, seemed genuinely shaken, admitting quietly, just to us, "That *is* from my desk . . ." He amended that statement uneasily. "Well, the desk I took over from Hank."

"Jack . . . ?" Ms. Parkins didn't seem to know what to say. But there was no doubt in the question. Just confusion over who would try to frame the guy she loved. "But who . . . ?" she finally managed.

Thank you, I wanted to tell her. *Thank you for believing he's innocent.*

There was no time to say that though. Detective Lohser was striding toward us, holding probably the first trophy he'd ever touched in his life, and telling my father, who was being circled by another officer, one who held *handcuffs,* "Jack Ostermeyer, you are under arrest for the murder of Henry Killdare."

The whole yard started to spin under the stars as my dad— seeming to realize that denial would only make things worse —wordlessly offered his hands, and those cuffs clicked shut. And I only vaguely heard the uniformed guy read my father his rights because my ears started ringing, too. But while the world reeled, I did manage to catch sight of a flash of long blond hair in the crowd that had gathered to watch Mayor-and-Coach Jack Ostermeyer being led away in manacles.

Pulling myself together, I abandoned my father, but only because I was confident that Ms. Parkins would take care of him.

I had other business to attend to, and I heard the rage in my voice as I stalked across the grass, snarling, "Vivienne Fitch. What the *hell are you doing here?*"

Chapter 78

T his is *none* of your business!" I snapped at Viv, who was lurking on the other side of the white picket fence that defined my family's yard. If she thought that little fence was protecting her from me—half pit bull, half Doberman —she was sorely mistaken. And I didn't care that a lot of lingering gawkers heard me threatening her, "Get off our property!"

"I'm not on your property, you nutcase." She gestured to her feet, showing me that her pedicured toes, peeking out from little windows in her suede shoes, were, in fact, on municipal-issue gravel. "This alley is public property. And this *is* my business."

"I repeat, what are you doing here?" I asked more calmly, but still with an edge to my voice.

"I got a message telling me the cops were going to dig for gold in your backyard," she informed me. "An anonymous text."

"You have to show that to the police!" I said, getting excited. "They can trace it."

Which would give them the identity of the tipster, who was probably responsible for burying the trophy. But Viv was shaking her head and making a mock pout. She pulled her cell phone out of her purse, holding it up high, like she wanted me to jump for it. "Sorry," she said right before I really did leap at the fence. "But I already deleted it." Dropping the phone back into her bag, she waggled her fingers at me. "It's gone bye-bye."

"You can't . . . They could still retrieve it . . ."

I was sputtering—and Viv wasn't about to help. "I'm here as a *reporter*, Millicent," she advised me. "The texter contacted me because she knows I write for the *Honeywell Gazette*—objectively, unlike some people. I wouldn't give up my source even if the police subpoenaed me, let alone turn over my contact voluntarily!"

"Millie . . ."

I turned to see Ryan opening the gate, letting Laura and himself into the yard.

Of course they'd stayed for me, and although my evening was pretty crappy, I couldn't help thinking that, between me and Viv, only one of us had friends on her side.

"What's going on?" Ry asked. "Huh?"

"Viv, here"—I jabbed a finger at my nemesis—"claims she's covering my father's *framing* for the *Gazette*. But I think she's full of bull."

As I said that, I wasn't sure what kind of bull, exactly, I thought Viv was filled with. But all at once, I was struck by this sneaking, if slightly insane, suspicion that Viv might've planted the trophy herself — and called in the tip. That there'd never been an anonymous text at all.

I still think she might've killed Coach Killdare, in a rage over that video.

And she's furious about me and Chase, not to mention can't let go of her dad's failure to beat mine in that old election.

What if she saw a way to take down my whole family?

I was thinking all that, but was still pretty shocked when meek, mild Key Club officer Laura Bugbee, who'd apparently had enough of Viv, too, said, "You probably sneaked over here and buried that stupid trophy in Millie's yard yourself. You've *always* been jealous of her and her whole family!"

"You are all deranged," Viv said with a sniff. She looked down her nose at Ryan. "I thought you, at least, had some sense, even though you hung out with these two. But I guess not."

Unlike most football players, Ryan wasn't in Viv's thrall and couldn't have cared less about her opinion of him. "You should follow everybody else and head home," he told her, so I realized that most people had wandered off. "Don't you have a car wash to run tomorrow morning? To buy new pompoms?"

"I'm not going anywhere until I get a story," Viv shot back. She pulled a notebook out of the bag that held the cell phone I still wanted to get my hands on. "I'm not leaving until I have what I need."

I'd been too upset to even think about covering the night's events for the paper, but when Viv made that announcement,

I realized that once again I had an advantage over her. One that I wouldn't squander. "Gee, Viv," I said. "I'm going to write a story, too. And"—I gestured around the yard, where police officers were still sniffing around—"I just happen to be inside the fence, with all the *quotable* people who actually know something."

For once, Viv seemed at a loss for words, and two red spots formed on her cheeks. "I'm going to get good quotes from people who saw your dad *get led away,*" she finally grumbled. "And the police will *never* talk to you."

I didn't wait to watch her chase after the last few rubber-neckers meandering down the alley. Although I didn't have a notebook handy, I turned to drill the remaining police officers for every bit of information my memory could handle before they got away. And I *would* get facts.

"We'll help you," Laura promised, grabbing Ryan's arm and tugging him toward the house. "We'll get you a pen and paper. Then we'll try to find out what's up with your dad. Where he's at, and when he'll be home."

"Thanks," I said, but absently, because I'd suddenly noticed one last person standing in the alley, at the very corner of the fence.

Chase. He stood with his arms crossed over his chest, and I saw a loop of leather around his left hand. As our eyes met, I caught, in my peripheral vision, Baxter's wrinkly head popping up over the fence, like he'd forgiven me for the bubble bath and wanted to say hello.

I was in a hurry, but I took a few steps in their direction, drawn to both of them. Especially, of course, to Chase, who gestured to the gate, asking, "Can I come in, Millie? I'd like to help, too."

Part of me really wanted that. And part of me wanted Chase to be there when everybody else left. It would've felt amazing to be able to just rest against him if I was alone later, as I expected. I had a feeling that my dad wasn't coming back anytime soon, if he even returned at all, that night.

But Chase had kept a *huge* secret from me. A *life-and-death* secret. And maybe what he'd done back in Philadelphia really was unforgivable, and he should be punishing himself forever.

Chase kept standing at the fence, waiting for my answer.

"No," I told him, shaking my head. "Not you. Not now."

I gave them both one last, conflicted look, then ran across the yard and took the notebook that Laura was offering. And, of course, Viv was right. The officers were reluctant to talk with me. But I was a good reporter, and—as a student of philosophy—I knew how to confound people with logic, and before long, I got two of them to crack and give me some decent quotes. Or maybe they talked because I bugged them until they'd do just about anything to make me go away.

Regardless, I actually learned quite a bit that night. Enough to write a good article.

But there was one detail that I didn't put in my story.

One factoid that I just socked away in my brain so I could mull it over later.

Namely, the way Viv had slipped and called her "anony-

mous" texter "she," in a world where, let's face it, most people still usually defaulted to "he."

Was Viv referring to someone that she knew?

Or did Vivienne Fitch use "she" because she was subconsciously implicating *herself*?

Chapter **79**

I sat in my glass booth at the theater the night after my father's arraignment—apparently we were now a family that understood what "arraignment" was—staring blankly at the dark street, eyes open but seeing nothing.

Chase knows what "arraignment" means. He's been through that. Has sat in a courtroom and maybe heard the word "manslaughter" applied to himself. What a horrible word. "Manslaughter . . ."

"Will you be watching the movie with Chase tonight?"

I shook my head, snapping out of my trance to realize that a wrinkled hand was slipping money through the slot. "Oh, hey, Mrs. Murphy." I banked her neatly folded five-dollar bill in my till and slid her a cardboard ticket. "I don't even know if Chase is coming tonight. And I don't think we're going to watch any more movies together."

"No?" Chase's alternate date sounded profoundly unhappy, and I realized that I probably shouldn't be burdening a little old lady with my romantic disappointments.

"It's, like, theater policy," I added. "I really am supposed to man the snack bar while the film plays."

Mrs. Murphy made a sad face. "But I brought both of you cookies." She pulled a plastic bag out of a tote that advertised her support for public broadcasting. "Chocolate chip — still warm!"

If ever there was proof of how down I felt, it was my response to *that*. "Thanks. But I don't think I could eat anything tonight."

I had barely choked down my dinner, even though Ms. Parkins had brought me and Dad homemade lasagna. But how could I eat when my father had aged about seven years overnight? The night he'd spent in a *jail cell* because they hadn't been able to get a district magistrate to set bail late on a Saturday night. And when he'd finally come home, about two hours before my shift, his shoulders had hunched in a way I'd never seen before.

"Hey, you've got that game with the Fruitville Eagles this Friday," I'd reminded him, trying to cheer him up by invoking one of his favorite rivalries. "That'll be fun, huh?"

But Dad and Ms. Parkins had shared a grim look, and my father had told me, "I resigned from coaching, Millie. I can't really lead the team under the circumstances." Then he'd added, "I may have to relinquish my post as mayor, too. I'm meeting with the borough council tomorrow."

Sitting in my uninsulated booth, I shivered.

Would my father really be jobless within twenty-four hours?

What would happen to us?

And had I ever really thought that writing a few positively spun stories for a high school newspaper could help anything?

"Enjoy the movie," I told Mrs. Murphy, suddenly desperate to do my job better in case we Ostermeyers needed to live on my minimum-wage salary. "Let me know if you need anything."

"Thank you, Millie," she said with a smile. I wasn't sure how she knew my name, since I didn't have a tag on my uniform. Had Chase mentioned it the night we'd watched *The 400 Blows*? Or did he and Mrs. Murphy talk about me when they sat together? The older woman seemed to read my thoughts. She noted as she shuffled off, "I hope you'll change your mind and join Chase if he comes tonight. He's such a lovely boy, and says such nice things about you."

It was pretty heavy-handed matchmaking. The kind of meddling that an actual grandmother might do on behalf of her grandson.

Is Chase a "lovely boy"? Would Mrs. Murphy bake him cookies if she knew his past? And yet, he's made an old lady happy.

Sighing, I resumed staring at the street, this time more alert and watching, with mixed emotions, for a tall, athletic guy who still, in my eyes, wore an imaginary question mark, even though I'd kissed him and nearly blurted out three words that I couldn't seem to say to anybody else in the entire world.

But he didn't show up, maybe because we were showing Hitchcock, and I knew he wasn't a fan. Or maybe he didn't want to see me after I'd literally fenced him out.

And when it became apparent that nobody else was com-

ing to buy tickets, I went into my post at the snack bar, retrieving my backpack from where I'd stashed it under the
candy counter. As usual, I pulled out a book. But that evening, I hadn't brought one of my philosophy texts. Instead,
I'd impulsively grabbed one of the Nancy Drew novels I'd
read with my mother.

Studying the cover, which featured Nancy in her usual
businesslike attire, I suddenly wondered if my mom had cho-
sen to read the books with me for a reason. Not because they
were both campy fun and yet compelling stories, for a nine-
year-old, at least, but because she'd known I'd be motherless
in my teen years—just like Nancy—and had wanted to give
me a role model. Wanted to show me a half-orphan who'd
grown up more than okay, and who looked out for her father,
her friends, and her dorky, straight-arrow boyfriend.

I turned the book back and forth in my hands, as if it was
a clue not to a murder mystery, but to . . . my whole life. My
past and my future. And I found myself wondering, *WWND?*

What would Nancy do?

Not to solve a murder and save her dad, but if she one
day discovered that dweeby Ned Nickerson wasn't quite the
"nifty," innocent frat boy he'd led her to believe.

Would preachy, straight-laced Nancy ditch him? Or—
given that she was also loyal and pragmatic—would she look
at the person he was now, and forgive him?

I was pretty sure I knew the answer. She'd ditch him—
kindly, but firmly.

And yet, I realized that I couldn't do that.

Chase had done something terrible in the past, and he

hadn't been forthright with me at first, but I still liked—more than liked—him, and had to at least give him a chance to explain why he'd kept stuff from me, and what, exactly, had happened on the night he'd wrecked that car and taken a life.

Unfortunately, by the time I tried to approach him at school, he had reasons to hate *me*.

Or so he thought.

Chapter **80**

"I was very pleased to see your latest story in my inbox this morning, Millie," Mr. Sokowski said, joining me at my locker on Monday morning. "I really think you have a chance at another Pacemaker this year." Then he frowned. "Although I'm sorry about your father."

"Thanks." I did appreciate the support, but I tried to peer around my lanky advisor.

Where was Chase, who should've been at his locker, too?

Was he skipping school?

"Millie? Are you listening?" Mr. Sokowski sidestepped, blocking my view. "Because—ironically—I'm trying to tell you that I'm very impressed with your focus lately."

"Oh, I'm superfocused," I said distractedly. I again tried to peek around him. "Like a laser."

I need to find Chase. Need to at least know if he'll talk to me after I shut him out, or if it's too late. And I just . . . need him today, too. In case things go wrong for my father with the borough council . . .

I heard Mr. Sokowski sigh, and I finally forced myself to

look at him just as he said, with clear annoyance, "Well, keep up the good work for the paper, Millicent. At least keep your head in the game there."

"Sure. Will do."

Mr. Sokowski left, and I resumed watching down the emptying corridor, just like I'd watched for Chase at the theater the night before. But once more, he was a no-show. At least, that's what I thought until I felt a tap on my shoulder and heard a familiar voice say, "Millie?"

I wheeled around, at once excited and relieved that Chase had approached me. Then I saw his face. "What's wrong?" I asked, without even greeting him.

He didn't greet me, either. He just looked at me with disappointment—and anger—in his usually beautiful blue eyes, demanding, quietly, so other kids couldn't hear, "How could you do that to me, Millie? I know you're done with me, but how could you betray my confidence? Tell *everyone* my story?"

What?

"I . . . I don't know what you're talking about."

Chase crossed his arms. "Really? Because everyone's talking about my time at Mason Treadwell—and you're the only student who knows . . . or knew . . . about that. Until *today*."

My heart sank to the floor. "But Chase . . . I didn't . . ."

He didn't believe me and rubbed the back of his neck, talking more to himself than me. "All I wanted was to be left alone. To finish out my senior year." He addressed me again. "Then you had to interfere and . . ."

He didn't have to finish. Two kids walked by, gave Chase

funny looks, and whispered the moment they thought they were out of earshot, "He was in, like, *juvie* . . ."

I turned back to Chase, begging him to believe me. "I swear . . . I didn't say a word! Not even to Laura or Ryan!"

"Yes, Millie." His voice dripped with sarcasm. "I'm sure it's just a coincidence that we kiss, I confess something, and you completely shut me out." He held up a hand. "Which I get. I didn't say I deserved understanding or forgiveness. I don't give those to myself." Then his eyes got even harder. "But you didn't have to go out of your way to make me more miserable. Believe me, I punish myself, every day of my life. I don't need anyone's help with *that*."

Before I could defend myself again, Chase walked away down the hall, his back straight, and opened his locker. I could see the picture he kept there—part of his punishment.

"But I didn't . . ." I said softly, not understanding how word about Chase's past had gotten out. I was seriously wracking my brain, trying to figure out if I'd somehow slipped up and said something, because it *was* a strange coincidence, his confiding in me and the whole story spreading. But I hadn't mentioned Mason Treadwell, or anything Chase had done, to anyone. Heck, I wouldn't even know how to start a rumor. I only had two friends.

It was almost like someone with better connections than me had suddenly decided to snoop into Chase's private life, which I couldn't imagine anybody bothering to do. Especially since nobody'd really asked questions for over a year.

Who in Honeywell High would go to great lengths to dig up dirt on Chase?

And then, all at once, I solved the riddle. Or, more accurately, someone else straight out answered my question. A witchy girl who couldn't keep the laughter out of her voice as she noted, "I think your boyfriend's really mad about his big secret coming out, huh, Millie?"

Chapter **81**

Who had connections?

And a propensity for malicious gossip?

And the will to put her irritatingly formidable brain to work if the purpose was diabolical enough?

Viv.

I wheeled around to find her standing right behind me, her boobs looking especially overinflated since she was puffing out her chest with pride at having screwed Chase over.

"He didn't want you, so you had to make him miserable," I accused her. I glanced down the hall, but Chase was gone. In fact, Viv and I should've been in homeroom, too. I turned back to her. "You just couldn't leave him alone. And now he thinks I sold him out!"

"Yes, watching him lay into you was an added bonus," she said, looking extra pleased. "I take it you knew that he's a closet delinquent."

"You don't understand," I said, defending the guy I'd recently turned my back on. "He just wants to be left alone."

"I would, too, if I my previous school was a *prison*," Viv agreed nastily. "I wouldn't go bragging about it, either."

"How did you even find out?"

"I always suspected there was something up with him," she said. "I mean, who refuses to party with the *cheerleaders*?" She uttered that with genuine disbelief—although I was tempted to raise a hand. Not that I'd ever been invited to a "cheer" party. "And when he took *you* to the formal," Viv continued with a mock shudder, "I *knew* he was totally off. So I sneaked into the guys' locker room—into the office —opened a desk drawer, and read Killdare's file on him. And there it was. Chase's last school, and his transfer papers." She examined her manicure and sighed with self-congratulation. "It was pretty simple, really."

Yes, simple—if you were the kind of person who sneaked around locker rooms.

I caught myself.

Well, I was that kind of person, too. But I didn't act *maliciously*.

"Look, Viv." I tried to appeal to whatever humanity she had. "He's sorry—"

Shark that she was, she smelled blood in the water, and bit. "For what?"

So, at least she didn't know why Chase had been at Treadwell. Needless to say, I ignored the question, repeating, "He really just wants to be left alone. He doesn't even expect people to understand, or want their friendship. He's just sorry . . ."

My voice trailed off, though.

How could I explain the complex, private, tortured person who was Chase Albright in a few sentences to a girl who, let's face it, didn't care, anyway? And who probably still wanted him, too, even though she pretended otherwise, telling me, "Whatever, Millie. You're lucky I saved you from one felon —although you're stuck living with another. At least until *he* goes to jail, too."

I knew that Viv was nearly crazed by jealousy. That she really was like a shark thrashing in the water, lashing out at anything that moved, in a total feeding frenzy of envy over the fact that, on top of everything else, I'd taken the guy she wanted. Clearly, that had been the last straw. Maybe I even should've felt sorry for her, because sometimes things did seem to fall my way. But that wasn't happening then—in fact, my life was a shambles—and I wasn't about to take her crap for one more second. She definitely wasn't going to get away with calling my dad a felon. And just as the bell rang, sending everybody spilling into the halls, I raised my foot, glad that I was wearing an old pair of Doc Martens, even if they weren't stylish—had never been stylish—because ballet flats or some other girly shoe wouldn't have made Viv yowl like she did when my giant boot met those wussy, peep-toed suede jobs she seemed to love so much.

And I finally didn't care that a ton of kids heard me say, with my finger right in her twisted-with-pain face, "I think *you're* the felon, Viv. I swear, I think you killed Mr. Killdare, and Mike Price, too. And if you mess with my family or my friends one more time—so much as show your face near our house again—my Doc Martens are going to do more than stomp your foot. They're going to *kick your skinny ass!*"

I'd always thought Viv was popular. I mean, I guessed she was, by most standards. But apparently a lot of kids secretly felt the way I did about her—believed she was nothing but a bully—because as I strode down the hall a bunch of students applauded.

Not Chase, though.

I couldn't tell what he was thinking when I stalked right past him, so close that our shoulders brushed.

I couldn't help but touch him. He stood in the very center of the corridor, feet planted wide, and I thought he meant to stop me. But I had other business to attend to.

First, I had to go to Mr. Woolsey's office to accept my inevitable detention for "inciting a disruptive incident."

Then I had to figure out how the heck I could prove that Viv had walked out of the boys' locker room with more than a nugget of damning information about Chase. I needed to think about how, on her freakishly emaciated frame, she'd smuggled out a trophy, too, and buried it in our yard.

Chapter **82**

D ad!" I jumped off the couch when he finally came into the house, late. And right away, I knew that his day had been worse than mine. He hadn't just gotten detention. He'd lost another job that he'd loved. First coaching. Now mayoring. I stopped in my tracks, my heart breaking to see him pull off his tie and ditch it on a chair. Something about the way he performed that familiar gesture seemed final, like he'd never do it again. And all at once, I wasn't worried about how we'd get by. I was only sick for how unhappy he was. "Oh, Dad . . ."

"Sorry, Millie." He dropped down onto the couch, rubbing his face with both hands, and I sat down again, too. "We . . ." His voice was muffled, and he seemed to have trouble getting out the news. "Borough council and I agreed that it's best if I take a leave of absence."

"A leave? That's not so bad, right?" I ventured.

He didn't say anything. He just exhaled with a whoosh and fell back onto the cushions, staring straight ahead—no doubt at a bleak future.

He doesn't believe he'll ever be mayor, or a coach, again. Maybe he even thinks he's going to prison.

"Dad, do you have any idea who might've planted the trophy?" I asked. "*Any* idea? Because I have suspicions."

He closed his eyes and shook his head. "No, Millie. I'm baffled. And I want you to leave it alone. A boy has been killed. Please. Don't give me cause to worry more by nosing around."

"Okay," I promised. But I had my fingers crossed. "Just don't worry, all right?"

He didn't answer, and although it felt strange at first, I moved closer and rested my head against his shoulder, just being there with him. I swear I half expected him to edge away. But I guess one good thing was coming out of the whole mess we were in, because for the second time in a few days, my father and I were close. Not only physically, which was weird enough, but—at the risk of coming across as too gushy—emotionally. It was like we were finally the team that my mother had no doubt hoped we'd evolve into.

We sat that way for a long time. I didn't try to tell him things would be okay, because I was afraid it would make him feel weak to be reassured by his child. And more to the point, I had no clue what was going to happen. We just hung out. Being quiet.

After about a half-hour, the door opened and Ms. Parkins slipped into the house quietly, as if she already knew the news and expected the grim mood. That was my cue to get up, and I went over to meet her at the door, since I was on my way out.

"I'm really glad you're here," I whispered with a glance at my dad, who was rubbing his face again. "You know. For all of this."

"I'm glad I can be here," she told me. "Thanks for letting me."

I looked down at my arm, which was being squeezed by fingers laden with cocktail rings. A gesture that wouldn't have happened if there'd been a library counter between us. She let go of me, and I reached for my jacket. "Guess nobody can stop true love, huh?" I joked. "Not even Millie Ostermeyer can stand in the way of *that*."

I said that to lighten the mood a little. But as I made my way through town, headed toward Coach Killdare's house, I wondered if I'd already proven that I did, indeed, have the power to wreck—if not true love on Chase's part—what sure felt like love on mine.

Chapter **83**

I wasn't sure how I knew that Chase would be at Mr. Kill-dare's house. Maybe I just figured that if I'd had a sucky day — and a key that would give me access to a grotesquely cute, nonjudgmental dog — that's where I'd go.

And Chase didn't seem incredibly surprised to see me, ei-ther, when he opened the door at my knock. He just stared at me for a long moment, then stepped to the side, saying, "Come on in, Millie. I think we have a lot to talk about."

Chapter **84**

Viv spread the rumor about you," I told Chase, who sat next to me on the kitchen floor, our backs resting against Mr. Killdare's cabinets, just like we'd once sat against the tub. At least the view was a little better this time. "The whole thing was her."

Chase drew in one long leg to kick, lightly, at my foot. "Yeah, I figured that out when you crushed her toes with those big army boots. I heard the tail end of your tirade."

I overlooked the dig at shoes that had served me very well that day, thank you—although I did appreciate his use of the word "tirade." *Jock geek*. "She found out about Treadwell by snooping in the football office," I explained. "Mr. Killdare had some old file with papers about your transfer. But she doesn't know what you did . . ."

I didn't quite finish that thought because that was still a bad topic between us.

Chase rolled a rubber ball across the linoleum floor, giving it a halfhearted toss, and Baxter gave equally unenthusiastic chase. "I guess you know all the gory details by now," he said, accepting the slobbery ball—and Baxter's head across his legs. It was clear the game was already over. "I'm sure you've read about it online."

"Yeah. I have."

Chase shifted to finally meet my eyes. "And . . . ?"

"I don't know." I was the first to turn away. I couldn't think straight when he looked right at me like that. We were having this terrible, uncomfortable discussion, but I couldn't control how I felt for him. No wonder Ms. Parkins and my dad hadn't been able to stay apart. "I just wish you'd told me."

"I do too." Chase began stroking one of Baxter's long ears, avoiding my eyes, too. "I just started to . . . like you so much. From the first time we really talked, on the walk from the cemetery. I didn't want you to think I was a monster."

"I could never think that, Chase." Well, not for more than a few minutes. Or maybe days.

He also knew I wasn't being completely honest, and he laughed—but not in a "ha-ha" way. "You ran away from me, Millie."

I couldn't deny that, and we got quiet for a while. Then I asked a question that I wasn't sure I wanted answered. "Did you, like . . . love her?"

It was a *huge* question, and I barely got it out. My stomach twisted into knots as I voiced it. And there was really no right way to feel about Chase's response. At least, it seemed that way to me.

"We just went out a few times," he said, shrugging—although I knew he wasn't taking our talk, or his relationship with the girl named Allison, lightly. He finally looked at me again. "And that actually makes it worse, doesn't it? I didn't even like her that much, but being with me cost her her *life*." He swallowed hard. "And then, when I started spending time with you, liking it—liking *you*—a lot . . . I felt like I was doing something incredibly wrong. I mean, how could I think I deserved to be with another girl? To kiss someone else, when Allison will never get that chance?" He rolled his head back to stare up at the ceiling. "Millie, I don't even know how to describe the guilt I feel every day. I really don't. And yet, I wanted so badly to go to that dance with you, and kiss you . . ."

I knew right then that Chase and I . . . It wasn't going to happen. Even though I forgave him, he was a long way from being ready to have a relationship. Maybe he'd never have one—although I doubted that. I had a feeling that, as time passed, he'd find a way to not exactly let himself off the hook, but to live with what he'd done.

And maybe, just maybe—even though I had this new dull ache in my chest—I could help him start to move forward.

"Chase?"

He faced me again. "Yeah, Millie?"

"Maybe you could begin to atone . . ." That sounded too biblical. "Maybe you could start to do some good—honor Allison, even—by telling your story. To everybody at school."

Not surprisingly, Chase seemed skeptical. He arched one eyebrow. "What?"

I shifted on the floor, curling my legs under myself so I could face him—and convince him. "Let me tell your whole story, in the *Gazette*."

He moved to face me more squarely, too, dislodging Baxter, who was asleep, even when his head sort of thunked on the floor. "You're kidding, right?"

"Chase, everyone is already wondering what you did to get sent to Treadwell. Why don't you answer their questions in the paper? Tell the truth, in black and white. Not only will it thwart Viv's attempt to make you a pariah via rumors, but you can tell everybody how sorry you are. Discourage them from making the same mistake. Because we both know a lot of kids at Honeywell party and drive. I'm sure some of them have just been lucky so far."

Chase took a moment to consider this. A long, long moment. Then he nodded. "Okay, Millie." He smiled faintly. "But don't screw this up, Ostermeyer. Get the story right."

"I will," I promised. "I'll get it right." Hesitating, I tried to decide how far I should push him. Then I added, "But first, before I do my official interview, there's something else I think you should do."

He already seemed slightly less burdened, like even anticipating his confession had eased his soul just a tiny bit. He smiled again. "What's that, Millie?" I could tell he thought I was bossy—but he sort of liked it. "What, exactly, do you think I should do?"

Standing up, I offered him my hand to pull him up, too. "I'll tell you when we get to school."

Chapter **85**

I'm not sure about this, Millie."

Chase stood in front of his open locker, staring at the photo of the girl whose life he'd taken. I finally had a chance to really look at her, too. She was as gorgeous as I'd expected, with long, dark hair and delicate features. She looked like she'd have good manners, too, as I'd also guessed. You could just tell by the polite way she smiled for her formal portrait.

How odd that she really was my competition — but in a way I'd never expected. She hadn't taken Chase from me by using the right fork at some country club "luncheon." She'd accidentally laid claim to him in a much more terrible — and irrevocable — way. A fact he confirmed by adding, "I've looked at her photo almost every day since the accident. It guarantees I'll never become that person I was."

"Chase, that would never happen, even without seeing her picture."

I sincerely believed that he punished himself enough without seeing a ghost smiling at him every day. I was pretty sure he carried Allison's image at the forefront of his mind.

"I think it's okay to take it down," I urged him. "Keep it. But take it down."

He didn't move.

"Chase." I said his name firmly enough to make him look at me. "I know this isn't the same, but for a while, I used to keep this shrine to my mom on the desk in my bedroom. With her picture and all this stuff from her funeral, like the program and some dried-up flowers. After a while, I kind of wanted to take it down, but I couldn't. And then one day, I spilled a blue raspberry Slurpee all over the whole thing, and had to throw most of it out. I kept the photograph—duh—but I didn't make as big a deal out of it. And I certainly never forgot Mom. In fact, I think I could remember her better when I wasn't always picturing her in a casket."

"Wow, Millie." Chase studied my face closely. "I don't know if that story's the same at all. But you've definitely been through some intense things, too."

Although I would never argue with that, I shrugged. "It's like Schopenhauer said, 'Life is short, questionable and evanescent.' In other words, stuff happens. To everybody."

Chase didn't seem to know how to respond to that. He just kept watching me in the nearly empty hallway, where only a few other kids in farmer and cowboy costumes, for some reason, were wandering late after school. Then he finally said, with genuine appreciation, "Millie, you are undeniably fascinating."

Yeah, but it's too late. It was too late about two years ago, when you crashed that car.

"Chase, take down the photo. Put it someplace safe, at home. But take it down."

He didn't say anything. But he did reach inside his locker and carefully removed the picture. Then, because he didn't seem to know what to do with it, I held out my hand. "Here. I'll put it in my backpack and give it to you later."

Chase gave me the photo, and, unzipping my pack, I tucked the picture into a book so it wouldn't get bent or stained.

"Why do you have your backpack, anyway?" he asked. "I don't suppose we're stopping by your locker to get your French textbook."

I was glad that he was already joking a little. "No." I zipped up my pack. "We're going to search Viv's locker." Slipping a strap over my shoulder, I added, "My inner pit bull/Doberman has been dozing for too long. It's time to take off the leash and go on the attack."

Chapter 86

H ow did you figure out Viv's combination?" Chase asked, watching me pop open her locker. "She's a lot more complex than Mike."

"Well, if I'd had to guess, I would've ventured 'six, six, six.'" I felt the back wall, in case there might be a secret compartment. Or a portal to Hell. "But I actually just heard her bark it to Mike a thousand times when she'd order him to run and get stuff for her at the end of French class. Luckily, he had a terrible memory and needed it repeated, over and over, while my powers of recollection"—I tapped my head with my index finger—"are pretty good."

"And yet, you can't conjugate '*demeurer*' after four years of study."

"I didn't say I was perfect . . ." I lost my train of thought because a junior with the unfortunate name Philip Foos strolled behind us, wearing a flannel shirt, cowboy boots, and a bandanna around his neck. I followed his progress down the hall. "And what is up with the farmer duds? I know this is Amish country, but this is ridiculous."

Chase seemed confused, too—by my ignorance. "Millie, haven't you seen the posters for the fall musical? *Oklahoma!* It starts on Saturday. That's why the whole cast is here so late." It must've been apparent that I was still clueless, because he reminded me, "Ms. Beamish has encouraged our class, every day for a month, to come see it. She's directing."

"O-o-o-o-o-h, yeah." I acted like I knew what he was talking about.

Chase wasn't buying it. "Did you not understand *that,* either? How are you not failing?"

Maybe I was. A little bit. "Let's just search this locker," I said, resuming my perusal of Viv's possessions. She also had photos inside her door. Of herself. Alone. Posing in different ways in her cheerleading uniform. I stepped back, in part because the collage was creeping me out. "You're tall," I told Chase, pointing to a shelf at the top of the locker, where, in mine, I kept inkless pens, an Einstein bobblehead, and a pair of socks. "Feel around up there. If she's got something secret stashed away, it's probably there."

He reached into the locker. "What, exactly, are we looking for?"

"A cell phone would be great. But I know she keeps that glued to her icy palm."

Chase gave me a curious look. "Why her phone?"

"Because when Viv was stinking up my backyard on the night my father got framed, she said something that made me believe she either was, or knew the identity of, the anonymous tipster. And I'm going to dig through her life until I find out what she knows—or *did.*"

Chase pulled a pink plastic basket down from the shelf and handed it to me for inspection. "What'd she say, exactly?"

I rooted through the contents of the basket—which essentially held Viv's false face. Lipstick, gloss, blush, more gloss, more blush . . . *Who wears all this stuff?* I shoved the container back at Chase, signaling that he should put it back. "Viv called the tipster a 'she.' And something about the way she said it . . . I got the impression that she knows exactly who buried that stupid trophy in our yard."

"Un trophée? Avez-vous gagné quelque chose, Chase?"

Both Chase and I turned around slowly to find that Mademoiselle Beamish—also wearing flannel, which was not a good look for her—had somehow stolen up behind us, even though she was wearing cowboy boots, too.

Is she directing? Or playing the role of lonely, disturbed farmhand Jud Fry?

"Um, no . . . I didn't win anything," Chase responded in English, probably to be polite to me. "We were talking about a different trophy."

Okay, I might've missed the gist of Ms. Beamish's question, but I was smart enough to realize that she'd assumed Chase had won something—not me. *Merci beaucoup, Mademoiselle!*

"Oh, goodness . . ." Ms. Beamish got pale and for once seemed to forget about speaking French. She rested her hand on a row of pearlized buttons running down the front of her western-style shirt and addressed me. "You're talking about what they found in your father's yard . . . It's been on the news, of course . . . I'm so sorry!"

"And it'll be on the news again when my dad is exonerated," I said. "So stay tuned."

"Of course he will be," Ms. Beamish agreed. But her gaze darted to her prize student, in a way that told me she was humoring me, even though she repeated, with a shaky smile, "Of course." Then she cocked her head. "But what are you two doing here so late? And why are you in *Vivienne's* locker?"

For a second, I wasn't sure how she knew that. Then I looked again at all the pictures of Viv—not to mention a sweater that she always wore, which was hanging in there. And, most tellingly, a notebook that read, in big, black Sharpie-d letters, "Property of V. Fitch! Hands off!" Then I glanced at the photos of Viv again, including an eight-by-ten in which she was doing her best Great White impression, each tooth polished to perfection.

"We're catching a killer," I muttered, sort of forgetting that Ms. Beamish was with us as I examined those teeth. And Viv's dead eyes, in spite of her smile. "She knows something. Something big."

"Millie!" Chase's sharp warning brought me back to reality. He shut the locker and took me by my shoulders, smiling at Ms. Beamish—but shoving me down the hall. "We were actually borrowing a book," he told our teacher. "But Viv must have it at home. We're leaving now."

"*Au revoir.*" Ms. Beamish gave us a wave—without moving from her post in front of the locker I hadn't searched well enough. "*Bonsoir.*"

"Well, that was a bust," I said when we were outside in the chilly night. "A total bust."

We walked toward Chase's car, which was parked on the street, and as he opened the door for me he reminded me, "Not entirely, Millie. Not for me. And we still have work to do. On my story."

I'd almost forgotten that, but I would never forget the next few hours. And when I was done talking with Chase, I thought we were both sort of spent. I was also confident that if he really had been my boyfriend, I wouldn't have had to worry about any more secrets coming out.

No, I could finally fully erase that question mark from Chase's chest.

If only I could've scrubbed him out of my mind and my heart, too.

Chapter 87

I wish, every day, that I could change the past,' Albright said. 'Not because I served time for involuntary manslaughter, but because I can't bring Allison back.'"

Laura finished reading out loud and set the week's copy of the *Gazette* on the cafeteria table. "Wow." She shoved one finger under the lenses of her eyeglasses, swiping at her eyes, which had teared up halfway through the article. "I can't believe that's really Chase's story. It's so sad, for everybody."

"I think it took guts to come out like that," Ryan added. "And I know something about coming out. He could've just kept lying low, riding out the year, even with the rumors. It can't be easy to admit to manslaughter in front of the whole school."

"He's doing an assembly on drunk driving, too," I informed them. "Mr. Woolsey asked him to talk before the next dance, and Chase agreed. I guess he's found a way to start redeeming himself."

"Millie?"

I'd been twirling spaghetti around my fork, not hungry,

because, in spite of helping Chase start to put his life back together, my father was still in big trouble and my heart was still broken. I knew that time would heal the really bad pain, but I couldn't imagine ever finding a guy like Chase again. One who befriended little old ladies, and kissed me in a way that I'd felt down to my bare toes, and who made me want even a glimpse of him . . .

"Millie?"

I heard my name spoken again and looked up to find Laura watching me. "Are you okay with Chase, after all this? It's a lot to swallow."

"It doesn't matter how I feel," I said. "We're not really hanging out anymore."

So why did I give in to the impulse to turn around and find Chase at his regular table, alone as usual, nose in a book? I didn't think kids were shunning him because of the stuff in the paper, though. I was pretty sure Chase still just believed solitude was best for him. One article wouldn't change everything—including how he felt about dating me. He'd made that clear, telling me, at the end of the interview, "I think I should put some distance between us, Millie. I still don't feel right seeing someone. I'm really sorry."

I turned back to my friends. "Besides, I have to focus on my dad now. He needs me."

"Is he really going to stand trial?" Ryan asked. "Because that seems crazy."

"Yeah, to me, too," I agreed. "But it looks like there's enough evidence to at least try him for Mr. Killdare's death, between all the public fights they had, and Mr. Killdare having cancer, which—let's face it—would've messed up Dad's life if word had gotten out. Not to mention the fact that the murder weapon was in our yard."

I looked around for Vivienne and found her at the cheerleaders' table, drinking her daily Diet Coke and eating air so she wouldn't gain a pound. But she had muscular arms, a calculating mind, and no soul . . .

Viv must've felt me watching her. She met my eyes—and I once again firmly believed she could've committed homicide. Heck, she'd threatened me, just that morning, when the story about Chase had been printed. I could easily recall our entire conversation, verbatim.

"You went behind my back to Mr. Sokowski." Viv glares at me, *slapping the paper against her hand. "I didn't authorize this."*

"It's a good story—and Mr. Sokowski knows who his ace reporter is now."

Viv practically growls. "If you think you've helped your murdering boyfriend by telling this sappy tale, you're sorely mistaken. He looks *worse* now.*"*

She was wrong, though. Kids were talking about Chase, but they weren't making up crazy stuff, and before long the whole story would fade away. Plus I'd made sure everybody understood how guilty he felt and why he preferred to remain aloof. Viv knew I'd smashed her rumor mill—and she was seething.

"Is it really the weapon? The trophy?"

I returned my attention to my own table, where nobody was shy about eating, to find Ryan opening a bag of Doritos, a worried look on his face.

"Well, it was wiped clean before it was buried—meaning there weren't any fingerprints or blood on it." I watched Ryan and Laura carefully, wanting to gauge their reactions when I revealed something I hadn't shared with anybody so far. "But they found these microscopic flecks of metal in Mr. Killdare's wounds. Although, according to my dad's lawyer, there's not necessarily a positive match between the specks and the coating on the trophy."

The evidence might not've been conclusive, but I could tell that the news concerned Ryan and Laura. Just as it did me. Still, they were supportive friends, and both said, almost in unison, "It's gonna be okay, Millie. It'll work out."

I wished I could have believed them.

I looked at Viv again, watching her toss her hair over her shoulder and take a dainty sip of soda, like she was afraid to ingest a molecule of *that,* even though the bottle clearly promised it was zero calories.

What was I missing?

Why wasn't I smart enough to link her to the crime?

Chapter **88**

I t took guts for Chase Albright to admit to his past and still
stand tall on a football field Friday night, rifling passes to
guys who probably thought *murderer* every time they looked
at him. Or maybe some of them were thinking, *That could
be me. Maybe I shouldn't down a gallon of beer at the after-game
party.* I hoped that was the case.

And—I gave my father a sidelong glance—it took a lot of
courage for former coach and former mayor Jack Ostermeyer
to come to a stadium that he practically used to own in a
town that he definitely used to dominate and watch a game
like the innocent man that he was.

I was superproud of him and wished I could tell him that.
But we were doing our best to pretend we didn't even notice
people giving him suspicious looks. Besides, he had a librarian sitting on his other side, and I thought the way she slipped
her hand into his, as if she was proud to be with him, too, was
probably all the validation that he really needed.

Everybody should have a librarian.

I thought I was also showing some spine by attending that

game, because watching Chase in his football uniform barking out orders and looking like a Greek god wasn't exactly helping my aching heart. Even when he simply walked to the sidelines during a break in the action, while some injured kid got the once-over by medics, I considered him pretty much breathtaking.

But he's hardly even talking to me anymore. Has closed himself off again. I got him to open up to the whole world—except me.

"Millie, do you want something to eat?"

I dragged my attention away from the field to find my father offering me money, which didn't happen every day. Still, I shook my head. "Nah. No, thanks."

Ms. Parkins leaned forward so she could see me around the bulky down vest Dad was wearing to ward off the late-October chill. Her eyes, behind her glasses, registered concern. "You're not hungry?"

"Not really."

She and my dad exchanged worried glances, then my father leaned close and said very quietly, because the stands were packed, "Millie, don't waste away because of a broken heart."

I reared back. "What?"

There was understanding in my father's eyes—but some of his characteristic flint, too. "Whatever happened with you and Chase, don't let it devastate you," he urged. "You're an Ostermeyer. You're stronger than that."

I'd had no idea my father had thought about me and Chase since the formal. In fact, I'd assumed he was even more distracted than usual and unaware of anything going on in

340 * BETH FANTASKEY

my life. And he'd never talked with me about boys—not that there'd been boys to talk about.

"Go ahead." He offered me the cash again. "Get all of us something to eat." He pointed toward the visitors' end zone, where I saw a folding table manned by Ms. Beamish, who apparently couldn't get one of the few Language Club kids to help her with what must've been a fundraiser. In truth, my Philosophy Club was almost as popular as that group. "I think they have doughnuts," Dad observed, craning his neck. "That sounds good."

"Okay." I plucked the cash from his fingers, thinking maybe I *should* eat something. I was probably losing all of the stomach capacity I'd built up, and while I might not have had true love in my life, I still did want to be on Sir Loin's Ye Olde Wall of Fame. "I'll be right back, okay?"

Walking down the steps, I scanned the field again, first finding Chase. He stood on the sidelines, helmet off, and even from a distance, I knew he was watching me, too. I almost waved—then stopped myself and made a point of looking at the cheerleaders, who'd taken to the field, entertaining the crowd until the real action started again. They all pretty much looked the same to me, like a string of paper dolls, but I did note that one normally vivacious—if you removed two letters in the very middle of that word—cheer queen was gone.

Where's Vicious Viv?

Missing her moment of glory to pee out a thimbleful of Diet Coke?

Then I hopped off the bleachers and threaded my way to

the Language Club table. But when I got there, Ms. Beamish had also taken off. However, there was a can for money, underneath a sign that read, "Support Our Trip to Düsseldorf and the Black Forest!"

"Have a nice time," I muttered, dropping in all the cash I had and taking what I hoped was about six dollars' worth of doughnuts.

"Don't take more than you've paid for, Millicent," a weasely voice interrupted my calculations. "Because that would be *a crime*, wouldn't it?"

Chapter **89**

W hat do you want now?" I asked Detective Blaine
Lohser, who was cramming money into the can,
too, and choosing a chocolate frosted. "Why are you even
here?"

"I'm here to get a doughnut—and watch the game," he
said, helping himself to change, for crying out loud. *Cheap-
skate.*

"Yeah, it's a likely coincidence, us meeting up," I grumbled. "I bet you don't even like football." *Because you couldn't
even cut it as a towel boy in high school.* "You're here to see people stare at my dad—and gloat," I guessed. "But if you think
my father cares, you're wrong. He's an Ostermeyer, and *we're*
tough."

"I do have an interest in keeping an eye on your father,
because *I* think he's a flight risk," Detective Lohser said. "But
I didn't really think he'd show up here."

I had turned out to be a little hungry, and I wiped pow-
dered sugar off my mouth. "Yeah, right. And you just happened to need a snack at the same time I did."

All at once, Detective Lohser seemed defensive. Maybe even *hurt*. "I just came to see the game," he repeated. "This is my alma mater."

I took a few seconds to digest that information and really look at him in this new setting. And although I wouldn't have thought it possible even moments before, I felt a twinge of sympathy. He was apparently alone at a football game, wearing an old Honeywell High sweatshirt that made his mustache come off as a desperate cry to be judged mature. In fact, without the 'stache, he probably could've passed as a student.

Was it possible that he'd approached me because he considered what we shared—a few dismal, contentious meetings—some kind of a . . . relationship? Was he that desperate for human contact?

I wasn't sure, but I found myself mumbling, "Sorry."

He seemed to understand how I'd just judged him. I could see it in his eyes—and knew that I'd been right. Then he puffed out his chest, getting officious again, and said, like we were at some school-safety assembly, "Just make sure you knock off the investigating, kid. Because while you might still want to protect your dad, life isn't a Nancy Drew book."

I could hardly believe he'd invoked the novels that I was finally, tentatively, reading again, even though doing that was still painful. I also recalled that—lonely or not—he'd persecuted my father all the way to a future court date. "*You* should read some Nancy Drew," I suggested. "Maybe you'd learn how to treat people—and how to solve a crime." I nodded to the can. "And put the change back, huh? Help some poor kids get to Germany already!"

Then, without waiting for his reply, I walked away—mentally high-fiving an imaginary Nancy, who I was pretty sure would've approved of the way I'd handled the whole situation.

It wasn't—unfortunately—until I'd fought my way back to my dad and Ms. Parkins, crawling over about fifty laps while balancing four doughnuts—and continuing to eat one —that something struck me as strange.

I couldn't quite put my finger on it or connect the dots, but all at once, standing there, blocking a bunch of Stingers fans' views, with a mouth full of Bavarian cream, something seemed off—and not just meeting up with a creepy detective, out of the blue, at a football game.

Viv, still absent, missing a chance to prance in front of hundreds.

Ms. Beamish abandoning her fundraising post.

A few words uttered at a locker.

Düsseldorf.

"Show Boat."

Wrestling.

Football.

Chicken clock.

"Oklahoma!"

Familiar handwriting . . .

I was acting on pure instinct, still not sure what connection, exactly, my brain was trying to make. But as I shoved a pile of pastries into my puzzled father's hands, crashed through a row of people who were getting pretty disgruntled with me, and ran down the steps toward the school, I knew where I was going.

The Honeywell High library, of course.

It might not've possessed the collected works of Montaigne, but it would have exactly what I needed that evening.

Chapter **90**

I was normally very respectful of books and librarians' efforts to keep them filed in orderly fashion, but that evening I yanked copies of the Honeywell *Historia*—was that even a word?—off the shelf in the special part of the library where they kept yearbooks dating back to about 1950 and tossed them to the floor.

Dropping to my knees, I began to leaf quickly through the 2009 annual, licking my fingers to get the pages moving and searching for pictures of the Language Club—while my brain did its level best to recall the knickknacks on Mr. Killdare's bookshelf. And there it was. A photo of smiling kids and chaperones against a backdrop of Greek ruins.

The Acropolis.

Ditching 2009, I snatched up 2010 and restarted the process until I found more grinning kids—right in front of the Leaning Tower of Pisa. *Bingo!*

Then 2011. A caption that read *". . . tours charming Copenhagen . . ."*

And next 2012. London. *Big Ben.*

The pieces were starting to fall into place, and my fingers shook as I snatched up the most recent *Historia* and flipped through it, practically panting. "Where were they that summer?" I said out loud. "What's the missing memento?"

And then I found it. The photo of students, some of whom I knew—including club president Viv, wearing a very trite beret, *gag*—and Ms. Beamish, all crowded together at the base of the Eiffel Tower. Some of them were hamming it up with souvenirs they'd bought. Replicas of the tower, which they held aloft . . . almost like trophies. Presumably heavy metal copies of a big metal structure.

All at once, I also recalled an announcement made at the end of my junior year. *"Students traveling to Switzerland this summer must have parental permission slips and a deposit filed by Friday . . ."*

Lucerne. A postcard sent while Mr. Killdare was alive, but that arrived postmortem . . .

"Viv. I gotta find Viv."

Promising myself that I'd apologize to the staff later, I scrambled to my feet, jumped over the mess I'd made, and tore out of the library, for the first time ever excited—albeit in a bad way—to get to my French classroom.

Chapter **91**

I thought you needed help carrying doughnuts," I heard Viv complaining loudly as I ran toward the dark classroom. "You ordered me to meet you here before halftime to restock—which is causing me to miss a chance to be midfield for at least fifteen minutes while they work on that stupid linebacker's messed-up legs. It's not like there's a devastating injury every day! So where are the boxes? And let's turn on a light, huh?"

"Viv!" I called out to my archrival—to warn her that she might not want to piss off Ms. Beamish right then—then grabbed the door frame and skidded into the room.

But I was too late.

As I watched in horror—the whole thing silhouetted against the window in a Hitchcockian touch that I thought Chase would've appreciated, in spite of not being a fan—Ms. Beamish moved up behind Vivienne Fitch and clocked her with a big metal Eiffel Tower that I'd seen on my teacher's desk for weeks—at least since Hollerin' Hank's death.

The murder weapon. In plain sight. Taken from Mr. Killdare's house—after being used to kill him.

It was probably a mistake to run forward, instead of away, but I acted on instinct, maybe subconsciously trying to make up for the time I'd tried to peel drowning Kenny Kaluka's fingers off my arms while we both struggled to shore, nevertheless getting credit for saving him. Or maybe part of me didn't want to lose a girl I'd enjoyed hating for the better part of two decades. Me and Viv . . . We had something. Something awful, but something. One might call it *historia*.

"Viv!" I cried again, shoving aside Ms. Beamish in my effort to save my enemy.

But, of course, before I could drop down to my knees, I found myself in the grip of a woman who, unlucky for me, not only advised the Language Club and directed off-, off-, off-, off-Broadway productions, but who *coached wrestling*, too.

Chapter **92**

L et Viv alone, at least," I pleaded, struggling against what I thought was a headlock. "She didn't know anything!"

"You said she knew who sent the tip," Ms. Beamish countered. "I heard you, at her locker. I can't let her ever reveal that."

"I don't think she knew anything," I protested, stopping my pointless writhing, which, oddly enough, made Ms. Beamish release me. It was like the Chinese handcuffs principle, only on a grander scale. I might've also caught her off-guard by letting her know that she'd possibly just killed—I glanced down at Viv's inert form . . . *Please don't be dead!*—an innocent person.

But as I stepped away and turned to face my teacher, I realized that I wasn't exactly free. Her broad body blocked the door, and she still held the Eiffel Tower, her fingers flexing around it. Testing it—as if she hadn't used *that* before.

Instinctively, I raised my hands, but begged on Viv's behalf again. "Please. Viv probably didn't know a thing. Chase and I were just guessing."

Ms. Beamish hesitated, seeming uncertain. "I did think it odd . . . I used a disposable phone . . ."

For a second, I thought I'd defused the whole situation. But, of course, that was far from being the case. Her expression was already getting flinty and shrewd again. "*You've* figured out everything, though," she reminded me. "Or you wouldn't be here." Her eyes shifted, too, just for an instant, to look at Viv. Then she locked on me again. "And now you've seen too much."

Yeah, I definitely had. And I had no idea how to stall, except to bring up a subject that I was pretty sure no girl, not even a tomboy like Ms. Beamish—and, let's face it, to a lesser degree, me—could resist "dishing" on.

"You must've really loved him," I said softly, lowering my hands. "I mean, you had sports in common, and Broadway, and . . ." *You were both big and loud and not easily likable.* I wisely omitted that last part. I didn't need to say more, though. Ms. "BeeBee" Beamish's broad shoulders had already slumped, just a little.

"Yes," she said, more quietly, too. "But he would never admit we were together, in public. Kept me hidden from everyone." She frowned, seeming to forget I was there for a second. "It was always like he was ashamed of me, while I loved him, in spite of *his* flaws."

"You . . . you tried to be part of his life, huh?" I ventured, to keep the conversation going and stave off my *death*. "Gave him a nice chicken clock to brighten up his kitchen, maybe? Kept some stuff at his house?"

Ms. Beamish gave me a weird look. "How did you . . . ?"

I somehow thought I'd be worse off if I mentioned that I'd been actively investigating Mr. Killdare's murder — rooting through his drawers — so I brushed it off, saying, "What girl doesn't do stuff like that?"

Ms. Beamish seemed to accept that. I had a feeling she didn't really care what I knew — because she was going to kill me the second we were done talking.

"So what happened?" I asked, feigning sympathy. Gosh, maybe I did feel this slight touch of compassion for her. It must have really felt crappy to have a boyfriend — an *unmarried* boyfriend — who still didn't want to parade you in public and kept you a secret from no less than the dog sitter. "What went down in the end?"

That was obviously not a good question, because even in the dark, I could see that her eyes glittered. I'd made her angry again. "One day," she said, "I just couldn't take it. I'd asked him to finally let me sit, as his guest, in the reserved bleachers at the first home game, and he just laughed. Laughed at me!"

She still sounded incredulous, while I thought, *For the last time — what is the big deal with FOOTBALL?*

Then Ms. Beamish took a step closer to me, starting to raise her weapon — to either demonstrate what had happened next or to do me in. Or, more likely, to kill both of those birds — one of them a redheaded Ostermeyer — with one replica tower. "When he did that, something inside of me just snapped," she growled, as if she'd summoned those overpowering emotions again. "I couldn't take it anymore, and I . . ."

"Whoa!" I took a step backward. "No need to show me! I understand!"

"No, you don't," she shot back. I could tell she was ferociously mad, and I started to get incredibly scared. Still, I dared to take my eyes off Ms. Beamish long enough to check on Viv again. She remained lying on the floor, but I saw her twitch, like she was either coming to or playing possum, which wouldn't have been a bad idea, given the situation. Either way, I was glad she was alive, both for her own sake and because maybe she'd jump up at some point and be helpful. Then I returned my attention to Ms. Beamish, who was still standing there, weapon aloft, like she was starting to savor the process of killing. "Please," I said, hearing the fear in my voice. "Please, don't . . ."

"*None of you* respect me," she snarled, stepping closer again, so I moved back, bumping into a desk. "Especially *you.*"

How had this become about *me?*

"I . . . I respect you!" I promised.

"No, you don't," Ms. Beamish countered. "You never speak French during free dialogue! You *sleep* in class!"

Oh, gosh, I really wished I'd tried harder. "That's not disrespect," I insisted, my voice shaking because she *was* starting to enjoy eliminating her enemies. She was practically salivating. "I just genuinely suck at languages!" I informed her, backing away again. "Ask anybody! Chase'll tell you!"

"Yes, *your* little boyfriend."

Ugh, to the tenth power. She might've loved Mr. Killdare, but

354 * BETH FANTASKEY

she definitely had it for Chase, too. There was all kinds of messed up inside her bilingual head.

"Why'd you kill *Mike?*" I asked a question that suddenly popped into *my* head. "What did he do?"

"Caught me taking the trophy," she said, which explained when it had disappeared. "He just *had* to come back to the locker room to get his hand weights! Right as I was taking it!"

I had no idea what hand weights were, but I felt terrible for Mike. They definitely couldn't have been worth dying over. And speaking of dying . . .

"*Au revoir*, Millicent," Ms. Beamish said, stalking closer, with a creepy smile on her face. "I suppose I'll have to find a way to pin this on your father, too." She knitted her unplucked brows as reality struck. "Although it will be more difficult, since he inconveniently showed up at the game . . ."

I probably should've used her moment of doubt to dart away, because I did see her lower her hand, just slightly. But when she flat out admitted to framing my dad, I stopped being scared and got unbelievably mad myself. Both angry and mad in the traditional sense of the word, meaning I didn't exactly think straight.

"You'll never get away with anything—or pin *this* on my dad," I told her, jabbing a finger at her chest. "Trust me, if you do me in, I'll come back from the grave and bury your stupid tower in YOUR backyard, then ghost-call the cops and tell them to dig it up." My voice rose as it really sank in just how miserable she'd made my father and what she'd cost him. "Then I'll testify at YOUR trial via medium and crystal ball," I advised her in no uncertain terms. "I swear, I'll do it, you murdering, framing witch!"

"I HAD NO CHOICE," she thundered, so loudly that I wondered if they heard her on the football field. *"No choice!"*

"Millie!"

I heard Chase's voice coming from the door, and I turned for just a split second, not understanding why he was there when he was supposed to be quarterbacking.

Chase . . .

Then I spun back around just in time to cry out—for some reason uttering my last words in very pissed off, poorly con-jugated French, invoking a host of philosophers who believed strongly in the concept of free will, just like I did. *"TU AS UN CHOIX!"* I hollered. *"YOU **HAD** A CHOICE!"*

The words were barely out when I felt a really heavy clunk against my curls, and everything went black.

EPILOGUE

How's your head?" Chase asked, gently stroking my hair, barely touching me, because even though it had been nearly two days since Ms. Beamish had clobbered me, I still had a pretty big bump. "Does it hurt?"

"A little," I said, shifting on the couch so I could rest even closer against his chest. I wasn't sure what the future held for us, but for the time being, he didn't seem inclined to stay away from me. I had a feeling that saving me had expiated a little more of his guilt. Either that, or he was starting to realize that life was, indeed, short and unpredictable, and that you had to grasp the present, even if you'd screwed up the past.

All I knew for certain was that I'd awoken on a classroom floor—next to Viv, who'd seemed a little *too* alert, as if she had been playing possum, even when I'd been about to get killed—and Ms. Beamish, whom Chase had tackled, although that wasn't normally the role of a quarterback. And on that floor littered with semiconscious bodies, I'd felt Chase's hand under my head and heard him telling me, "Please be okay, Millie. I love you. Please wake up . . ."

I hadn't been drifting toward some celestial light or existential darkness, but those words had helped to clear the fog from my head and compensate for the throbbing inside my skull — which still lingered.

"I think some hamburger would help ease the pain," I suggested.

Chase took the hint and picked up my Double Bungee from a plate on the cushion next to him, offering me a bite.

Okay, I was admittedly taking it too far, getting fed, but I knew I wouldn't be able to milk my injury forever. I would enjoy the extreme pampering while I could.

"Why'd you come for me?" I asked for the millionth time, like a kid who enjoyed hearing the same bedtime story, over and over. "I couldn't believe it when you showed up."

"You tossed away a doughnut as you ran toward the school, Millie."

I honestly still didn't recall having done that.

"And to see you run, in general — which I never saw happen in phys ed," Chase added. "I knew something was wrong. I started to play again, but I kept screwing up, watching for you to come out of the school. Finally, I just had to go." He rubbed my head again, a little harder, like he knew I was starting to heal and maybe overplaying things so we could keep sitting so close on the couch. My dad would definitely put an end to any public displays of affection the moment the lump went down. "Thank God for this hair, huh?" Chase teased.

"I'm sure its spring action cushioned the blow and saved your life."

I pushed off his chest so I could see him grinning and rubbed my head, too, silently thanking my mother for sharing her genes with me. "Yeah. I'll never complain about it again."

I was pretty sure I was about to get a compliment—or a kiss. I could tell, just from the look in Chase's eyes. Unfortunately, my dad and Ms. Parkins came in the front door, right at that inopportune moment—along with Baxter on a leash.

"*You* are walking this dog, the minute you feel better," my father complained without even greeting us. Chase and I wisely moved a few inches apart. "And I don't care if you still have a concussion. It needs a bath *tonight*."

He was griping, but there was a lightness to it, since he'd resumed his post as mayor. Although he didn't intend to coach again. He said it just didn't have the same appeal anymore. But I secretly suspected he wanted to devote more time to the woman who was unhooking Baxter's leash—but winking at me. "I'll wash him, Millie. You just rest."

"I can't believe I'm letting you keep this thing," Dad added with a gentle—somewhat affectionate . . . or maybe not— kick to Baxter's rump as the dog loped to me and Chase. "In retrospect, you had a lot of nerve asking while you were in the emergency room."

"Thanks again, Dad." I smiled. "Love you!"

I said that last part like I was joking, but I really wasn't. I wanted us to start saying that to each other, even if it didn't come naturally yet.

"Love you, too, Millicent," Dad grumbled, but I knew he

meant it, too. He came over to the couch, offering me and Chase a newspaper that had been folded under his arm. "And I guess you both *do* deserve a reward for saving Viv — and me," he added grudgingly. He unfolded the *Honeywell Crier*, the town's daily. "Here. Read."

Chase accepted the paper, and we both saw that the story of our confrontation with Ms. Beamish was on page one. There was an unflattering shot of me wobbling out of the school with the assistance of a paramedic — and what looked like a model's headshot of Viv.

"She looks better than me," I admitted. "But she's going to be furious about the story. Ironically, it's killing her that I saved her." I grinned at Chase. "What if I actually win a Pacemaker on top of this?"

Chase's smile was uncertain. "I think I'll be worried. She already despises you more than usual for nearly getting her killed."

"Yeah, how about how she and Mike really were talking about Viv helping him cheat on a French test when I overheard them?" I mused, feeling a tad responsible for the goose egg Viv was sporting on her head, too. Then again, if Viv hadn't been so evil to begin with, I never would've thought her capable of homicide. I shrugged. "Who knew?"

"Just watch your back for a while, okay, Millie?" Chase urged.

I wasn't worried. Viv and I had a *historia,* and though she might stand back and let me get murdered to save her own butt, she'd never actively, physically hurt me. At least, I didn't think so. "I see there's 'no comment' from Detective Lohser,"

I added, shifting the conversation, because I was starting to get a little uneasy, too. "He 'could not be reached.'"

"Yes, he seems to have disappeared," Dad agreed. "Thank heavens."

"Speaking of which . . ." Ms. Parkins rested her hand on my father's arm and nodded toward the kitchen.

For a second, my dad didn't seem to understand. Then he got that she was trying to give me and Chase some privacy, and he frowned. "Isabel . . ."

But Ms. Parkins kept smiling in her infectious, persuasive way and tugging his arm. "Jack . . . Come on now. We're intruding on a dinner date."

"Oh . . . Fine." My father went along with *his* date, but gave me and Chase one warning look right before the kitchen door swung shut—behind a trotting Baxter, who'd clearly taken a shine to my father, even if the reverse wasn't true.

I still wasn't sure whether Dad was protecting me from Chase, or Chase from me. Either way, we both ignored that cautionary glance. The moment he and Ms. Parkins were gone, I moved closer to Chase, and he moved closer to me. We kissed once, just quickly, because we *were* under my dad's roof, then I rested my head against Chase's chest again, thinking that was good enough for now. More than perfect, really. Like a scene right out of Nancy Drew's life—if she'd ever worn Doc Martens and been lucky enough to get an AWESOME dog, and an even more amazing boyfriend, like mine.

ACKNOWLEDGMENTS

As always, I want to thank my family for making this book possible. Endless thanks to my husband, Dave, for believing in me and helping me carve out time to work. And thanks to my kids — Paige, Julia, and Hope — for learning to use the microwave and surviving on Lean Cuisines while I wrote. You girls are awesome.

I am also indebted to my parents, Donald and Marjorie Fantaskey, for your unswerving faith and support.

Similarly, I am eternally grateful to my in-laws, George and Elaine Kaszuba — and especially to my sister-in-law, Sandra Petrosky, who serves as my unofficial, but phenomenal, publicist. Your efforts to promote my books — including your surreptitious rearrangement of store displays — is much, much appreciated.

And, of course, I want to say thanks to "my" librarian, Elizabeth Maule, who let a geeky, book loving fifth-grader become a library "assistant," giving me a safe place to retreat when that first year of middle school got overwhelming. I know my shelving efforts created more work for you, but you never let it show.

Thanks, also, to my indefatigable editor, Margaret Raymo, and my dynamo agent, Helen Breitwieser. You always have my back—and push me in the right direction. You two are the best.

And how can I express sufficient gratitude to my friend Jackie Kelly, who asked the crucial question "If you want to be done with this book, why don't you sit down and write it?" You are too wise.

To Scott Manning—thanks for stepping in at the last minute with your French expertise. *Merci!*

Finally, a million thanks to all of you readers who support my books, especially those of you who have become my genuine friends, be it through cyberspace or face-to-face. High on that latter list are all the cool people at my gym, my kids' schools, and the businesses I frequent around my hometown—especially Denise Poust at the hardware store. Thanks so much for sharing my books from your personal "bookmobile"!